GENE
MAPPER

TAIYO
FUJII

GENE
MAPPER

TAIYO
FUJII

TRANSLATED BY JIM HUBBERT

SAN FRANCISCO

HAIKASORU
Published by VIZ Media, LLC
P.O. Box 77010
San Francisco, CA 94107

www.haikasoru.com

Library of Congress Cataloging-in-Publication Data

Fujii, Taiyo, 1971–
  [Gene mapper. English]
  Gene mapper / Taiyo Fujii ; translated by Jim Hubbert.
     pages cm.
  ISBN 978-1-4215-8027-2 (paperback)
  1. Genetically modified foods—Fiction. I. Hubbert, Jim, translator. II. Title.
PL870.J54G4713 2015
895.63'6—dc23

                              2015008033

Printed in the U.S.A.
First printing, June 2015

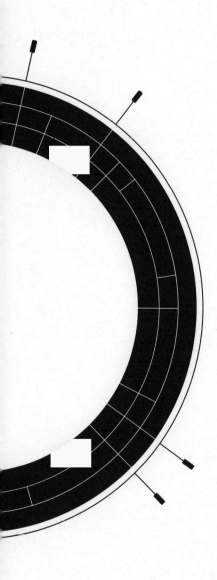

PART 1
AUGMENTED REALITY

1   Offer

The alert tone hummed deep in my ear.

I extended my right arm—already on the sheet out of habit—and cut the sound with a wave of my doubled index and middle fingers.

Rub face. Thumb eyelids open.

Two straight weeks of sweltering nights. Tropical Nights, in Meteorological Agency–speak. I felt the building's steel bones channeling the heat into the darkness of my loft in Worker's Heights.

Why was it dark? Did I input the wrong wake-up setting? What time was it?

Mamoru, you have one priority message. Shall I play it for you?

Message Manager was inside my ear, like the alarm. I rose up on an elbow and pushed away the hair plastered to my forehead. I always set messaging to Do Not Disturb/Discretionary Override. This was the first time the system had ever woken me up.

Still fuzzy. I nodded. Message Manager suspended my workspace where I could see it without getting up. Centered in the space was a thumbnail of a man with a ruler-straight part and thick-framed glasses.

> TAKASHI KUROKAWA :: TIMESTAMP 04:32
> FROM: MEGURO, TOKYO @ RESIDENCE
> MM CONFIRMS THIS MESSAGE PRIORITY/URGENT

"Hello, Mamoru. Sorry to ring you this early."

The familiar, gentle voice flowed from the workstation. With his twentieth century manners, Kurokawa would never have voiced me in the middle of the night unless it was a real emergency.

"There's something you need to hear about Mother Mekong. You worked on it last year. SR06 is mutating. They say it's gene collapse."

My right arm, outside the sheet, prickled with shock.

There were cases—in the lab—of distilled plants developing outside the design envelope, but they were vanishingly rare. L&B Corporation was synonymous with Super Rice, and SR06 was their most advanced formulation yet. Could it actually crash? I couldn't imagine it.

"I'm waiting for details. What I can tell you is that the logos and cert marks you mapped are disintegrating on the north edge of the site. L&B wants a report right away, with or without a verified cause."

Shit. What about all the other people who helped launch Mother Mekong? My intro to the project came from Kurokawa, my agent. He was just the conduit for L&B's developer kit. I doubted he'd had anything to do with site design. That would have been handled by a specialized construction outfit. Mapping the logos across the site was my job. I was certain this was Mother Mekong's screwup, but naturally L&B had Kurokawa and me in its sights before anyone else.

"I'm heading into a crisis meeting," said Kurokawa. "I'll confirm the report format and what they want from us, and collect any information I can from the Cambodians. Sorry, but I'll need to glass you tomorrow at the usual time."

"Glass" meaning an augmented reality meeting. Typical Takashi Kurokawa, as if we were back in the Internet era. Businesspeople— and freelancers like me—use contact lenses with embedded LEDs for image projection. Kurokawa had his glasses, but I always thought they were part of his salaryman look.

I checked the clock. A meeting at this hour? His plate was full. It was midday in San Francisco. That meant brand management would probably be in the meeting. It was only two a.m. at L&B's Central Research Lab in KL and Mother Mekong's headquarters in

Phnom Penh. TrueNet just gets better and better, but though it can erase distance it can't do much about time zones. I wondered what time they'd be holding the meetings between Tokyo, San Francisco, and Phnom Penh once they had more information about Mother's "mutation."

I was happy to leave L&B to Kurokawa, but what time were we supposed to meet exactly? Did "tomorrow" mean tomorrow or today? Nine a.m. was the usual time. Or was it ten?

Whatever. Make it a morning—breakfast, coffee, mail. Was there time for a run? No, didn't look like it.

The wake-up icon pulsed silently. Good. I lay back and traced the outline of my arm under the sheet, feeling the goose bumps subside, and sleep came again.

* * *

"I voiced you at an ungodly hour. Did I end up waking you?"

It was nine after all. The meeting started with Kurokawa, hands flat on the conference room table, bowing deeply.

The room was mine. The wind from the fan on the high ceiling rippled the blinds, throwing fractal slats of morning sunshine onto the white stucco walls. The light scattered and glowed. A Kandinsky lithograph hung on the wall behind Kurokawa. The arrowlike object in the frame pointed at his bowed head. All in all, the room was probably a bit much for a two-person meeting, but then again, it wasn't real.

The room, the artwork, Kurokawa bathed in light—everything was projected on my retinas by my contact lenses. The fan moved the blinds, but the only thing striking my skin was the thready stream of damp air from the cooling unit. If I slid my fingers across the "table" they would hit the urethane wallpaper. I left the detail settings at medium to save money. No footprints on the carpet, no fingerprints on the table, not a mark on the stucco.

Against this pristine backdrop, Kurokawa—his hands on the table that wasn't a table—looked uncannily real. His fingers were slightly bent, the tips bloodless from the pressure. Was he using an avatar today? He usually went with RealVu for augmented reality. With RealVu, you have to use multiple cams, but to get the fingertip effect, his own table would have to be the same height as the "table" on my AR stage.

"Yeah, I was dead to the world. Message Manager flagged it priority. Not your fault."

"Well, I'm sorry anyway." Kurokawa's face had a healthy sheen. The corners of his mouth were turned down apologetically. I realized that the subtle shifts in his expression were too good for an avatar. This was 3D RealVu.

Glasses with thick black frames perched on his baby-smooth face. His build was on the chubby side. The dark blue single-breasted summer suit was half unbuttoned, and the crimson knit tie was impeccably knotted against an expanse of white shirt. If he ever needed an avatar to wear this retro getup with as much aplomb—and a hairstyle so carefully arranged that it looked fake—he could've picked out something from LusionTek's Salaryman Series, but somehow he'd always preferred RealVu.

RealVu is a pain in the ass, frankly. You have to dress just right if you want to actually look "real," and multiple lighting sources are necessary to reduce inappropriate shadows on the real-time image. After an all-nighter, an avatar is just the thing to project the energy you wish you had. Yet here was the real Kurokawa looking fresh and rested after a night without sleep. It was vaguely irritating.

"Takashi, you must be tired yourself. I thought we'd be meeting tomorrow. I didn't think you meant in a few hours."

I knew he wouldn't catch the sarcasm, but I also knew why Message Manager had marked his voice mail priority. I decided to change the settings. This would be the last time anyone ever woke *me* up.

"Sorry to put you out. I hope you have time to walk through a few things with me right now."

The man was relentless. I sighed and rolled my eyes, but my avatar spread its arms in friendly accommodation. Behavior Correction is very handy at moments like this.

"Thank you, Mamoru. I'd just gotten the news myself. I'm not up to speed, but I thought I'd take the liberty of alerting you right away. I apologize for the absurd timing."

He bowed again and put a beige envelope on the desk. "These are aerial photos from the site."

He untied the flap, extracted a "contact sheet" and tossed it over with a practiced gesture. I heard the whisper of paper on the table and noticed that his movements were not FileShare animation. Even with an avatar, extracting something from an envelope with a physical operator tag and tossing it onto the right spot would be tricky without lots of practice. A sudden vision of Kurokawa alone in his room, practicing photo-tossing with a frown of concentration on his round face, cheered me up a bit.

He must have put in the time, because the sheet slid to a stop right in front of me. ACCEPT SHARED IMAGES? popped up, followed after a second or two by the security scan stamp. Even with the low-res thumbnails, the terraced fields were clearly visible, spread like fans over the site. The year before, I'd spent days and nights staring at photos of the same landscape until I was blue in the face. The file name was 070939-mekong-photos, which meant they were taken the day before.

"Three-D? Very nice. You came prepared."

The only reaction to this new stab at sarcasm was a puzzled blink and a "Yes, of course" nod. Time to pack it in. The war of nerves wasn't working.

There was no EULA. I tapped a thumbnail to extract the HD aerial photo. The contours of the site rose up from the table. I could see the orange L&B and Mother Mekong logos shimmering against the fluorescent green rice plants. Between the two giant corporate logos lay a row of star-shaped certification marks: FULL ORGANIC, WATER CYCLING, ACTIVE GROUND COVER, ZERO EMISSIONS, FAIR TRADE. SR06 was the first five-star distilled crop project. L&B wanted the world to know it.

Even the cert marks, which were far smaller than the logos, were several hundred meters across. Everything on the undulating, terraced terrain had to be visible from the air at any angle without distortion. That required a precise gene-mapping program.

My program.

"Look at the north side."

I flicked the top of the photo. At the higher resolution, I could see smearing in the logos across the terraces on the edge of the site. The blurred markings were flecked with patches of matte green, the color of powdered tea. Clearly the genes for color expression I had programmed into SR06 were not doing their job. Or were those patches of green something else? I couldn't remember seeing that weedy hue on the SR06 color chart.

"These green patches. Do you know what they are?"

"All we know is that they appear to be rice plants. As you can see, the color is distinctive. No distilled plant has that color."

"Are you sure?"

"That's not all. Mother Mekong found insect damage, probably because the site is Full Organic."

"Insects? Then it's some kind of wild grass. It has to be. Even if it's a mutation, it wasn't from my code. The zero-six style sheet won't let me alter traits for pest resistance even if I wanted to. Those sequences are all sequestered. Check my code. You'll see I didn't go anywhere near that stuff. Mother's crew have contaminated their own site, that's all."

"I certainly hope so." Kurokawa sat back and folded his arms. "But we still have to investigate. Don't worry, L&B's footing the bill. I'm sure it wasn't your hamartia, and as long as I'm right, I'll send them a big invoice for our services. In the meantime, I need you to start right away."

Hamartia? Almost before I had a chance to be puzzled, a subtitle appeared below Kurokawa's face.

HAMARTIA: 1. A MISTAKE OR ERROR. 2. A SIN FOR
WHICH ONE IS RESPONSIBLE. 3. A TRAGIC FLAW.

Not a common word. I had to keep AutoGlossary running when I talked to Kurokawa.

Our agreement with L&B specified As Is delivery, same as for software programming and similar work. If a problem shows up after your code passes inspection and third-party verification, you're still good.

"Takashi, I need you to define 'right away.'"

"I'll be sending you DNA data from samples of that unidentified vegetation. First you need to figure out what we're dealing with."

"Come on. It's an indigenous weed. When are they going to collect the samples? I need to know when the DNA data will be here."

"I told them to upload it to your public folder just before we got on. As long as the bandwidth out of Cambodia is no worse than usual, you should have it before noon."

At least he could have asked me if I was willing to handle it. "Really on the ball there, Takashi."

"I always try to be of service." He bowed again. His natural, real-time embarrassment made me regret the sarcasm. Oh, well. I never could wriggle away from such a tenacious negotiator, especially with a vanilla avatar. I promised myself that one day I'd use something more full-featured for meetings like this.

"I'll leave you to it then. As soon as you find something, let me know, no matter what time it is." Kurokawa smiled. He put his hands on the table, stood up and made a perfect, formal bow, and vanished.

The conference room vanished too. The room was replaced by the drab walls of my loft. My clothes went from semi-custom business casual to T-shirt and jeans, beat-up but comfortable.

The alert light strobed. SAVE VIDEO?

"New project. Mother Mekong Investigation. Register video and photos to this project."

New project created. Name: Mother Mekong Investigation. I have registered the aerial photo file 070939-mekong-photo and the meeting video to this project.

I had to say, Kurokawa looked good. The thought crossed my mind that maybe I should get RealVu too...but no, avatars were more my speed.

Avatars gave you an edge: Behavior Correction. If you lost your temper in a meeting, your avatar wouldn't show it. That wasn't all. With an avatar, your feet were on the floor no matter who was running the stage. You looked where you were supposed to be looking, and your words were timed to compensate for transmission delay. With RealVu, I'd end up doing a new variation on the trending meme of that Japanese CEO who finished a press conference by bowing until his face was buried in the table.

I checked to make sure the video was registered to the project and adjusted my butt in the chair. I had to get some work done before I went off on a tangent.

"Show new upload in shared folder."

One file found. File name: 070939-collapsed-SR06. Registered by Thep@Mother_Mekong.

"Open file."

The upload is in progress.

"What?"

Confirming...The upload is in progress.

I checked the folder. The progress bar wasn't even up yet, just the revolving wheel and PREPARING UPLOAD.

"Okay then, tell me when it's done."

I will notify you when the upload for file 070939-collapsed-SR06 is complete.

The guys at Mother Mekong must have their own headaches this morning, but couldn't they handle a simple upload? Were these the people I would be working with?

So, we wait. I decided to review where I stood so far. "Search last year's projects for Mother Mekong. Map all Kurokawa meetings onto the calendar. Add summaries."

The calendar for 2036 appeared in the center of the workspace. I pinched the ends in both hands, stretched them to arms' width, and swept the video thumbnails into a row arranged by date. AR let me stretch my workspace to fill my field of vision. You have to be your own boss to have this kind of freedom. It's pathetic that salarymen are limited to the width of their cubes. How do they get anything done?

It took a few more seconds for the summaries to fill in. The virtual Post-its floated into place on their thumbnails, each in a different position to make it visually distinct from its neighbors. Now I could easily survey the whole timeline.

I use my contact lens–projected workspace every day, but it never ceased to amaze me. Everything—the interface, the virtual Post-its, the other widgets—was shaded as if real ambient light were falling on a real object. The sense of physical presence was seamless.

"Play third movie."

Conference for October 15, 2036. Topic: Final project specifications.

The interface disappeared, and the wall pulled back. I was a fly on the wall of a spacious conference room with Kurokawa to my left, on the near side of the table. My avatar was on the far side. The video was nine months old, but other than the weave of his suit, Kurokawa looked identical to the man I'd talked to just a few minutes ago. Everything was the same down to the length of his hair. We each had a binder open to the same agreement.

"Just so you know, Mother Mekong SR06 is going to be the world's first five-star distilled cultivation site," said Kurokawa.

"Five? Then there's a lot on my plate."

"Yes. Mother Mekong is guaranteeing Full Organic and Water Cycling certification. L&B is funding site construction for the Active Ground Cover and Zero Emissions certificates. The project guarantees local hiring, so they get Fair Trade too. You'll be mapping all five marks and the logos for both companies."

I understood why L&B was ready to hand us a blank check. Mother Mekong was a test bed to prove that synthetic biology could drive sustainable yields to new heights. The logos and cert marks could be monitored with TerraVu's satellite imaging service. They would stand as proof, on a twenty-four/seven basis, that this synthetic life-form was under total genetic engineering control. If the logos were disintegrating, L&B would panic, that was certain.

In a few more days L&B's competitors, the certification agencies, and the FAO would wake up to what was happening. If we didn't pinpoint the cause of the mutation and come up with a way to knock it out, L&B's position at the top of the distilled crop heap was going to be in jeopardy.

"Play logo color meeting. Start with the specification chapter."

Conference video for October 27, 2036. Personal profiles are available for any individuals mentioned during playback.

The video started. Again Kurokawa looked the same. It could have been a continuation of the previous meeting.

"Mamoru, the partners want fluorescent green."

"Excuse me, did you say 'fluorescent'?" Even with Behavior Correction, my stunned surprise was noticeable.

"Yes. This is a joint request from L&B and Mother Mekong. Please use the GFP protein listed in the style sheet. That should give us a nice fluorescent green effect."

Now I remembered. That vile hue was another example of Barnhard's meddling.

I could understand having fluorescent green in the daytime as a genomic control indicator. But the protein they wanted to use was derived from jellyfish DNA. The stuff actually glows blue-white. What the site looked like at night I couldn't imagine and didn't want to. A hundred square clicks of rice glowing in the dark.

I called up the profile for Lintz Barnhard. A text block and a 3D minikin about eight inches tall popped up, suspended above the table. The avatar had the full mane of swept-back white hair, the bespoke suit, and the perfectly hemispherical gut, as if the man was pregnant with a balance ball. Even in miniature, the aura of power—Barnhard was about six-foot-five in RL—was palpable. This was someone I wouldn't want to hang out with even in augmented reality.

Lintz Barnhard was legendary in the genetic engineering community for sheer tenacity. He was a genuine pioneer who had propelled L&B from a second-tier brewer to the king of distilled crops in under ten years. He was too senior to be down in the weeds with people like us, but L&B's commitment to feed the planet was on the line with Mother Mekong. This problem was too important to leave to the experts.

I watched the video and paged through the documents. The specs for the logos had been challenging, but nothing I couldn't handle. I sampled a few more videos but didn't notice any unusual requests related to the developer's kit L&B had delivered through Kurokawa. If someone screwed up, it looked like it wasn't L&B.

Was it me? I was a logical suspect, unfortunately. I pictured Barnhard bursting into a meeting, pounding the table, and grabbing my avatar by the lapels. The image was depressing. I had to prove that my mapping hadn't triggered a gene meltdown.

Upload for file 070939-collapsed-SR06 has begun. Estimated time to completion: forty-six minutes twenty seconds. I will notify you when the transfer is complete.

Was the pipe out of Cambodia that small? Anyway, the timing was perfect. It was time for a run. I needed to clear my head.

*   *   *

When I got back and checked the file, I rolled my eyes. Mother Mekong needed to hire better people.

The file was two hundred gigabytes. Now I knew why the upload had taken so long to start—the security scan was choking. Malware was getting worse all the time, and sterilizing two hundred gig would've taken a huge amount of time.

But the person who handled the upload—Thep, was that his name? He needed help. If he knew anything, he'd know that two hundred gigabytes couldn't be right. Someone had messed up somewhere.

The *Oryza* genome only has around three hundred million base pairs. Even the 3.2 billion base pairs of the human genome can be captured in a gigabyte. The entire genome, coded amino acids, and auxiliary information in a space-hogging format like gXML only takes up twenty-five gigabytes or so.

I wasn't sure how closely I'd be working with these people, but maybe that Fair Trade certification was forcing Mother to cut corners. Where were they getting their people? The concept was nice, but the least they could've done was hire someone with a degree from somewhere real to handle external liaison. Someone who knew what he was doing.

The file was gXML. Right now, this was all I had to work with. I had no choice but to get on with it.

"Gene Analytics. Open 070939-collapsed-SR06."

> INITIALIZATION FAILED
> INSECT AND PLANT CODE GROUPS FOUND
> SELECT TEMPLATE AND OPEN IN MANUAL MODE

I didn't have the voice plug-in, so the messages appeared in text. Gene Analytics could handle everything from fortune-telling via blood type to biological weapons design, yet for this genome it couldn't decide whether the Kingdom was Animalia or Plantae. That meant the sample was contaminated—I was dealing with a mix of different organisms. The Cambodians had probably contaminated the mutated DNA with genetic material from grasshoppers or some other insect.

I mean, shit. No matter how primitive their equipment was, the basic protocol for handling samples was the same.

"Schedule. Include request for second round of samples in next Kurokawa message."

New smart task created. Request for new DNA field sampling to be included in next Kurokawa message.

It looked like I was going to be spanking Mother Mekong a lot. The tasks were piling up. Who knew when they'd be able to deliver the next data set? I decided to see if I could get something out of what I had on the bench before I touched base with Kurokawa again.

I didn't know whether I was dealing with rice or some other grass species, but if I could isolate the Plantae DNA buried in the sample, I could prove there was no connection with SR06. That would shoot down the gene collapse theory and give Kurokawa a bigger stick to beat Mother Mekong with.

"Gene Analytics. Open code using Oryza template. Send messages to workspace voice output." The program drew a bar across the workspace and started reading out the data. The bar was six inches high and six feet long at least. I watched it fill in with *Oryza* DNA in green. Junk—duplicate data or anything the program couldn't recognize as plant DNA—was gray.

The bar was coming in mostly gray. I wasn't surprised. I watched the program do its best to take an impossibly long gene sequence and process it as if it were a single organism. "What kind of life-form has a genome fifty or a hundred times larger than Homo sapiens?" I muttered.

Reading data as Kingdom Plantae, Angiospermae, Monokots, *Family* Poaceae, *Genus* Oryza.

"Duh. That's what I asked for."

WARNING. LETHAL EXPRESSION SEQUENCES.
MODELING OR EMBRYO-PRINTING PROHIBITED.

"Wha—?"

A clutch of vertical red sectors flashed around the center of the bar. I hadn't seen a warning like this outside the classroom. I winked at the first red line and triggered another pop-up.

VULNERABLE FOR MALM-PUCCINIA ORYZIAS

"Bull*shit*!"

A plant with no rust resistance in the middle of Mother Mekong's precious SR06?

By the time the red rust blight ended its long burn through the Asian rice crop in 2022, tens of millions were dead of starvation. The same year, the WTO had banned cross-border trade in nonresistant cultivars, and in less than two years most legacy cultivars had pretty much disappeared. If transmission had been happening through soil microbes or insects, it could've been eradicated with pesticides, but red rust was transmitted through swallow droppings. It had soon spread all over East Asia.

For free agents like Kurokawa and me who depended on distilled crops for a living, red rust and the Great East Asian Famine had a special significance. Natural strains of rice—leaves mottled with red-brown spots, seedless stalks slowly withering—were replaced by the first generation of plants that paid our bills.

L&B had always been an aggressive genetic modifier of rice cultivars for brewing beer. It soon turned out that some of their modified strains lacked the receptor gene for red rust. In fields of brown-spotted, dying plants, a few stood tall above the rest, heads heavy with golden grains.

This was an opportunity Barnhard was born to seize.

L&B was mainly known for beer, but thanks to his abrasive personality, Barnhard had been sidetracked into L&B's sake sales division. He had no understanding of genetics, but when he heard about the resistant plants that had just been found on an L&B plantation, he convinced the government of Singapore, which was just getting back on its feet after the Internet imploded, to foot the bill for the development of a new variety of Super Rice Zero that would be safe for direct human consumption. Barnhard ran the project with a whip hand, and in less than a year L&B had a release candidate ready to launch.

Everyone in the industry knew about Barnhard's presentation to the UN's Food and Agriculture Organization. His performance shed more heat than light, but his aggressive approach put distilled crops—rice, and later wheat and soy—on the map. "Our distilled rice, SR01, is more robust and safer for human consumption than cultivars produced through crossbreeding or mutation selection. It's evolution-proof. We know every base pair in this genome. Every trait is under our control. SR01 is just the first drop from the distiller's pot, but we're certain it will be a very fine blend."

Barnhard hammered away with "distilled" everywhere he went, and after a while the name stuck. "Distilled" became a brand that symbolized the difference between full-scratch genetic design and the GMO crops of the 2010s, which took natural plants and selectively modified them for traits like secondary infertility and resistance to pesticides.

L&B's genetic "distillation" made such methods obsolete. Genetic engineers investigated every base pair in the target genome, jettisoned everything unessential, and added new traits. When SR01 burst on the scene twenty years ago, it was almost an artificial organism. The latest generation, SR06, had been scratch-designed with synthetic biotechnology and bore hardly a trace of its natural ancestor.

The scramble to adopt the new crops and farming methods spawned a huge industry. Organizations were set up to monitor and regulate protein content and allergens from the design stage.

Specialized construction firms carved out growing sites configured for the crops. One-man research labs used embryo printing for high-speed prototyping, and for leaf and flower color, there were gene mappers like me.

I wondered how Barnhard would feel if he knew that SR06, which he probably thought would be the summit of his career, was contaminated by a legacy plant with *no resistance to red rust.* Would he explode with anger, his face turning crimson the way it did at the FAO? Or would he turn white and clutch his spherical gut?

"Gene Analyst. Task complete?"

I am completing my analysis of the data using the Oryza template. The data includes a complete natural genome for Oryza sativa *subspecies* japonica.

"Sativa japonica?"

Oryza sativa japonica *was a family of rice cultivars formerly grown on islands off the east coast of Asia.*

So the plant that had invaded Mother's sanctuary was a legacy cultivar vulnerable to red rust. I couldn't fathom how this might have happened, but as long as I could demonstrate that the sample had no connection with the genome I delivered, I'd be in the clear.

"Gene Analyst, search the file for Mamoru Hayashida."

Found. There is a crop header in the file 070939-collapsed-SR06 with this name. I will display the header.

The very data I was praying I wouldn't see scrolled across the workspace. It was the header for SR06.

> VENDOR: L&B CORPORATION/FLO CERTIFIED
> PRODUCT: SR-06/FLO CERTIFIED
> VERSION: 6.01.5
> CONTRIBUTOR-PUBLISHER ACCOUNT: ENRICO
> CONTI @ L&B CORPORATION

And bringing up the rear, in the position of honor...

There I was. Enrico was listed too. He had been the project manager.

This DNA wasn't just a mix of insect and legacy plant DNA. DNA from SR06 was present too. The second round of samples would prove this was no case of gene collapse. But either way, I had to find out exactly what was contaminating Mother Mekong's site.

"The intruder." That's what I decided to call it. How was I going to go about collecting information? TrueNet would probably have almost nothing helpful.

The Lockout hit two years before red rust. The collapse of the Internet not only wiped out nearly all of the world's server data, it erased most data on personal computers and phones.

That was in 2017. I still remember the day it happened: the streams of meaningless characters on my mother's monitor and the live news broadcasts with no text inserts. The rolling blackouts. My father coming home early from work and watching television for weeks.

In high school I took a class on the history of technology and learned that the Internet's biggest search engine had gone bonkers, hijacking every computer it could reach.

It took several years to get a new network up and running. That was TrueNet, and it was no Internet free-for-all. All programs and data on TrueNet are closely vetted and administered. Nothing non-essential is allowed. After red rust and the great famine hit five years later, most of the legacy rice plant data accumulated over the years was no longer very useful, and very little of it had made it onto TrueNet.

Still, there was plenty of data out there. The problem was getting to it. I needed a specialist—a salvager. That meant another Kurokawa meeting.

If all I needed was authorization for another DNA sample or

Mother's cultivation logs, a text would have been enough. Finding the right salvager was going to be more complicated.

"What a mess..."

Since I hit thirty, I'd been talking to myself more. Then again, my workspace was the only "one" who heard me.

"So we're back to the Internet."

I sent Kurokawa my distress rocket.

2   Café Zucca

"Meeting someone? Care for a magazine while you wait?"

I lowered my iced espresso and saw the Perfect Smile above a blinding white shirt.

She knew how to strike a pose. Lean in at an angle, shoulders cocked, chest out, forearm parallel to the floor with a basket of magazines on her elbow. And The Smile. My cast member waitress was real, but what I was seeing was her avatar.

This was the first time I'd called a meeting with Kurokawa at Zucca. It was a popular spot. For the price of a drink you could hang out at the cutting edge of augmented reality. The place was close to packed out, but most of the customers were avatars logged in from outside. When I walked in, the physical café was fairly empty— I could still see the "real" seating—but by the time my lump of sherbet floating in iced espresso arrived, I'd almost forgotten how it looked.

The waitress was walking from table to table, handing out magazine widgets to help people kill time in the late afternoon. Last time I was here, it had been Old Master widgets that let you sketch like Rembrandt. Another time it was ship-in-a-bottle widgets. All you had to do was move your tweezers around a bit and you could build something pretty amazing. Or chess, complete with avatar opponent. Café Zucca worked hard to get the most out of their stage.

"Looks good. What's the house special?"

"I'd go with *Times of the World*. Sascha has a special feature."

The banner popped into the space in front of me, beckoning in large letters. *The Horror: Linuxpocalypse 2038!*

"Is this for real?"

"Sascha scooped the story. She says we're going to have a crisis next year. I think she's right."

"Sascha?"

The waitress pointed to the banner subtitle: *Sascha Leifens Reports: Engineers Gone Wild!*

"Sascha is a founder of World Reporting Network, Mamoru. She's terribly popular. I'm a fan too."

I'd never interacted with this cast member before, but she knew my first name. She pulled the July 11 issue of *Times of the World* from the basket and presented it with a flourish. The perfect smile, the model posture, the personalized banter—Zucca's Behavior Module was top notch.

"Be sure and tell me what you think. Enjoy!"

She winked and waved. As she headed to the next table, the "breeze" blew through her hair. The blinding summer sun was off the zenith, its light creating a halo around her white shirt. As I watched, a river of perspiration started cascading down my spine.

It was 39°C in the shade, a typical midsummer Tokyo afternoon. The tables had umbrellas, but the spaces between were in full sun. No one but an avatar could walk around outside like this without having her shirt plastered to her torso with sweat.

Zucca's powerful AR stage was full of cast member avatars who were indistinguishable from the real thing. My real waitress was walking around in this melting summer heat wearing the same white shirt, long slacks, and a garçon-style apron, but no way could she have looked as fresh as the avatar she was "wearing" on the stage.

The paper copy of *Times of the World* was heavier than I expected. I couldn't remember how long it had been since I'd held a physical magazine in my hands.

Out of habit, I poked the title with my index finger and flicked left, but all that did was move the paper a little. I carefully grasped the upper right corner of the page—the feeling took me back—and

peeled it to the left. The familiar PLAY button was waiting under the
LINUXPOCALYPSE banner on the next page. Zucca's stage had inserted
an AR projection into a physical magazine. I was probably just holding
a bundle of blank pages. So you got the luxury of real paper but a
familiar way to enjoy the content. Nice. I tapped the playback button.

"Shut up and listen, bitch!"

I heard a snarl of anger. Something white flew at me from out of
the page. I automatically ducked. Luckily I wasn't holding my espresso.

It was 3D video. A red-faced old man was sitting up in a hospital
bed. His breathing was ragged, and his arm was stained with blood
where the IV tube had torn loose. It was hard to watch. The object
that flew off the page at me must have been a pillow.

"I told you, we fixed it!"

"Oh, dear. You mean you fixed it on *your* computers. Isn't that
right? Why didn't you think about the hundreds of millions of *other*
PCs around the world?"

The interviewer was off-screen, her voice dripping with sarcasm.
Baiting her subject didn't seem like the best way of getting useful
information. Was this the famous Sascha?

"Was the whole world my responsibility?"

"So you don't feel responsible after all. Such a shame."

"I *told* you, we upgraded TIME_T support from 32- to 64-bit
almost immediately. Weren't you listening? We had a 64-bit patch
as soon as the processors came out. It was there for anyone who—
What's so funny, you piece of shit?"

The old guy pulled the IV bag off the stand and fastballed it at
the camera. The video reframed. Now I was looking at a TV studio,
with the man in the hospital frozen on ranks of monitors along the
walls. The World Reporting Network logo revolved slowly in the
lower right corner. A woman in a short jacket and slacks was perched
on a tall chair, legs crossed. I guessed she was in her early thirties.

SASCHA LEIFENS was subtitled across her chest. So this was the
reporter my waitress liked so much.

Sascha shrugged her shoulders and tossed her bobbed red hair as she stepped down. I knew she was an avatar when her hair returned to exactly the same position. Most casters use RealVu to at least give the impression that they're communicating facts. Not Sascha.

"There you have it. What do *you* think?" It was the voice from the interview. "The operating system he coded in a trance, while ignoring his responsibilities to society, has an astonishing flaw."

A large chart appeared above her head with a string of thirty or so ones and zeros along the top. Below the ones and zeros was a date readout: years, months, days, hours, minutes, seconds.

"These are time values for Unix. Look closely. He used a 32-bit integer to express these values to the second, even though he knew very well that Unix would have to be viable for at least decades. The way he coded it, the time value will reach its overflow point next year—at seven seconds past 3:14 a.m., January 19, 2038."

The time count on the chart rolled toward the overflow point. Now almost all the numbers were ones. Sascha made a pistol with her thumb and index finger and took aim at the chart.

"Bang!"

The last zero changed to a one, and all the ones rolled over to zeros. The time readout flipped to January 1, 1970, and the chart shattered into a million pieces.

"I'd like to invite everyone out there to ask software engineers and corporations what will happen when our PCs can't handle time signatures correctly. I did, and this is the answer I got."

Sascha lifted a corner of her shapely mouth and faked a male growl. "Well, miss, there won't be enough 32-bit computers left in the world to matter."

She shrugged. "When I asked how many computers will be affected, they couldn't answer. Why? Because they don't know. But for some reason, they *do* know there *won't be any problems*. That's techies for you."

The sugar in my espresso couldn't mask the bitter undertaste.

Zucca's coffee wasn't very good. I felt like blaming Sascha. I couldn't believe that a major information conduit like *Times of the World* would stoop to this kind of tabloid agitation.

First, nearly all CPUs are 128-bit now. Maybe there are some 32-bit devices out there that can't be patched, but the programmer Sascha spoke to was right: there couldn't be enough devices like that to make a difference one way or the other.

"Want to hear something even *scarier*? This flaw will affect programs that control forces powerful enough to threaten our very existence." The studio monitors switched from the guy in the hospital to images of mushroom clouds over nuclear power plants, ICBMs popping out of silos, and fusion reactors melting down. Sascha frowned, shook her head, and turned both palms upward in a "Whatcha gonna do?" gesture.

"If this was a problem the human species never faced before, we might cut those programmers some slack. But in the year 2000, during the Internet era, the man in the hospital and his friends created an identical problem. They never learn."

Video from the early oughts rolled past on the monitors. There was a red-faced kid with curly hair wearing a hoodie in a cubicle crowded with toys, then a guy with a bowl cut and old hippie-style clothes hunched over an old fliptop PC.

"These men developed one Internet service after another that violated our rights, especially our right to privacy. Worse still, they ignored the lawful ownership of intellectual property with their 'Open Source' movement, which brought billions in economic losses."

As I half listened to Sascha's anti-programmer tirade, I was thinking about something else.

The genetic engineering that had led to distilled crops used programming techniques developed during the golden age of the Internet. We isolate every gene that expresses specific traits and use object-oriented programming methods to manipulate these strands of DNA as black boxes. When we get the output we're looking for, we capture it in genetic algorithms. The number of algorithms is sufficiently large that no one engineer can master them all.

My crop style sheets are based on methods originally developed to specify the look of websites. I don't need to know everything about the genome itself. I just apply the extracted code for physical features to design the look of the plant.

I wondered what these young programmers were thinking when they first connected computers on a global scale, opening one door after another to the unknown. When he designed his operating system, the aging developer Sascha interviewed knew very well that his 32-bit timestamp would be obsolete in a few decades. He knew the risk, but he had other issues to juggle. The conflicts with human rights, privacy, the economy, national security—each new idea opened another door, a door they couldn't close. But opening doors was always more important than the possible consequences.

"I'm sure you all remember what happened in 2017. The computer network known as the Internet collapsed because of built-in flaws, and the rest of us were locked out. This was a warning."

Sascha peered intently into the camera and clasped her hands. Her tirade was about to peak. With apologies to the cast member who put me onto this, I had to say, it was all pretty trite.

"We must be vigilant about the relentless advance of science and technology. There's no guarantee that programmers share the same dreams as the rest of us. What damage will their latest blunder bring? We'll have our answer in six months. The apocalypse is coming."

"Sorry to keep you waiting, Mamoru. Now what is that, a printed magazine? How retro. What are you reading?"

As I lifted the page to pause the video, Kurokawa was leaning over my shoulder, still dressed exactly as he had been this morning. It was four o'clock. He was right on time.

"Some kind of journal called *Times of the World*. It's pretty awful."

I opened the page again and put the "magazine" on the table. Sascha had already launched into her next piece.

"Synthetic rice is close to certification for worldwide use. But how long will these artificial organisms remain under human control? Is the 'distilled' development process really safe? We bring you the frightening truth."

Now she was dumping on distilled crops.

"What a bi—"

I closed the magazine. I felt like the old guy in the hospital, but I caught myself. Maybe not appropriate for the café.

"You mean, what a bitch? I agree."

Kurokawa smoothly finished my sentence for me. He signaled one of the cast members and ordered a cappuccino.

*　　*　　*

"I like this café."

The sun was lower. The shadows of buildings were falling across the avenue outside. Kurokawa blew on the foamed milk in his big mug of coffee. The steam rose and fogged his glasses. It was hot as hell. Kurokawa was probably in a nice air-conditioned room somewhere, but at least he could have ordered something cold for my sake.

"The stages you pick for our meetings are always pleasant and peaceful. I liked the room this morning, but this café is very tranquil. Sorry, my glasses..."

Kurokawa took his glasses off and wiped them with a handkerchief from his pocket. I thought the fogged lens effect was another Zucca touch, but apparently he was actually drinking something hot from a mug the same size as those used by the café.

"Are you home right now?" I asked.

"Home office." Kurokawa put his glasses back on. Now I noticed that his hair, always as carefully arranged as a doll's, was slightly out of place here and there.

"Did you even get any sleep?"

The contact from Mother Mekong couldn't have come in later

than ten last night. Kurokawa was conferencing with L&B at four-thirty a.m. Then he conferenced with me, and this meeting was scheduled through half past four. Which meant he hadn't slept. No wonder he looked tired.

"I'll get some sleep after we're done. I've got another meeting tomorrow morning at four. If I don't sleep, I won't be in any shape to talk."

He put his hand to the back of his neck and shook his head from side to side. A waitress with a tray of empty cups and glasses came over quickly, smiled as she took his mug, and walked away. He returned her bow casually.

Zucca offers full service combined with total augmented reality, but people's need for human contact is another reason it's popular. I started coming here after work with friends from my polytechnic, but the chance to communicate with some pretty nice-looking people adds a bit of color to the drabness of everyday life.

"Sorry to take your time, but before we get started I need you to get me up to speed for tomorrow. Enrico is going to be there, and if that weren't enough, the VP is sitting in. We're going to talk about the SR06 package you delivered."

"You mean Barnhard?"

I had a sinking feeling. There was no way I could isolate the intruder's DNA before tomorrow. Kurokawa would catch the heat instead of me, and he'd be hung out to dry, if not by the industry then at least by L&B.

"Yes, the one and only. It's not that he doesn't trust Enrico, but it was Lintz who managed to grow Mother Mekong into a five-star project. It's getting lots of attention from all over the world. He's worried, of course."

"Do you need me to back you up?"

"It's all right, Mamoru. Get a good night's sleep and keep working on your analysis. That's the most important thing right now." He sighed. "I'm sorry to say this, but Lintz is becoming a problem.

He really ought to leave everything to Enrico. He knows the project in much better detail. Recently Lintz has been all over every little thing..."

It was rare to see Kurokawa grope for words. His face darkened. He closed his eyes, knitted his eyebrows, and grasped his lower lip between thumb and forefinger. Suddenly he looked very young. His glasses and seemingly painted-on hair had always drawn most of my attention, but with his flawless skin and darting pupils, I realized he could easily pass for a teenager.

"I'm sure Enrico's livid, but Lintz has taken over the investigation. At least that's what seems to be going on. A few people have seen him chewing Enrico out over the last few hours."

I'd heard about Barnhard's political savvy. If he decided Enrico wasn't making the cut, he'd not only make sure he was out, he would make sure no one in the industry remembered him after he left. Good thing I was a freelancer. We were usually insulated from corporate politics.

"If Barnhard starts stirring things up, people on the front line will lose their motivation," said Kurokawa. "I want to prevent that by making sure he isn't worried about the technology. I hope you can help me."

"All right. What do you need to know?"

"Let's keep it short. If I can explain the principle behind color mapping, and why we weren't able to do L&B's logo in full color, I can get over tomorrow's hump. That's all. Go ahead."

"That's all" was a lot. Where to begin? For a moment I was stumped. I had hardly understood the principles myself when I first encountered them as a polytechnic student.

"Well, let's see. As the leaves and blossoms of distilled crops grow, color expression genes trigger development of receptors for chemical messengers—plant hormones. When the messengers are dispersed from towers in the right concentrations, color expression genes are activated and promote cell division..."

Kurokawa's wide-eyed expression said *I don't understand.* I didn't get it either at first, and I had a lot more background at the time.

"Let me draw you a picture. Sorry, could I have something to write with?"

The waitress returned with a tray full of writing widgets. The tray was just a prop, another nice touch from Zucca to make you feel like a customer in a "real" café. There was a full selection, everything from quills to drawing pens. Everything links with your workspace drawing app—they're all the same AR widget.

I chose four highlighting pens in different colors. Kurokawa leaned forward and picked up—I couldn't believe Zucca had something so primitive—a red lead pencil.

"Draw anywhere you like. Use the tablecloth or a napkin," said the waitress. "If you need 'paper' to take your work away with you, just let me know. Oh, one more thing"—she pointed to the space between me and Kurokawa—"If you write anything here, just remember you can't print it out. Have fun!"

"Thanks. I'll let you know when we're done."

She hoisted the tray onto her shoulder, winked, and walked away. I was impressed with the natural way she handled the tray, which was of course empty.

"Shall we begin? Let's say our crop responds to only two chemical messengers, orange and green. When both messengers arrive in the right concentration, the leaves of the plant change color. With SR06, the style sheet would look like this." I wrote a style sheet selector, *.leaf(orange==green),* in the air over the table. "Now let's see how the color is expressed when the messengers arrive."

I drew two small crosses on the tablecloth about eight inches apart. One green, one orange.

"These are the messenger towers. Mother Mekong has a few thousand, but two is enough for this example. The chemical messengers are dispersed from these towers."

I looked up to make sure he was with me and drew a circle

centered on each cross, about two inches in diameter in matching colors.

"Mamoru, what do they use for messengers?"

"Mostly leaf alcohols. Other compounds are used too, but most of the time it's something with the same chemical structure as a natural attractor."

"Is that to comply with the Full Organic protocol?"

"I don't know. But if they stay natural, they don't have to worry about nature addicts tramping around the site."

"Do these messengers use—what are they called—optical isomers?"

This was an old term. I wasn't sure how Kurokawa came up with it. He was talking about chiral molecules—molecules that are mirror images of each other but nonsuperposable, like left and right human hands. Some very weird effects can happen when big molecules, like sugars or proteins, are switched with their optical isomers.

"We usually just call them isomers. Where'd you get that anyway? Now that I think of it, L&B has a policy of not using them with their distilled crops. The competition stopped using them too after the fifth generation."

"Thanks. Just wondering."

"Let's keep going."

I put a fingertip to the orange circle. Handles popped up for resizing and dragging, mimicking my workspace environment. I pressed on the resizing handle and set the animation parameters. The circle started expanding.

"The tower releases a pulse of the messenger in aerosol form. It spreads out over the field." The little circle, oscillating gently as it expanded, did a good job of replicating the way the aerosol moved out from the tower.

"Now, if we send pulses from both towers simultaneously—" I touched the orange circle to stop the animation, copied its attributes, pasted them onto the green circle, and restarted the animation. "The orange and green circles expand, and eventually they have to overlap, right?"

Kurokawa watched intently. The red pencil he'd been toying with had migrated to a perch behind one ear. That was the first time I'd ever seen someone do that with an AR widget. Zucca...

"That's how you draw a straight line."

"Just a second, Mamoru. Where is the line drawn?"

"Between the towers. Let's slow down the animation and mark the intersections of the circles."

I adjusted the controller to slow down the animation. The two circles kept expanding and finally touched at the midpoint.

"The messenger pulses join midway between the towers. The plants in this location receive both messengers at the same time. That activates the genes for color expression."

I stopped the animation and drew a red X where the circles touched. Kurokawa nodded. Now he had the pencil wedged between his nose and upper lip.

I restarted the animation, and the circles began to overlap. "When the messengers are released simultaneously, color genes are activated in plants that are the same distance from both towers. As the crops change color, they draw a line right down the middle of the space."

I ran the animation four times, adding four more marks above and below the first mark where the edges of the overlapping circles touched. Now I had nine marks lined up vertically between the towers.

"Short pulses produce narrow lines. Longer pulses—several seconds, say—produce thicker lines. In this case, two circles have drawn a single line."

"I see. So it's as much about controlling the environment as controlling the genetics. But..."

Kurokawa was rolling the pencil between his palms, head cocked to one side. I knew how he felt. The first time I heard this explanation, I couldn't figure out how gene mappers made the jump from straight lines to the complicated figures being produced in the real world.

"Bear with me a bit more, Takashi. If we want a curved line, we just delay one of the messengers."

I reset the animation, this time with the green circle starting later. The orange circle moved outward to contact the green circle a bit closer to its tower. I used the blue marker to mark the contact points. Now the plot was a curve.

Kurokawa leaned forward and started helping me, adding marks to the plot here and there, more or less at random, but accurately. He was getting the hang of it.

"All right, I understand. With only two towers, you can draw straight lines of different widths or curved lines."

"Right. Say you add another orange tower to form an equilateral triangle. Release the messengers at the same time and you can draw right angles. Vary the timing and you can trace a variety of curved lines."

I got to work adding more towers and circles. Soon the table was covered with overlapping waves tracing complicated patterns. Both of us were busy adding marks to the intersection points when Kurokawa said, "So far so good. I think I grasp the principle. But can you really use this to draw a logo? The towers are fixed, and the terrain is uneven. I still don't see how you could draw complicated figures like logos and letters."

"What I do first is build a kernel of the design with a few towers. I guess it's easier if I show you."

I opened my workspace and pulled a preliminary sketch from the Mother Mekong project file. Zucca's stage rendered it as an old-style blueprint. The layout showed fifty or so towers surrounding the letters *L&B* depicted in spidery lines. The design was far from a logo—all I had at this point was the size of the design and the rendering topology. For L&B, *L* had no enclosed space, while *&* and *B* each had two enclosed spaces.

"The mapper has to specify the initial layout manually. First I create a sketch like this. Then I let the program figure out the timing needed to draw it with these towers."

Kurokawa wrote an equation in midair above the table—an exponential function that had an astronomical number of possible solutions.

"Mamoru, with only four releases from each tower, there are several billion possible combinations. But there are a lot more than four towers. Fifty trillion combinations? No, even more. How do you derive the sequence you need?"

"Gene expression programming. You break the random patterns into 'genes,' score them for fit, and make them compete. As stronger genes emerge, you add system noise and keep pitting them against each other."

"And what you're hoping is that the release sequence to draw your logo evolves out of the noise?"

"Right. It's not accidental. Even with only fifty towers, the search space that contains all the possible messenger release patterns is practically unlimited. The solution is to apply selection pressure to drive the process in the right direction. Different gene mappers have their own selection algorithms."

"Interesting. Manipulate the evolution process to speed up the search. Okay, I've got it." Kurokawa laid his pencil on the table and nodded. "Next question. Why couldn't you render the logo in full color?"

"They had to limit the number of towers to get Organic Covered Certification. The whole site only has about two thousand towers. With that, I have to render two logos and five cert marks. Even L&B's total computing capacity probably couldn't handle all the rendering calculations, and as the logos get more complicated, butterfly effects start becoming a problem."

"That makes sense. All right, I think we're done. You're an excellent teacher."

"You're a fast learner. I'm surprised. It took me a whole semester to wrap my head around it."

"I'm ready for tomorrow. I owe you one. Now let's deal with your request."

Kurokawa took an envelope from his briefcase. As he laid it on the table, I felt a slight pressure in my throat and ears. The environment turned grainy, like old 35mm film. That, and the AR feedback I was feeling, meant Kurokawa had switched to Private Mode. Zucca's rendering approach was beautiful. It was like being in a Technicolor movie.

The babble of voices around us faded to a soft, unintelligible drone. Private Mode in public spaces is usually dead quiet, but Zucca's production values include background noise that sounds like people speaking Japanese. The customers were replaced by avatars instead of gray silhouettes. Zucca had a reputation to maintain.

"Mamoru, I have the Mother Mekong cultivation logs and TerraVu photos you asked for. I also asked them to collect another sample. Thep wasn't very happy about that, but she said she'd send you DNA from a full-grown SR06 plant too, just in case."

"Thanks, Takashi."

Kurokawa tapped the envelope, and it morphed into a standard folder. The security scan ran, and SCAN COMPLETE popped up.

"They sent me the cultivation logs when they told us about the mutation. I should've given them to you then. Sorry about that. I thought it wasn't necessary, so I held on to them."

He was right. The records didn't contain much that was helpful. Everything jibed with the reference schedule. The intruder had been discovered about ten days earlier. Until then, the crop had been expressing the logos and cert marks exactly as specified.

"I was hoping this was Mother's mistake, but these logs look pretty professional. Lots of detail, well-organized."

"Thep is still young, but she used to do environmental agriculture consulting out of her own lab at Nankai Institute of Technology in Singapore. She knows her stuff. Mother Mekong couldn't have gotten all five certifications without her help."

She knew her stuff? Two hundred gigabytes of DNA data?

"So Thep is a woman," I said finally.

"All I needed from you was the style sheet. You didn't need to deal with her."

"Yeah, I was too busy coding the damn plants to glow at night." I held up one of the TerraVu satellite shots. The L&B logo stood out black against the faintly glowing fields.

Kurokawa laughed cynically. "No one wanted that except Barnhard."

"Sorry, I'm off topic. I'm grateful for the materials, but this won't tell me what caused the mutation. Without knowing the nature of the intruder, there's nothing we can do."

" 'Intruder'? I like it. Let's call it that until we know what we're dealing with. No one expects you to come up with the answer right away. There's something more important."

Kurokawa put the envelope under his arm and steepled his fingers. He peered at me intently.

"Mamoru, one thing we'll probably be discussing tomorrow is the investigation team. Sorry, but I need you to clear your schedule for the next month. Can you do that? I'm authorized to offer you at least twice your standard rate. You can push back the work on the SR06 sites in Hangzhou and Wakkanai till we're through."

"A month? You think we'll be finished that soon?"

"There's only a month until the first harvest takes place. If we don't pinpoint the cause and figure out a solution before then, Mother Mekong's five-star project will be a failure. SR06 will be discredited and discontinued. L&B itself could be threatened. Prototype SR06 sites are already being constructed in Vietnam, Laos, and Myanmar. If those go..."

"Barnhard's head will be on the block."

"This is no time for complacency. Did you forget that your name is in the credits?"

I felt suddenly dizzy. My avatar would not betray the effect this reminder had on me, but it knocked me back physically.

"I guess I'd be finished as far as this industry goes."

"Let's do everything we can to make sure that doesn't happen. My job is on the line too."

"Okay. Now I've got something for you. I need to salvage some data from the Internet. Know anyone you could recommend?"

I explained that the intruder was a legacy cultivar with no resistance to red rust blight. As a first step to figuring out how to deal with it, I needed to salvage information buried on the Internet and compare it with the Mother Mekong data.

"A salvager? I'm sorry, I can't help you there. All I can suggest is to go to CoWorkingNet and make a backchannel offer. Internet salvage is strictly for freelancers. I don't mind if you handle it yourself. You'll be dealing with public information, so just cut an OpenNDA with a reasonable use-by date."

A faint shadow fell across the grainy "movie" table. Someone said something I couldn't make out.

The waitress was peering over my right shoulder, pitcher in hand. In Private Mode, she would see an alias avatar instead of the "real" me. *More water?* was probably what she said. The alias waved her away with the practiced gesture of a stage actor. The shadow of its "hand" transited the table.

"If that's it, I'd better be going," said Kurokawa. "If I don't get some sleep, I might doze through the meeting tomorrow."

"Take it easy, Takashi. Get some rest."

He stood up, bowed, and disappeared. He must have logged out from within Private Mode. The film grain effect dissipated and the surrounding conversational buzz faded in gently. Kurokawa's alias was still sitting across from me. Zucca's selling point was its AR stage. It wouldn't do to have customers vanishing abruptly.

The alias gestured invitingly toward the cake cart, stood up, and melted into the foot traffic on the avenue. I had no reason to stay now that the meeting was over, but I decided to write my recruiting ad then and there.

One month. It wasn't much.

I guessed that Thep would collect the second sample carefully. Even if she hurried, I'd be waiting a few days. That would use up a week, more or less. If she was such a hotshot, I figured I should go ahead with the data I had to see what I could get.

First I had to find a salvager.

3   Internet Diver

My call tone beeped again. It was late afternoon of the following day. The sun was turning the rear wall of my "conference room" a warm gold. The next appointment was a salvager who went by the handle of Ya-God-Oh. His screen name was an attempt at Japanese, at least.

My call for salvagers generated a few dozen responses. I winnowed the field to five after checking track records and specialties. All the candidates used handles, unlike the mappers I was used to dealing with. I didn't care what they called themselves if they could do the job, but this morning's conversations with Bull's-eye and Jackpot 7 had pretty much wasted my time. I'd had more than enough hacker bullshit for one day.

Why did these guys spend so much time harping on the tools they used? The old Internet was fenced with cyber razor wire to keep it from contaminating TrueNet, but you didn't have to be a genius to get onto it. What was left of it depended on which country or even which city you were in, but from Tokyo you could still reach old servers through any Meshnet wireless node run by Anonymous.

Bull's-eye was completely full of himself. "Leave it to me, old buddy. Give me the search term and I'll track down whatever it is you want. What was it again? Right, DNA. Find it for sure. For sure, no problem. Give me the model number or some unique ID. There's a cache somewhere. I can get it for you. Just give me a week or so."

If all I needed was to input search terms to a zombie server and fetch something from a twenty-year-old cache, I didn't need a salvager. What I needed was a hell of a lot more complicated. I needed a specialist, not a script-kiddie.

Ya-God-Oh claimed to have some background in genetic engineering. I wasn't sure what to believe, but he had to be better than the two guys I interviewed that morning.

"I've been waiting for your call. I'll be recording, if you don't mind."

I was sitting across from a dog.

He had a red bandanna around his neck. Big and brown. Golden retriever? His front paws were on the table. He looked slowly around the room and smiled, if that was possible for a dog.

At first I thought, *This can't be Ya-God-Oh.* An assistant? Maybe an agent. Still, I was amazed by the resolution. I go out of my way to make my stage presentable, but this dog made it look like a cheap video game. The rendering was astonishing. At first I almost thought I might be looking at an actual canine in RealVu, but the long golden fur, with the tip of each hair glowing in the sunlight, was waving gently in the breeze from the air conditioner. If the fur was complying with my physics settings, this had to be an avatar. Maybe a commercial setup like Zucca's could hit this level of realism, but I didn't know it was possible to render so many frames per second in my environment. If he was sending his assistant with an avatar this good, I wondered if my system would choke when *he* showed up.

The dog noticed the flashing AGREE button on the table and tapped it with a paw. He looked up and smiled.

"Nice to meet you, Mamoru. My name is Yagodo. If you want to tape, go ahead. Sorry for the unorthodox avatar. I hope it won't be a problem."

With their mouths open, dogs tend to look like they're smiling anyway, but I had a feeling the man on the other side of the stage was actually grinning. So this was Yagodo's avatar, and that's how his name was pronounced. I'd heard about nonhuman avatars—animals, cartoon characters—used by some members of Anonymous and every one of the No ID fundamentalists who refuse to even connect to TrueNet.

I'd been hoping to avoid one of those types. It looked like I'd drawn another low card. This was worse than empty bragging about hacker tools. Yagodo was spoofing me—in a job interview no less. He had to be fake.

My avatar concealed my sigh of disappointment. Instead it motioned Yagodo to continue. Sometimes Behavior Correction does the opposite of what you want. Functionality comes with a price.

"I guess you've never chatted with a dog before."

I froze. There was something wrong with my commstat bar. No information on where Yagodo was, which provider he was using, his nationality, nothing. Jackpot 7 used multiple cutouts to screen his identity, but on TrueNet you know your caller's location, always.

Now the bar was empty except for YAGODO, the elapsed time in minutes and seconds, and the charges, which were adding up way too slowly, it seemed to me. Maybe he *was* using RealVu, which costs almost nothing to deliver to an AR stage. Or was his avatar so cutting-edge that it was hogging system resources and slowing everything down? It was spooky.

"I'm sorry if I've unsettled you, Mamoru. Would I be right if I guessed you've never dealt with a salvager?"

The voice was fiftyish and seemed to be native Japanese. It had a professional tone that didn't fit the nonhuman avatar approach.

"Yes, first time. I never needed to, until now."

"First time. I see. Well then, welcome to the lost world of the Internet. TrueNet has its points, but I've been poking around the ruins of the Internet too long to leave it behind. Almost thirty years, in fact."

"Not so fast. I haven't made my mind up yet. As the ad said, I'm looking for legacy crop plant data. Let me give you some details and you decide if you're up to the task. How you respond will affect my decision. Are you sure you want to do this interview as a dog?"

"I know it complicates things, but I have my reasons. I just finished a job, and my new assistant told me there was an interesting project out there. I haven't done any DNA salvaging for a while. Crops, is it?"

I gave him the basic details: I was looking for data on an unidentified contaminant infesting a field of distilled crops, and the bizarrely large DNA sample in my hands contained, among other things, a complete *Oryza* genome. I was careful not to mention Mother Mekong, L&B, or SR06. Even if I had, my avatar's NDA filter would probably have kept Yagodo from hearing.

"I need to know what this intruder is. Almost all the data on legacy cultivars with susceptibility to red rust blight is somewhere on the Internet. For a start, I need you to find a DNA match with the intruder, and tell me the cultivar and where it was grown. Information on efficient ways to eradicate it would be a plus. Too tough? Maybe it's over your head."

While he was listening, the dog kept tapping his front paws rhythmically on the desk. I could hear his tail as it kept hitting the back of the chair. His face was mostly unreadable, but he didn't seem upset by my skeptical attitude.

"Rice...hmm..."

The dog lifted his nose and puckered his lips—at least it looked like puckering. His paws were side by side on the table. Now he looked like a philosopher-dog. Yagodo probably had his arms folded.

"Rice, now there's a hard one. With wheat, you could just pull the genome transcript and references from Cambridge Open Resources. Wheat wasn't hit by a disease like red rust that made cultivar information irrelevant, so everything on the Internet is on TrueNet too, including DNA information for all the cultivars. It would be easy to narrow down the field by calibrating the genetic distance between what's online and your intruder. For soy, with all the GMO variants, you could get modification location and sequencing data by accessing patents and academic papers. Then you'd compare them with the standard genome. You wouldn't have to go Internet diving at all."

This was not the bullshit answer I'd been expecting. No one without specialist knowledge could have tossed that off without prepping first. It also hit me that if Yagodo was as old as he sounded, he might have a better grip on the state of things around the time of the Lockout than even Kurokawa and I did. He also handled the terminology correctly from the point of view of managing a data search. Progress in synthetic biology had changed the meaning of "GMO" since the period Yagodo was describing, but he used the term correctly, the way it was used at the time. This sort of contextual awareness would be critical for the salvaging work I had in mind.

"Rice genome." Yagodo's avatar tapped his nails rhythmically on the table. He was probably using a keyboard. "Here's something. The *Oryza* genome was decoded in 2004. It was a big MAFF project."

A caption popped up below the dog's muzzle.

MAFF: MINISTRY OF AGRICULTURE,

FORESTRY AND FISHERIES

PRECURSOR TO MINISTRY OF

ENVIRONMENTAL PRODUCTION

Another extinct period term used naturally. This was no run-of-the-mill salvager. I thought Yagodo might turn out to be a real "jackpot."

"But I don't think this will help much," he continued. "There are too many varieties. It would take a full day just to search for thirty or forty matches."

"Hold on. All I need is a match to *Oryza sativa japonica*."

"You don't get it, do you? Well, I guess it's no surprise. You're young."

The dog gave me a sidelong look and batted his eyelashes. Yagodo was probably grinning at my lack of background, but for some reason it didn't bother me at all.

"You would have to search through rice cultivars on the books of agricultural research stations, farmer's coops, organizations like that. We're talking several thousand."

"Were there really that many? But maybe that's good. There should be collateral data from the allergen and toxic isomer reports."

The dog shook his head. The beads on his bandanna tinkled.

"We're talking twenty years ago, Mamoru. Registered cultivars were tested carefully, but farmers all over Japan were doing their own cross-breeding, cultivating mutated versions, you name it. And the kind of really detailed testing you're thinking about—testing that covers the whole genome—wasn't required until distilled crops came along."

"So they weren't monitoring for mutations?"

"Probably they were. On a sample basis, sure. But the approach was totally different from the designed—whoops, I guess it's still 'distilled' in Japanese—the distilled crops you're used to dealing with. Check digits to kill off mutated seedlings? Full scratch design, to define nutritional yield to the microgram? Not with legacy crops."

So Yagodo not only had a handle on genetic engineering in the old GMO era, but he checked out with today's tools. Up to the fourth generation of distilled crops, genetic engineers used natural plant DNA as a scaffold to hang new characteristics on. Full scratch design—synthetic biology—only kicked in with the fifth generation. Yagodo knew this, otherwise he couldn't have corrected his own slip. I still didn't know how he stacked up as a salvager, but in terms of genetic engineering and crop science, it didn't look like I'd have to teach him much.

"I just picked up something interesting from the Internet. Take a look."

The dog pushed a document across the table. It was something I hadn't seen in a long time—an electronic document formatted for hard copy output, with page numbers at the bottom. A "PDF" file.

"That's a summary of agricultural testing standards, 2012, salvaged from MAFF's old website."

"What, you mean now? Mr. Yagodo, you did what?"

I was so astonished I lost control of my tongue. My avatar repaired my broken sentence, but it probably couldn't hide my startled surprise.

"Salvaged it. You can access the current version on TrueNet, of course."

I flicked through the numbered pages. They looked like scans of an internal ministry document.

"Since 2022, all go.jp documents have been digitally watermarked to prevent tampering. You don't see the watermark, do you?"

"You're right, it's missing." If Yagodo had somehow altered the document to conceal the signature, there would have been a security warning. This was no contemporary document. Maybe he counterfeited it somehow, while we were talking?

"Very good, Mamoru. Never trust anyone." My Behavior Correction setting wasn't high enough to conceal my look of doubt. "But in this case, you can. I'll even tell you where to get your own copy. Don't worry, no charge for this one."

The dog pushed a new file across the table. Under the "Web-Archiver Pro" banner was a screenshot from what looked like an old web page. Parts of the image were blank and the resolution was grainy. On the timeline indicator "2012" was flashing. It looked genuine.

No one would have the skill to fabricate something this suited to the context while we were sitting there. It had only taken Yagodo seconds to pull it off the old World Wide Web.

"What do you think? A simple example of salvaging. I don't usually recommend trusting a dog, but this is just a taste of what I can do."

"I'm blown away. I looked into what salvaging involves before I posted that ad. I interviewed some salvagers too, and they told me what you just did would take days, maybe a week. But you did it while we were sitting here talking. I'm impressed, to say the least."

"I'm glad to hear that, but it wasn't that difficult, you know. Public documents aren't hard to salvage." The dog raised a paw and laid it over his eyes, a pose like one of those cat toys in Chinatown. Yagodo was probably scratching the back of his head in embarrassment, but the dog's forelimbs weren't flexible enough for that.

"If the genome for your intruder isn't in some public corner of the Internet, finding it is going to take work. And I have a feeling you want me to do more than just find it."

"You're right. Identification is the first step. I need to know how it got there, figure out a way to get rid of it, and keep it from coming back. I'd like you to get started as soon as you can."

I'd already made my decision. I could always keep looking, but I had a feeling I wouldn't find anyone better. "If you went to work now, how much time do you think you'd need?"

"I'll be honest—I don't know. A standard search for public sources of matching *Oryza* DNA might take two, three days. If I don't come up with it that way, it means going to a deeper level."

"What deeper level?"

"Let's just say a deeper level. Listen, I hate to sound like I'm dictating terms, but I have a request."

The dog put his paws side by side and peered closely at me. I wanted to hear more about Yagodo's "deeper level," but I was more anxious about his request. We'd be operating on L&B's dime, but I didn't have a blank check. If he was expecting some outrageous fee, I'd have to pass.

"Could we do this project in person?"

"In person? You mean physically in person?"

This was a surprise. I'd worked with Kurokawa for several years and never actually met the man. Sure, I got together with friends, but AR had made physical presence almost completely unnecessary for work.

"Yes, in person. I'd like you to come to my office. I have a slight problem with using TrueNet to interface with the same address too often. I know this sounds odd. It's not the usual approach."

"Well, I have two hundred gigabytes of data to deal with. It would be easier if we were in one place."

"Two *hundred*?"

"Yep, and I'm not sure why, but that's what they sent me. It looks like the sample is a mix of DNA from several organisms." The dog's brown eyes opened wide in surprise. "I'm waiting for a redo on the sampling, but I don't want to sit around waiting. Bringing you what I have and dealing with it on your end would be faster and more efficient. The thing is, I'd need my agent to sign off. Can you wait?"

"Of course. No problem. If you come, I can be your consultant. My knowledge should be useful overall," he said. "I promise not to charge much, especially if you take the trouble to travel."

It was an attractive proposal. With Yagodo's skills, I felt sure we'd identify the intruder that much faster. On the other hand, I still didn't know much about him. If he was a member of Anonymous— they mostly hated TrueNet—I could still work with him. If he was a No ID fundamentalist, I wouldn't be able to cut a contract with him. It was L&B policy: no dealings with "antisocial" people or groups.

"Thanks for offering to consult. It's just that my client doesn't let me do business with people who follow a certain philosophy."

"Rest easy, Mamoru. I'm not Anonymous, certainly not No ID. You'll see when you get to Ho Chi Minh."

"Ho Chi Minh?"

"Vietnam. Oh, forgot my location data." The dog dipped his head and raised a paw in the universal gesture for "sorry." The avatar concealed Yagodo's expression, but I was starting to like the man on the other side of the stage.

By now I was really looking forward to meeting him. I knew I was dealing with a talented salvager, maybe astonishingly talented. I didn't even care whether he gave us advice. If all I had to do was fly to Vietnam, get what I was looking for, and be back within a week, I'd be satisfied.

I also liked the idea of seeing Ho Chi Minh City. Meeting in augmented reality is enough for just about any type of work-related communication. Opportunities to get out of Japan and get paid for it are almost nonexistent.

VIETNAM/HO CHI MINH appeared in the commstat bar. I couldn't understand how this was possible.

"Doesn't TrueNet display location data automatically?"

"Sorry, I didn't know it was required for your stage. I'll input it next time."

Input it. If Yagodo had access to system-level resources, he could input anything he wanted. If so, he was off the charts in terms of network expertise, on top of his professional-level genetic engineering background and virtuoso salvaging skills. The cliché "hacker" was crossing my mind when his avatar suddenly started breaking up.

I was looking at compression artifacts. His right leg jumped from one point to another and back again, as if the image were running backward. The next instant, I heard my avatar speaking, though I hadn't said anything.

"My contact will probably come along."

"Will you be bringing anyone with you?"

Yagodo's voice arrived after my avatar's response. I almost responded, then I remembered: my avatar had already spoken...?

"Thank you." My avatar again. Yagodo's video feed kept blurring and jerking. The hair on the dog's head rose, then lay abruptly flat again. He looked at me, then the image jumped and he was looking off into space. What was going on?

"I'll send you an estimate for my services right away."

I opened my mouth to say "Thank you," but my avatar was already answering. It was as if time were running backward.

Yagodo says he'll send an estimate, and I thank him. He asks about the number of hotel guests, and I answer. That was the only correct sequence for the exchange.

"I'm not in a hurry, but you must be. I'll start getting things ready. That way you can be here anytime starting tomorrow."

The dog began to lower his right paw, then looked left and right as if noticing something. "Damn, I think we're out of sync."

"My avatar is responding on its own. What's going on?"

The dog popped back into focus. Now my avatar spoke when I did.

"Too many censor spiders on that circuit, so I switched us through Taiwan. This circuit has a lot less latency. I think it confused your delay sensor."

He switched the circuit? How did he do that?

"Are you all right, Mamoru? No dizziness or headache?"

"No, I'm fine."

"Then there's no need to worry. There was around a second of latency before I made the switch. Your avatar was timing your responses. The new circuit has almost zero latency, which put your avatar out of sync for a few seconds. You were coming through normally on this end."

So it was the delay sensor. I was unconsciously used to communicating with the delay; my awareness of what I was hearing was fouled up by the change in latency. At least I guessed that was what happened. I knew the stage corrected for delays to make the conversation sound as if it were unfolding in real time, but that also meant you might remember something out of order from the way it happened. It was hard to believe, but what remained in memory was a conversation that took place in reverse order.

I was starting to wonder about my dependence on an avatar. Was this why Kurokawa insisted on using RealVu? Maybe I needed to dial back my behavior settings and work on my communication skills a bit.

"Yes, I think I'll be coming with my agent."

"Sorry to keep asking favors, but would you mind if I text you the details and my budget? I'm enjoying our talk, but I've been on too long."

"No problem. I'm pretty sure we'll be asking you to handle the job. I'll get back to you as soon as I can about the trip schedule."

The dog put four legs on the chair and jumped to the floor. "That's right, I forgot." He wagged his tail.

"Listen, Mamoru. The DNA, the data they sent you for the intruder. That two hundred gigabytes—was it a single data set?"

"Yes. It looks like the samples were contaminated with insect DNA and DNA from the distilled crop plants."

"Insects? How long did it take them to extract the DNA after gathering the samples?"

"Less than half a day."

"Then the samples weren't contaminated. That's a single continuous genome from a single organism."

"But it's two hundred gigabytes. An organism with a hundred times more DNA than humans—"

"Is impossible? We'll think about that when you get to Ho Chi Minh City."

The dog winked and bounded off.

*　　*　　*

I closed the stage and opened my workspace. The message from Yagodo was already in my inbox. His fee was eight thousand "Common World Dollars"—eight grand was the target I listed in my recruiting ad—and another two thousand for consulting. It was just like a salvager to send me a quote in an imaginary currency, even though my target was US dollars. Anyway, I guessed L&B would agree to the fee.

What surprised me was Yagodo's resume. It was complete, straightforward, and digitally signed. Isamu Yagodo, resident of Vietnam. The contact number and account he used for the meeting matched the numbers in the status bar. He might be a member of Anonymous, but he was no fundamentalist. Still, his knowledge of network architecture and ability to manipulate the digital domain meant that I couldn't trust him to be exactly what he seemed.

I played back the part of our meeting where the conversation had seemed to flow backward, but there were no compression artifacts and nothing odd about the sequence. I was already having trouble remembering what I'd experienced.

"Add comment to archive: avatar delay sensor malfunction."

I decided not to just make a note of it. Part of my problem was that I was relying too much on my avatar.

"Disable avatar Behavior Manager and set Behavior Correction to Weak."

Mamoru, if you lower Behavior Correction to Weak, your mumbling and incessant eye blinking will not be filtered. You want to look your best in meetings, don't you?

"I don't care; lower it."

Yagodo's avatar made it hard to judge, but I suspected he wasn't using Behavior Correction. I didn't feel like going to the same lengths as Kurokawa, but I thought I'd better learn to show a little more of myself to the world.

"Message to Kurokawa. Attach Yagodo's text file and an edited summary of the video."

If I could get Yagodo on our team, it would be only a matter of time before we identified the intruder. Running across someone so capable so early in the investigation felt like a good omen.

Then there was the chance to actually travel—what did they used to say, "take a business trip"? To physically go to a foreign country to complete a task, in an era when there was hardly anything that couldn't be handled over TrueNet. I was looking forward to it.

Kurokawa got back to me in record time.

OKAY TO USE YAGODO AND TRAVEL TO VIETNAM. TAKASHI

There was an attachment. It was an air ticket to Ho Chi Minh City. The challenge ahead was going to be tough, but maybe Kurokawa was as eager as I was to get out for a change.

I checked the departure date. My eyes widened.

The flight left the next morning.

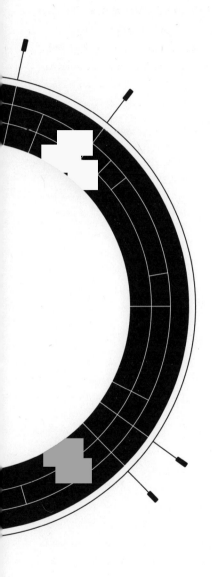

PART 2

HO CHI MINH CITY

4   Miss Nguyen

I noticed the runway as I descended from the Boeing at Tan Son Nhat International. The apron was marked with green and white lines that looked like fresh paint. To my still-sleepy eyes—I was out from the takeoff roll until just before landing—they looked almost too fresh.

These pristine markings on the flight apron were another achievement of genetic engineering: sustainable cement excreted by designed coral. They were unmarked even after being scuffed all day by shoes and vehicle tires. Mother Mekong used the same technology to get their Active Ground Cover certification. The terrestrial coral digested air pollutants and waste stuck to the concrete, keeping the apron and its markings spotless.

I looked more closely at the unnaturally vivid markings and remembered the propaganda images I'd seen of small animals being "eaten" by "carnivorous" pavement. Nature addicts hated this kind of engineering.

The sharply defined lettering and details expressed by the coral looked classier than the huge logos I mapped onto grass species. I'd heard that the coral could do a complete redraw overnight. The color-expression technology was probably not all that different from the techniques I used for logos, but it was a different specialty, and I couldn't quite picture how the mapping was done. Watching the coral as it redrew might give me ideas, but I didn't have many chances to visit an airport in the middle of the night.

I had arrived at Narita International at five a.m. to pick up everything I thought I might need for a trip to Vietnam. I couldn't believe that the "business trip" I lucked into would mean a six a.m. check-in. All I'd had time to do the night before was format the data for analysis and pack the gear I needed to run Gene Analytics. I understood why Kurokawa was in a hurry, but sparing a day for prep—a day, at least—would've been great. I was worried I'd get to Vietnam and discover I'd left something critical behind.

I was mentally checklisting my suitcase as I turned into the corridor that led to passport control. A man in a neatly tailored suit was ahead of me, pushing a huge four-wheeled suitcase. There was no mistaking the clothes and the neatly parted hair.

"Takashi!"

Kurokawa swung the bag around skillfully so he could look at me and keep it moving. I felt suddenly dizzy. There seemed to be something wrong with my sense of perspective.

The round, smooth face, the doll-like hair, and the dark irises peering steadily from behind black-framed glasses were a mirror image of the Kurokawa I knew from years of augmented reality meetings. The deft way he handled his luggage was familiar too. But his body was completely different.

"Nice to see you in the flesh, Mamoru."

The voice and steady gaze were coming from somewhere below the level of my breastbone. The man was tiny: four foot six, seven at the most. His body had the proportions of a full-grown adult, with perfectly formed feet and hands. He reminded me of those artifacts you see on low-quality stages where the scaling is screwed up.

"I'll be joining you on this trip to Ho Chi Minh City. Thanks for having me along."

Kurokawa placed his arms at his sides and executed a picture-perfect bow. He looked like a salaryman in an old movie. Actors don't know how to bow like that anymore. With hardly any chances to meet face to face in work settings, I wondered where he'd learned to bow so smoothly.

"The pleasure is mine." Caught up in the moment, I did my

version of a bow. Naturally my shoulder strap slipped off, almost dumping a load of delicate gear on the floor. I made a grab for the strap and hoisted it back on my shoulder. My bow left me looking down on Kurokawa from directly above, which felt even more unsettling.

Maybe it would be better to shake? By the time my hand was extended, Kurokawa was holding out a small paper rectangle with both hands. It was printed with his name, contact number, and network account. I turned the rectangle over. The other side displayed the same information in English.

"Takashi, what is this?"

"It's called a business card. Please keep it on file."

Since we weren't in AR, I didn't have AutoGlossary to help me out, but then I remembered. Business cards were a kind of physical media used to exchange personal data. I'd only seen them in movies.

"Interesting." While I was wondering what the polite thing would be to do with it, someone behind me yelled in English.

"Hey, you!"

I spun around and saw a cart stopped in the corridor, piled high with luggage. The suitcases were plastered all over with red FRAGILE stickers. A skinheaded woman stuck her head around the luggage mountain and glared at me.

"Out of the way. Your ass is blocking the corridor." Yet more English.

I wasn't exactly in her way, but it must've been hard for her to see. I gave her some space. As she pushed past us, she stared at Kurokawa from behind dark sunglasses.

"Sorry, kid. Didn't see you."

I was still processing this statement in English as she walked away. Then she laughed derisively, and the nickel dropped.

"You—!"

"Mamoru!"

Kurokawa was on tiptoe with his hands raised to block my line of sight. The woman turned, glared again, and flipped me off before striding away.

"I appreciate your support, but I'm used to this kind of thing. You don't need to feel bad about it."

"Okay, but..."

"At least I don't look my age." He smiled and looked down at his knit tie, carefully tucking it into place behind his jacket button. He took his time with it. Maybe this was how he absorbed the pain. Even if he was used to being singled out, it still had to hurt.

"Aren't you going to be hot? The tie, I mean."

"Not at all. I'm dressed for the heat."

With a smooth motion, he undid the button and opened his jacket. The light behind him showed through the single unlined layer of cloth.

"But didn't you hear the announcement? It's thirty-five degrees outside."

"Don't you know it's cooler to wear a coat when it's hot? I bet you're the one who sweats when we get out there." He glanced at my T-shirt and jeans.

*　　*　　*

I waited next to the baggage carousel while Kurokawa dealt with the telecom services agent. He was arranging a local flat-rate stage. He would need it. He had to be ready for L&B anytime day or night.

Kurokawa was on tiptoe, clutching the edge of the VIET ARV counter with one hand and gesturing animatedly with the other. He was a veteran international traveler, but from where I stood he looked like a child trying to keep his balance.

Why was he so small? He always had a healthy glow. Even after meetings that ran far past midnight, he was at work the next day with as much energy as anyone. He certainly wasn't weak. His precise movements and gestures in our meetings—I'd never seen him use an avatar—proved that his motor coordination was above average.

Maybe he'd had some major illness as a child? I was curious, but I couldn't see asking him straight out.

As I was mulling this over, Kurokawa came back with an actual paper receipt in his hand.

"Sorry to keep you waiting. I can't believe how cheap their stage is. Five dollars a day for unlimited use. Why don't you get one while you're here? I'll bill L&B for it."

"I'm covered. I have roaming."

"Isn't that expensive? By the day, it must be—"

"Twenty dollars if I max out. Remember, I'll be stuck in Yagodo's office almost the whole the time."

"Yes, I forgot."

Before I hit the sack the night before, Kurokawa had confirmed that Mother Mekong was already collecting the second round of samples from the intruder and SR06 at multiple locations across the site. He was expecting the new data today.

Yagodo wouldn't be on the case until tomorrow at the earliest, but once he started salvaging I'd have my hands full looking for matches. Since Yagodo was an excellent salvager, I might have to comb through dozens of genomes a day. It didn't look like I'd have much time to get out.

But I wasn't in Vietnam just to sift through suspect genomes. We still had no idea why the mutation—or intrusion—happened and only a month to figure out how to stop it from happening again. If Yagodo's advice didn't turn out to be helpful, I'd have to head back to Tokyo as soon as the salvaging was done.

"I guess all we have today is our meet and greet with Yagodo?"

"Yes, and I'm looking forward to it. I watched that video closely. Yagodo is a real find. Even L&B doesn't have many people with that much talent."

"Yeah. That dog avatar took me by surprise though. Hey, it's about time."

My suitcase was finally coming along the carousel.

*   *   *

"This person who's meeting us. How do you pronounce that?"

Yagodo had texted that a "Miss Nguyen" would be waiting at the airport. The gender was clear, but the name was a mystery. How did you say it?

"It must be something like 'Gwen,'" said Kurokawa over his shoulder. I was pushing a cart loaded with our luggage while Kurokawa walked ahead. We emerged from the baggage claim area into the lobby and a sea of faces, all yelling at once.

"Hey mister! Over here!" "Taxi, very cheap!"

A waist-high fence ran the length of the lobby, separating us from the taxi and hotel touts, people holding boards with passenger names, and throngs of waiting people. The touts shouted in Japanese, probably because of Kurokawa's suit.

I stopped in my tracks, stunned by the noise. In a few seconds the T-shirt under my shoulder strap was damp. The low-ceilinged lobby must have had air conditioning, but it felt five degrees hotter than back by the carousel. The aroma of chicken broth and cilantro filled my nostrils, reminding me that I'd missed lunch on the plane.

The crowd behind the railings seemed incredibly diverse. I kept noticing a man in a short-sleeved Mao jacket and black slacks with a bored smirk on his face. He was holding a sign at chest level that said "Gorph Robertson" in fancy calligraphy. I walked the length of the railing slowly, but no one was holding a board with our names on it.

I reached the far end of the lobby and headed back. The skinhead who had called Kurokawa "kid" was walking toward the central exit, followed by a straw-haired guy pushing her luggage cart. The cart was now piled even higher with luggage that she must have checked. The mound looked like it was about to topple. The pair passed through the exit and out of sight.

"They must be journalists. That's quite a load."

I heard Kurokawa, but my attention was nailed to the exit. A young woman with long black hair was standing just inside, next to the automatic door.

The lobby was crowded with people reuniting with loved ones, hugging and chatting happily. Others crisscrossed the lobby, turning their heads constantly, searching for someone. In the middle of all this the woman stood motionless, holding a board with something on it, staring intently at the baggage claim exit.

She was wearing a close-fitting white silk tunic with trailing flaps front and back over pants of the same material. The sunlight glowed through the loose cuffs of her sleeves and the fabric of her pants, gently suggesting the outlines of her body. Whenever the door slid open, a puff of air stirred the flaps of her tunic, which reached almost to the floor. Her long limbs and petite head were a contrast with the women around her. She stood with her weight on her right leg, upper body turned slightly like a model. The pose reminded me of an avatar.

"I think that's her." Kurokawa pointed. Now I saw that the board she was holding had our names in ink-brushed characters. It was upside down, which was why I hadn't noticed it before.

"Excuse me, are you Miss Nguyen?"

She turned and stared. After a beat, her face blossomed into a smile.

"Sure, I'm Nguyen. Assistant of Yagodo-san. You are Hayashida-san and Kurokawa-san, right? Welcome Ho Chi Minh City!" She slipped the board under her arm, held it against her slender torso, and stood at attention to welcome us, head slightly cocked. I liked the rhythm of her English and her ever-changing expression.

"Nice to meet you," I said in English. "Um, your board is upside down."

"Really? I apology to rotate your name. I'm not familiar for Japanese." She snatched the board from under her arm, hurriedly turned it the right way, and held it out to show us. "Is it okay? I'm so sorry."

Kurokawa smiled and shook his head. "Ok-kay, u-ee doan u-orry bauts. Dikkimura u-raitto itsu?"

"Yes, Yagodo-san write this."

I couldn't believe it. She understood him. Is this how he spoke English outside augmented reality? At least they were communicating. I just wasn't sure how.

The pleasing rhythm of Nguyen's English totally belied the impression of coldness she'd given when I first noticed her. If she was going to be around the office, this visit—business trip—was shaping up to be more fun than I'd expected.

Kurokawa nudged me in the hip.

"What?"

"Oh . . . nothing. I'll tell you later." He pointed to his glasses.

"We'll go to your hotel by taxi. Are those all your baggages? Okay, follow m—"

Nguyen spun around, spinning the flaps of her tunic in opposite directions, and thrust an index finger toward the automatic door, but it didn't open fast enough. She jammed her finger against the glass.

"Đau!

Charming, but a bit ditzy.

*   *   *

We hit the traffic jam as soon as we got onto the main artery heading downtown, after the soccer stadium. The four-lane road was a sea of immobilized electric vehicles with just enough space for electric motorbikes with two (or three) riders and throngs of jaywalkers to weave between. Children pinned flyers behind windshield wipers. Beggars followed, plucking the ads off and wiping down the windshields before motioning for tips. There were a lot of missing limbs and people on crutches. Nguyen dismissed them all with a wave from the front seat, but everyone was smiling, no one seemed stressed out. It made the whole scene easier to take.

Kurokawa and I sat in the back. I felt cramped, but Kurokawa had plenty of space to cross his legs. He leaned toward me and smiled. "Don't you envy me? I'm always in business class."

I got the joke, but it was hard to think of a response. I wondered how my avatar would've handled it in augmented reality.

Kurokawa chuckled at my dilemma and pressed his palms against his cheeks. "Don't feel uncomfortable. There's nothing I can do about it. In AR, I can put myself across as normal size, so it's not that inconvenient."

Maybe his tiny size was why he used RealVu. No, it would make even more sense for him to use an avatar. It's easier to relax around people when Behavior Correction has your back.

"While we're on this trip, I might have to ask you to help me reach things now and then. I hope you won't mind. Oh, and also—"

Kurokawa pointed a finger toward Nguyen's back and made the invitation gesture, lifting his glasses slightly off his nose.

I blinked twice to enter his stage. Kurokawa was suddenly "normal" size. Now the back seat really felt crowded. He put a finger to his lips to indicate Private Mode.

I accepted the invitation. Everything outside the back seat turned murky. Nguyen and the driver became gray avatars. This was about the best you could expect from a portable AR stage.

I felt the subtle pressure shift in my ears and throat signaling the switch to physio-feedback mode. Now our bodies would give no indication of our conversation and gestures to outsiders.

Kurokawa pointed to a sticker on the window. It said in Japanese, LET OUR BEAUTIFUL INTERPRETERS ASSIST YOU AT NO CHARGE!

"I was going to mention this at the airport, but Chinese characters and Japanese signage are all over the place here. Why didn't she know her sign was upside down? She must've known what she was doing."

"Maybe she just goofed. Yagodo used calligraphy. You saw her jam her finger. She's a bit of a space case."

"I don't know... Oh, I guess you're right. Sorry. Please forget it."

Kurokawa managed a bow in the cramped space and deactivated the stage. We had only been in Private Mode for a few moments, but I was hoping I would see slightly different scenery when we came back out. No luck. At this rate we wouldn't get to the hotel until after dark. It was getting ridiculous.

I leaned toward Nguyen. "How long to drive?"

"I guess forty-five minutes since now."

"Nosso long," said Kurokawa. "Itsu bam to bump. Iz itsu yujual?" He pointed at the traffic. I liked his attempt at "bumper to bumper."

"Not so usual. It's second of three heavy traffic time in a day. It will finish soon."

How did these two manage to communicate? Maybe they just had the timing down.

We chatted with Nguyen about her job, starting with her hiring a few months earlier and moving on to the purpose of our visit. I was hoping she'd have some information about what Yagodo had accomplished so far, but she had nothing to offer.

When we asked about Yagodo himself, she became very talkative. Yagodo was a "wizard" with technology. He knew just about everything, and when it came to computers he could do anything. He was based in Vietnam because of its easy access to the Internet, particularly to old Google cache servers.

When I ventured a bit of skepticism about the existence of such servers, Nguyen told me something "special" she'd heard from Yagodo. Just a rumor, of course, but just after the Lockout, a group of hackers had commandeered a container ship moored off Singapore that was serving as a backup server farm for Google. After a few years the ship showed up at Saigon Port. It sounded preposterous, but I had to admit that it was also a bit more plausible than some of the rumors I'd heard about the fate of the vast pools of data from the Internet era.

As we were chatting, the traffic finally started moving again. I spotted women walking along the road who were dressed in the same style as Nguyen. I asked her if it was some kind of fashion trend.

"No, we call it *ao dai,*" she said proudly. "National dress of Vietnam."

As we continued chatting about nothing in particular, the taxi emerged from a district of shops and food stands and arrived at a huge traffic circle.

"Here we arrived. Thanks for your patient for long driving. We hope you to prefer this hotel, Ambassador." She pointed to the colonial-style entrance of a hotel facing the circle.

*   *   *

I tossed my bags in the room, changed my T-shirt, and headed for the lobby. Kurokawa hadn't even gone up. He was sitting on a sofa next to the luggage trolley with his briefcase on his lap. Nguyen was across from him. The beautiful girl in her ao dai and the tiny salaryman were a conspicuous pair.

We followed her out the revolving door into a sunlit furnace heavy with the scent of coriander. The heat and glare made me dizzy even in the shade of the awning. The sun seemed to hang just a few yards above the sidewalk. The light bounced off the concrete and hurt my eyes. Activating my stage would have cut the glare, but it was a waste of roaming fees. My contact lenses didn't have UV filtering anyway. I needed sunglasses.

The traffic circle was ringed with scattered palms that gave scraps of shade to the food and drink stands. One stand had a shiny aluminum box filled with ice and canned soft drinks. Another mysterious stand seemed to be selling something in small, unmarked chrome cans. Another was piled with freshly baked baguettes and what looked like the makings for sandwiches. It was well past noon, but the benches were crowded with people lounging.

The coriander scent came from a noodle stall a few feet from the hotel entrance. Just seeing the clouds of steam rising from the huge pot made the sweat run down my back. A man on the bench slurping noodles stood up and said something to Nguyen. She waved a hand irritably, and the man sat down again. He lifted his chopsticks but didn't give up on us. "Taxi cheap for you. Two dollars."

"Không cần!" Nguyen snapped and looked quickly away, apparently embarrassed at the sharpness of her reply. Still looking cool and comfortable in her tunic, she pointed out the entrance to a street on the far side of the circle.

"So, let's walk."

She had to be kidding. In this heat? "Isn't it too far?"

"Only ten minutes!"

Kurokawa followed her without hesitation. Nguyen was a local, but Kurokawa's willingness to stroll around under these conditions in a long-sleeved shirt and blazer was baffling. He must have left his nervous system back at the hotel.

I trudged after them. After only a few steps the perspiration was pouring down my forehead. The shade from the sparse fringe of trees along the roundabout did nothing to cut the heat from the sidewalk.

We finally reached the opposite side and turned off onto a street guarded by the biggest palm tree so far. As we turned the corner, my chin dropped in astonishment.

The street was lined with tall concrete poles strung with a dozen or so bundled cables. The bundles must have been two feet in diameter, each with tens of thousands of cables a few millimeters thick. Here and there a bundle sagged into a huge loop under its own weight. A few were touching the ground.

The cables had been crudely bound together. Many were broken and protruding from the bundles like frayed hairs. The bundles had been patched all over with vinyl tape. They looked like cables in an old data communications center that I saw once in a video.

Kurokawa stopped and pointed at a frayed cable. "Mamoru, this is a telecommunications cable. Look, it's *metal*."

I could see copper color peeking from the broken cable ends. This was no optical fiber system. I'd never heard of using copper— which has only a fraction of the bandwidth of glass—to handle the huge amounts of data exchanged by TrueNet's interactive services.

"You found very funny thing. It's D...DSL cable. Vietnam is in developing term for next generation of network yet." Nguyen seemed slightly embarrassed at our interest, but what was DSL? Some kind of communications protocol? I'd have to ask Yagodo later.

We followed the cables along several blocks of shacks and make-shift housing before reaching a district with small souvenir shops, boutiques, and hair salons. There were more people here. Many of them were tourists.

At each corner, smaller bundles branched off and disappeared among the clusters of buildings. With so many shops in the same area, a wireless network should have been much more user-friendly. There had to be a reason people were clinging to such an obsolete technology.

Nguyen turned right into a narrow street where the shopping district petered out. The next intersection had a stand on each corner. We stopped in front of one with an electric kettle and more of those mysterious chrome cylinders on a canvas tablecloth. A sweet milky aroma, like melted butter, wafted from the stand. Kurokawa nudged me.

"That's Vietnamese coffee. Let's have some later."

"Sure, if there's time."

"We should make time to relax on this trip. We still don't know how long we'll be stuck here." He adjusted his tie, though it already looked adjusted.

Nguyen waved cheerily to the woman running the stand and went behind it to a stairway that ran up one side of the building. I looked up and saw a broad terrace on the second floor, ablaze with red and purple flowers.

5   Yagodo

When we reached the terrace, Nguyen was pushing open the big
sun-drenched door to the office. The door was a single heavy slab of
timber with a complicated grain that might well have been real wood.

"Welcome to Yagodo-san's office."

There was a whisper of air and the scent of fresh-cut blossoms.
The room with its cream stucco walls was pleasantly cool, though I
couldn't hear an air conditioner. The floor was dark and glossy. A pair
of sofas with hill tribe motifs faced each other across a table that was a
smaller version of the door. At the far end of the room were two plain
desks with chairs. The afternoon sun from the terrace lit the spacious,
airy office with a soft brightness.

A man was writing at one of the desks. He wore an open-neck
short-sleeve shirt the color of the walls. He stood and came toward
us, a large man with an intelligent face, strong nose, high forehead,
and long white hair combed straight back. His eyes were light brown.
I could see he was enjoying our fascination with his exotic office. He
spread his arms in welcome and smiled.

"Welcome to Ho Chi Minh City. I am Isamu Yagodo." No mistake, it was the voice of the dog.

"It's good to meet you, Isamu. Thanks for inviting us." I extended
my hand. His grip was surprisingly strong. The bunched sinews of his
forearm looked like the cables we'd seen outside.

"No, I should thank you. For taking the trouble to come here."

"I never dreamed we'd be conferencing one day and meeting the
next." The warmth from his hand penetrated my palm.

"And your companion...?"

"My name is Takashi Kurokawa. It gives me great pleasure to meet you." With the same sleight of hand he used at the airport, Kurokawa produced a business card. Yagodo received it with a practiced gesture, using both hands. To my astonishment, he had a card of his own ready.

"I haven't exchanged business cards with anyone for a long time," he said.

"Well, this is the first time I've ever gotten one in return, to tell the truth. Ah, this is handwritten."

I peered at the card in Kurokawa's hand. "Isamu Yagodo" was written with a flourish, followed by his telephone number. And that was all.

"I didn't know a salaryman would be visiting, otherwise I'd have had some printed up. Handmade will have to do this time. I'll give you my full resume once we're *there*." Yagodo lifted invisible glasses with a fingertip. "You'll want to know who you're dealing with. But first, I'm sure you're tired. With that flight from Narita you must've hit the afternoon traffic." He pointed to the sofas. "Have a seat. Let's enjoy some of that famous Vietnamese coffee." Then he switched to English. "Nguyen, order coffee for our guests and for yourself."

She called the order in Vietnamese to the coffee stand below. Yagodo settled onto the sofa with his back to the door. I sat facing him. Kurokawa half climbed onto the sofa next to me and fidgeted a bit, searching for the best position.

Yagodo waited until Kurokawa was comfortable. He leaned forward with elbows on his knees, supporting his chin with clasped hands.

"I saw the aerial shots of Mother Mekong. You've got a problem, don't you? You can see it in the night photos. Is that GFP you're using? It's the new SR06 color, I think."

How did he figure that out? I never mentioned Mother Mekong

or SR06 during our meeting. Even if I had, my avatar's NDA filter would have blocked it. Kurokawa looked slowly from Yagodo to me.

"Takashi, it wasn't me. I never mentioned the site."

"Yes, you're right. My apologies. I checked when I watched the video."

Yagodo nodded. "Sorry if I surprised you, but all I had to do was search for distilled genome credits with Mamoru's name and then sift through the latest TerraVu images until I found the site. The satellite passes overhead every four days. Your logos are smudged on the north edge of the site. So that's where the mutation is."

For a few seconds I was speechless. If an outsider like Yagodo could find out so much so quickly, it was only a matter of time before the whole industry knew what was going on.

"Mother Mekong is a five-star project, so there's a lot of information out there. It was easy. You must have some serious street cred to be on this project, Mamoru. SR06 is going to make history."

"You're overestimating me. All I did was the logos."

"Don't be modest. Your name has the place of honor as the style sheet designer. I'm surprised a big player like L&B would give an open credit to outside consultants. Usually the in-house designer and the PM hog all the credit."

He turned to Kurokawa.

"And you were the producer, right? There were a lot of project partners. The site had to be specially constructed to get those certifications. I bet you had your hands full."

"True. I handled all the third-party liaison work." Kurokawa bowed slightly with his legs crossed. He had finally found the right position on the sofa, though his feet weren't touching the floor. "I'll also be coordinating this investigation. For public consumption, L&B is responsible, but the actual work will be done by three people: me, Mamoru, and you as our advisor, starting today. Of course, L&B is collecting information too, but their hands are full just covering the legal and sales issues. They need to prepare their explanation of the situation for Mother Mekong and the Cambodian government. They've also started bringing the FAO up to speed."

Just the three of us? This was news to me. I wondered if we could do it alone, but if Yagodo could glean so much from published information, his skills would be a big asset.

"A tough challenge then. Ask me anything you want. You have my full support. If we don't succeed, global agriculture could be set back a generation."

"You're absolutely right. Thanks for coming on board."

"Set back a generation?" I looked from one to the other. "You mean back to natural plants?" Yagodo's comment had an ominous ring.

"That's how it looks to me. Isn't it true, Takashi?"

"Mamoru, I'm sorry. L&B's press releases for the investors use the same argument. I didn't want to put too much pressure on you, but that's what we're up against."

Kurokawa shook his head in resignation and launched into a summary of the mission and milestones of Mother Mekong's five-star project. SR06 was going to prove that distilled agriculture could actually help the environment and give farmers a sustainable business model. That made the certifications important. Outsourcing style sheet design to a freelancer and assigning responsibility to Thep at Mother Mekong to make the final site construction decisions was part of L&B's plan to assure the public and regulators that it was not going to monopolize control and keep all the profit.

This was not the first time I'd heard these talking points. They were included in the promotional material that came with the Mother Mekong contract for my files. Still, I had dismissed most of them as the kind of noble bullshit you find in every corporate mission statement.

"L&B is working on ISO certification for Mother Mekong–style sustainable farming. Many governments are still refusing to allow distilled farming within their borders, and ISO certification is the only way to break through that wall. Thailand and a dozen or so other countries have canceled bilateral agreements with the FDA to keep distilled crops out. L&B wants to get Thailand on board so it can break into the opposition camp.

"Then there's the Middle East. Islam forbids the consumption of 'unnatural' GM food. If we can get ISO certification, we have a chance to bring Mother Mekong's sustainable farming to the Middle East. I don't think the lobbying to get distilled crops certified as halal is going to make much headway soon, but Thailand is starting to come around."

"I see commercials all the time aimed at farmers here in Vietnam," said Yagodo. "'Isn't it time you considered Mother Mekong sustainable farming?' Not since yesterday though."

"Advertising is on hold until we find the source of the problem." Yagodo clasped his hands over the knee of his crossed leg. With his feet in the air, he didn't look stable, but his movements were natural and relaxed. "The campaign was going well, at least before yesterday. Lintz Barnhard is the main mover and shaker. He gives the project a face that governments can relate to, which has been useful. Barnhard is synonymous with distilled crops."

Yagodo sat back with a twinkle in his eye. "If he doesn't fix the problem quickly, that face will be a liability. He'll be synonymous with failure... Sorry, that was a bit harsh."

"I'm afraid you're right. I don't think there would be an immediate ban on distilled cultivation, but distribution could be affected. If distilled crops can't be exported, in the long run it's not much different from a ban."

Yagodo still had that twinkle in his eye. Kurokawa gave him a questioning look and continued.

"When this problem becomes public knowledge, will sanctions come down on SR06 only? Maybe they'll apply to all L&B products. Or maybe to all distilled plants. Or maybe even to all genetically modified foods. We don't know. The answer will depend on how the media react and how L&B responds."

Yagodo stroked his chin. "In other words, how Barnhard responds to media attacks?"

Kurokawa laughed cynically. "Lintz Barnhard doesn't take criticism very well."

"Takashi, are you saying that the future of distilled crops—our future—is riding on how Barnhard deals with the media?"

The image of Barnhard struggling to deal sensitively with journalists baying for his blood was amusing, but from the stories I'd heard and the way he was supposedly treating Enrico, he wouldn't be able to resist going ballistic, like the man in the hospital I'd seen the day before. The thought of losing my income because of someone else's lack of self-control was depressing.

"No, Mamoru. Basically it all depends on our investigation. If we can't pinpoint the cause so L&B can get something out to the media immediately, and if we don't find a way to fix the problem soon, then all these negative prospects could become real very quickly."

I realized that my mouth was completely parched and not just because of the sweating on the way here. Yagodo was about to add something when there was a knock on the door.

"Master, sau đây là cà phê."

Nguyen stood up from her desk and walked quickly to the door, tunic flapping. The door didn't seem to have a latch, but I heard a soft tone when she touched the handle.

"Cám ơn."

The woman from the coffee stand entered with a tray. The sweet aroma I noticed earlier filled the room. Nguyen pointed to the low table. The woman set the tray down and held out her mobile phone. Nguyen touched the screen of her own phone with an index finger before they touched phones. The woman's phone made a sound like a coin falling into a piggybank.

"I bet you've never seen HMC for making payments," said Yagodo, noticing our puzzled looks. He explained that Nguyen had transferred funds to the coffee stand from a prepaid account with her mobile carrier. Credit cards had never caught on in Vietnam. During the Great Recovery after the launch of TrueNet, prepaid accounts had become ubiquitous.

I knew that only the developed economies used postpayment systems, but seeing a prepaid deposit payment with my own eyes, fused with the aroma of sweet Vietnamese coffee, made it a vivid experience.

Kurokawa was fascinated. "Payment with HMC? I have a contract with a local carrier here. I'd like to try it. But doesn't it interfere with feedback? I have quite a few implants. As you can see, I need to compensate. Most environments weren't designed for me."

"I don't see why it would. I've got about twenty myself, but I've never had a problem."

"Twenty implants? Well, I'll give it a try. It looks useful."

"Oh, I nearly forgot. The office door is HMC too. I'll register you two so you can come and go. Is this your first encounter with Vietnamese iced coffee?" Yagodo pointed to the tray. "It's drip filtered."

Small chrome cylinders were perched on metal disks that covered the mouth of each cup. "After the water filters through the coffee, add some condensed milk and toss it in the glass with ice. If the filter gets clogged, wiggle the rod inside the filter."

As the coffee kept flowing down into the cups, the aroma became even stronger.

"I think we're ready. Drink up."

I took a straight sip of the freshly filtered coffee. The combination of strong bitterness and sweet aroma put me off. Two spoonfuls of the sweetened condensed milk made all the difference. Now the taste matched the full-bodied aroma.

Yagodo poured a three-second slug of milk into his cup and busily stirred the cream-colored mixture. That had to be too sweet. The man might know his stuff technically, but I wouldn't want to take his advice on taste.

"You should try our sandwiches too. It's too bad the wheat they use these days tastes like plastic."

Kurokawa had imitated Yagodo's coffee preparation to the letter and was now sipping from his glass. The taste didn't seem to bother him, but when he heard Yagodo's comment he put his glass down. I stopped drinking too. Yagodo had just insulted distilled wheat.

"You don't care for it?" said Kurokawa evenly.

"Well, if you've never had the real thing it's hard to judge, but it's not as good as it was. Food should have complex flavors. But they still bake bread the way the French have for centuries. It's better than in Paris, in fact. Ho Chi Minh City is like a time capsule."

If Yagodo thought coffee that was mostly condensed milk tasted good, I wasn't sure I could trust his judgment. Maybe he just didn't like the concept of distilled grains?

"Time capsule—that reminds me." Yagodo moved his lips wordlessly, placed the tips of his thumb and little finger on his temples, and lifted the usual invisible eyeglasses. He was inviting us to enter his AR stage. The lip movements must have been his activation gesture. He was already there waiting for us. I blinked twice to activate augmented reality.

"Whoa!"

Kurokawa—rendered full size—gaped with surprise. "Isamu, I'd love to know where I can get a stage like this. It's amazing." He extended his full-sized hands and slowly lowered them to the table. The complicated reflections in the polished grain of the table were completely free of artifacts. The stage was as real as the one at Café Zucca. No, it was better.

"Do you like it? That's great. This is my homebrew stage. It only needs to work in this room, so I focused on making it realistic. It wouldn't be fair to compare it to an off-the-shelf stage."

Yagodo seemed overly modest, but I had never heard of one person handling all aspects of stage development—camera positioning, image processing, and real-time feedback with results that were not just functional, but better than any commercial system. It didn't seem possible. His system was configured for one environment, but so was Café Zucca's. Even if it had started as a commercial platform, an AR producer would still have had to customize it.

"Please use it as much as you like. Takashi seems more comfortable, I see."

Kurokawa nodded enthusiastically. His hands were on the table and his feet were on the floor. His center of gravity was stable on the sofa.

"Thank you. The chance to work on a stage with this kind of real-time rendering is priceless. Pardon me while I fine-tune my size."

Yagodo motioned "be my guest" and turned toward the door.

"John! Paul! Let's see what you have for us."

The door opened silently, and two huge golden retrievers bounded into the room with matching red and blue bandannas around their necks. The dog with the red bandanna looked like the model for yesterday's avatar. It had a Frisbee in its mouth. The other dog had a tennis ball.

The dogs circled Yagodo's sofa from either side and deposited their "gifts" on the table before taking positions on either side of him.

"Good boys. John is, let's see, from a farm in northern Japan, and Paul was on an agricultural testing station near the Sea of Japan—both were important sites for riziculture during the Internet era. Hey, I've got guests, you guys. Try to behave." Both dogs now had their front legs in Yagodo's lap and were happily licking his face.

"Mamoru..." Kurokawa pointed to the table.

The Frisbee and tennis ball were gone. Instead there were two folders. Yagodo nodded.

The dogs were avatars.

They were indistinguishable from real dogs, and to judge from Yagodo's reaction, he could "feel" them licking him. But real dogs can't carry augmented reality widgets around in their mouths.

"Isamu, you're making fun of our guests."

Nguyen was staring crossly at Yagodo with her hands on her hips. She was wearing glasses. For the first time, she spoke in Japanese.

"Nguyen, I thought you couldn't speak Japanese?"

She smiled and drew her hair back over one ear with a fingertip. An earphone was connected by a lead to the frames of her glasses. The light reflected off the lenses as she moved her head, making her look a little surreal.

"Isamu's stage has a very nice translation engine," she said.

You can hardly find AR glasses in Japan these days. They don't have the processing power to render something like Yagodo's stage without a lot of implants, and I doubted that Nguyen had any. Yagodo must have customized her glasses. In augmented reality, the two of them would have no trouble communicating.

"John! Paul! Get back to work!" The dogs looked crestfallen but trotted over to the door. Paul touched the handle with his nose and they bounded outside.

Kurokawa and I stared at each other, blitzed with amazement. Yagodo was enjoying our surprise.

"The whole dog thing started as a joke, but the more I played with the concept, the more I was hooked. Sorry about the ruckus. Anyway, here's the data I salvaged yesterday."

Yagodo slid the files toward us. One was labeled 2014 JAPAN AGRICULTURAL COOPERATIVE, IWATE BRANCH OFFICE, INTERNAL PC. The other was titled 2013 HOKURIKU AGRICULTURAL RESEARCH INSTITUTE ARCHIVE.

"Isamu, before I accept this data, I have to know where you found it," said Kurokawa. I was thinking the same thing. "Was this actually on the Internet at some point?"

"Yes, just as the file names indicate." Yagodo pointed to the first folder. "That was salvaged from a PC in a JA office. And I picked up that"—he pointed to the second folder—"from an internal server at a research institute. I couldn't find enough data published on the Web, so I had to dive deeper."

Kurokawa leaned forward. "So this information was never disclosed on any website. It was on someone's personal computer. Please explain how you did this. Within the limits of professional secrecy, of course."

"I salvaged this from an Internet cache server connected to Ho Chi Minh's network."

"But, Isamu—" I was getting impatient. "Cache data was up on the Web at some point. You can't use the cloud as a gateway to pull down data sitting on a hard drive somewhere, even if the PC was connected to the Internet at some point."

Kurokawa was shaking his head too.

"Well, I guess you'll have to know," said Yagodo. "You know how the Lockout actually happened? The data recovery software that protected the cloud during routine server maintenance somehow decided it needed to take control of every PC and mobile device connected to the network and do a clean reinstall of its internal search engine." Yagodo took a sip of his coffee. "When it did that, *all* data on the drives it reached was uploaded to the cloud."

"No!" I couldn't help it. I was too shocked.

"Why so surprised? Backing up your data before you reinstall your OS is the most basic of basic rules."

Yagodo continued his incredible story. The data sucked up from millions of PCs and other devices was routed to a fleet of seaborne data recovery centers. The center for East Asia was anchored off Singapore. That ship ended up getting hijacked, and after going missing for several years it appeared suddenly in Saigon Harbor.

"Since it docked, I've been able to use our local network to access data that was never up on the Internet. Of course, not anyone can do this. I had to find a way in first. You'll want to confirm that the data is genuine, but the organizations I got it from are still around. Go ahead and contact them. They must have backups, probably on tape, or even hard copies."

Kurokawa stroked his chin thoughtfully. He was probably thinking about what to do if we ended up with a match to something that was someone else's intellectual property.

"Takashi, it'll be okay. Let's not waste more time. We should take a look at this. At least we have something to work with."

My words shook Kurokawa out of his meditation. "Yes, I guess you're right. Okay, we'll take the data. Thanks for your help, Isamu."

Kurokawa skillfully manipulated the file to create a copy and pushed it over to me.

"Better get to it, Mamoru. Start looking for our match."

"Will do." I opened the folders for a quick look at what I'd be dealing with. Each folder held around forty files. I never imagined I'd be able to access data off someone's personal computer harvested through a network in Vietnam.

Still, something bothered me. "Isamu, haven't you ever tried to find out where this treasure trove of data is, exactly?"

He laughed. "Waste of time. You saw the trunk lines on your way here from the hotel. Those cables are old and brittle. They break all the time. People reconnect and reroute them every day. There's no way I could trace the physical location of the servers."

"He's right, Mamoru." Nguyen shrugged. "Here in Ho Chi Minh City, if you have trouble with your connection, you just go outside and connect your cable to somebody else's."

"It's not a crime," said Yagodo. "They still pay the monthly fees. And frankly, I'm not sure I want to know where the servers are. I don't want to scare them off. If they pick up and move, we're both out of a job."

The cables were all over the city, branching out like capillaries from fraying arteries patched with tape. If we'd been dealing with Yagodo remotely instead of in person, I would've laughed in disbelief, but I'd seen the cables myself. Who could say what kind of data was sloshing through them?

Yagodo slapped his knee and brought me back to reality. "Mamoru, why don't you put your search off till tomorrow? You too, Takashi.

The four of us should go out and see a bit of Ho Chi Minh, have a proper meal. The food here is unbelievable."

I remembered how hungry I was, but I also remembered Yagodo's taste in coffee.

"Um, sure."

Wait—Kurokawa was drinking it the same way, without batting an eyelash. I wondered if I could trust their choice in restaurants. Then again, if the food turned out to be as sweet as the coffee, I could always get Nguyen to take me somewhere later.

Things were looking up after all.

6   Office

A faint tone sounded from the other side of the heavy door as I touched the brass handle. The HMC lock recognized me immediately.

My first full day on the job.

The door opened smoothly, and the scent of okra flowers that Nguyen had decorated the office with wafted from inside.

"Morning, Mamoru."

Yagodo's cheery voice manifested from the vicinity of his desk. I blinked twice before I even saw him and entered his stage. The functionality was just like my workspace in Workers Heights. He had thought of everything.

There was a cloud in the middle of the room.

It was so thick I could barely see the desks on the other side. The cloud revolved slowly, shot through with vivid streaks of purple lightning. Each streak seemed to leave behind a small, bright point of red. Yagodo was working on something, obviously. But what?

"Sorry, things are a little messy. I'll have this cleaned up in a minute."

I could see him waving through gaps in the cloud. He was wearing a Hawaiian shirt.

"Isamu, can't you do this in your own workspace? How can the rest of us get anything done? We're sorry, Mamoru." I could hear Nguyen from somewhere behind the cloud.

"What is this?"

"A molecular model." Yagodo walked right through it. The cloud didn't react, which meant he wasn't using physical tags.

"If we'll be working with a two-hundred-gig gXML file, we've got to speed up the matching process. I'm just playing around looking for shortcuts. Want to take a look before I shut this down? I might be onto something. Hey, where's Takashi?"

"L&B collared him while we were eating breakfast. Another emergency meeting."

"It's well after dinner in San Francisco. They're keeping him busy." Yagodo laughed as if he thought this was humorous.

I remembered Kurokawa's look when he got the call. He'd come back to our table from the buffet counter with twice as much food as me. When the call came, he knitted his eyebrows and sighed, "I don't believe it." He'd gone back to his room to take the call.

They wouldn't leave us alone. I wasn't surprised. Four days had passed since Mother Mekong reported the mutation, and L&B still had no information to help them break the news to the world.

I dropped my shoulder bag. "It's already evening in San Francisco. I doubt the call will last long. Takashi keeps his stage activated, so he'll find his way here."

Bolts of lightning kept flashing inside the cloud. Each flash left a purple streak about six inches long. Yagodo reached into the cloud, took a streak by both ends and held it up to the light.

"Brute-force solution to a sixteen-character hash in zero point two seconds. Not bad. I'd like to multiplex the cell connections and up the bandwidth to the limit of cell-liquid potential, but I'm still trying to find something in my communications interface library than can handle it."

I looked closer at the streak Yagodo was holding to the light. I could actually see a tiny results log: A>B:LOREN_IPSUM. "Isamu, what are you doing exactly?"

He lowered his gaze and looked at me intently. "I didn't mention this, did I? I took a stab at designing a bio-nanomachine. I've been working on it since last night. The idea is to do a brute force hash calculation."

"You're kidding. You built this?"

"It was easy. Calculating machines are assemblies of simple input/output circuits. They don't have to be electronic. Proteins can do the job. If you have a set of operating rules, the approach is more or less the same. This setup isn't super efficient, but if I can make it work, we won't have to grind all the way through each data set."

Yagodo pointed to the cloud, a huge calculating circuit of virtual protein molecules composed of virtual amino acids. As I saw more and more of his technical chops, I was starting to feel embarrassed calling myself a gene mapper. All I could do was edit genome style sheets.

"This is impressive, Isamu, but the samples weren't collected properly. Mother Mekong's samples were contaminated with material from insects and SR06. I mean, two hundred gigabytes..."

Yagodo cut me off with a raised finger. "Mamoru, I told you two days ago: you have to assume the data represents a single organism. Now, let's get to work— Sorry, let me shut down this model."

He spread his arms wide and swept them together. The cloud shrank to the size of a basketball. He suspended it deftly over the coffee table. "Mother Mekong uses a serial DNA sequencer, right?"

I nodded. It went without saying. The holy trinity of genetic engineering was a serial DNA sequencer to read the data, an embryo printer to output the data in cell format, and Gene Analytics to analyze the data and model it with CAD tools.

"What an invention," Yagodo said, marveling. "Just touch a bit of tissue to the sensor and nanomachines unravel the double helix of the chromosomes in the cell nucleus. The DNA readout comes from a single cell." He winked. "No contaminated samples."

"What?" Suddenly, I saw what he was getting at.

"Sure, maybe you could get a contaminated readout if you took cells from more than one organism and ground them until the nuclei were crushed and mixed, but you'd have to go to a lot of trouble."

He was right. I had let the sheer size of the sample confuse me. If

Mother was using a serial DNA sequencer—which only operates on single nuclei—then the data couldn't be contaminated.

"Well, what do you think we're dealing with? What kind of organism would produce such a large amount of data?"

"What do *you* think it is? Most of the sequences are probably junk. This molecular model is designed to save us time, but it will only handle a two-gig sample. With two hundred gigabytes, we could be dealing with any sort of organism."

"You think there's something significant about the size?"

"I don't think anything. I hope it's mostly junk DNA, that's all. Anyway, let's see if we can find a match to the legacy DNA you abstracted from the sample. We need to know what it is and where it was cultivated. Without that we can't move forward."

There was a knock, and Yagodo turned toward the door. It went transparent. We could see Kurokawa reaching for the handle. There must have been a camera outside.

"Morning, everyone. Sorry I'm late."

Kurokawa was carrying his briefcase. He was already normal size.

"How did it go? I bet they're pushing us to work faster."

Kurokawa dropped his bag on the sofa where he'd sat the day before. He had the same look on his face that I'd seen at breakfast.

"Not exactly. They gave me a video message from Barnhard. It's for the two of you, actually."

"What, me? I've never even met anyone from L&B."

"I tried to talk them out of it. We don't need this kind of pressure right now, but they insisted. In fact they made a big fuss about it. Sorry, but you need to watch this now."

"Let's use the translation engine and listen in Japanese," said Yagodo. "English has a tendency to draw blood in situations like this."

"Thank you. I should warn you—Barnhard made me promise to play this back at life size. Sorry if it makes you sweat a little."

I sat next to Yagodo. Across from us, Kurokawa took a video file from his bag and laid it on the table. He paused, then tapped playback. Instantly, the huge man with the spherical gut was standing next to him. He was closer to six-eight than six-five. I almost had to look up at the ceiling to see his face.

"—No, this kind of message only works in RealVu. That's why you're useless when the going gets tough. You and your pathetic avatar." Barnhard was speaking scornfully to someone off camera. They must've been in a hurry if they couldn't take the time to edit.

Barnhard adjusted his collar. "Sorry. I am Lintz Barnhard. As you know, I am vice president of L&B. I am also leading the team that is investigating the mutation at Mother Mekong's site in Cambodia."

What about Enrico? He was the project manager and the liaison with Mother Mekong. I knew Barnhard was meddling, but now it looked like Enrico was completely out.

"Unfortunately, as I'm sure you've heard from Takashi Kurokawa, my hands are full dealing with clients and the regulatory agencies. I'm not involved in the scientific side of the investigation. Regrettably, I will have to leave that entirely to the three of you."

I'd seen Barnhard many times, though not in the flesh, but he never looked anything other than bored or irritated. I couldn't remember ever seeing him the way he looked now—apologetic, almost pleading. The mutation at Mother Mekong was eating him up.

"Mr. Hayashida and . . . Mr. Yagodo, was it? I'm depending on you."

Barnhard's projection took a step forward. Now he was embedded in the coffee table with both hands out in a supplicating gesture, staring at an empty wall with an expression of such intense sincerity that I almost burst out laughing.

Yagodo started to move the table, but Kurokawa stopped him with a quiet "That won't be necessary." He didn't seem to be taking it too seriously either.

"Distilled crops are facing an existential crisis," intoned Barnhard. "I am a vice president of this company, but to be blunt, I don't care what happens to L&B. There are twelve billion mouths to feed on this planet, and we can't rely on natural plants if there is any hope of meeting their needs. If distilled crop acreage reverts to these outmoded sources of calories, we'll lose more than half the world's supply of wheat, rice, and soy. The topsoil is already close to exhausted as it is."

Barnhard wrung his hands mutely. For a few seconds, he seemed to have lost the capacity to speak.

"If that weren't bad enough, a world dependent on natural food means unrestricted genetic modification. No one knows where that might lead." He looked down, closed his eyes, and shook his head.

"I'm sorry...Mamoru. Isamu." He sighed and looked up. "As I told Takashi, I want you to go to Mother Mekong. Find out what's happening. Takashi's..." Barnhard hesitated. "He is...different, as you see. He needs your support."

His head dropped again, pleading to a blank wall. The look on his face was close to agony. He didn't seem to be faking it. By now he had advanced to the center of the table and seemed to be growing out of it. I suppressed another chuckle.

After an awkward few seconds, Barnhard seemed to pull himself together. He patted his lapels, straightened up, and gave a brisk nod toward the wall.

"I'm depending on you, Mamoru. And Isamu, I thank you for your help."

Yagodo looked at us, openly puzzled. "Maybe the translation engine is too good. We could listen to the English." He stroked his chin and gave Kurokawa a sidelong look. "Takashi, you're not an L&B employee, are you?"

"No, I'm freelance. True, most of my work is for L&B."

"When Barnhard was talking about you, he made it sound like you were a member of his family. Maybe it was the engine?"

Kurokawa nodded, but his expression was hard to read. He put the video file in his briefcase.

"That whole thing about going to Cambodia sounded odd, you know? Like he was asking Mamoru to ride shotgun for his son."

Yagodo's voice had a slightly sarcastic edge. Kurokawa stared at him intently. From my angle, his glasses partially hid his expression, but his jaw was set.

"Maybe it did sound that way. As you say, it must be the translation engine. The original English didn't come across that way."

"Sure. That must be it. It's not like you could be his son. I mean, look in the mirror. And he's twice your size."

"Isamu, stop it!" Nguyen was fuming. "Stop being so insulting. That man is not twice Mr. Kurokawa's size!" She looked at Takashi. "Mr. Kurokawa, I'm so sorry. He just says whatever comes into his head."

Kurokawa's expression had assumed its familiar gentleness. He shook his head and smiled.

"Twice as wide, three times as deep, and four times as heavy. Isamu is right. Don't worry. I'm not offended, really."

I was concerned about Barnhard's request. If we struck out for Cambodia just as our search was about to get on the rails, it was going to kill our efficiency. Mother Mekong was out in the sticks. It wasn't like we could catch a cab from Phnom Penh.

"Listen, Takashi. Can't Enrico cover this? I know L&B is short-handed, but Enrico's the project manager. He was on this from the beginning. He knows the site."

"Enrico?" Yagodo was up and halfway to his desk when he heard me. "The SR06 PM, right? Didn't he go walkabout a couple days ago?"

Kurokawa paused before answering. "Well, I guess you know just about everything. I only found out about it in the meeting this morning."

"His wife wrote on her wall that her husband hadn't come home from work. Anyway, you just got here, and now they're shipping you off to rural Cambodia. I feel sorry for both of you."

Yagodo was in his chair, swiveling back and forth. I got the feeling he thought of everything that was happening as a comedy of errors.

"I didn't think we'd have to inspect the site." Kurokawa looked crestfallen. "If all we had to do was interview the staff, it would be easy, but I left the meeting with a list of assignments to execute while we're there."

"Is there anything I can do to help out?"

"We'll need some extra gear for fieldwork. A camera array to record what we do, a proper container to bring the samples back, and a lot of other things besides. Can you point us to a source that has everything? We'll need the array for night shooting too. No one has documented the mutation process yet."

"Why a sample container?" I was puzzled.

"Mother Mekong's serial DNA sequencer is down. There will be no second round of DNA data out of Cambodia."

"What? You're kidding me. We're not getting more data?"

"I just heard from Thep. We have to take samples ourselves and bring them back for analysis."

"Then you'd better go to Kim's shop," said Yagodo. "Nguyen can take you. Kim is Ho Chi Minh's go-to bio guy. He should have everything you need. He can do the analysis for you too. I could have everything delivered, but the problem is the suits."

"Suits?" Kurokawa and I spoke at the same time.

"You can't risk contaminating your samples. We need to do a proper analysis as soon as possible. I'm sure Kim has some biochem warfare suits in his inventory. Mamoru should be easy to equip, but I'm not sure if he has anything small enough for Takashi. We'd have to check."

"Do we really have to go that far?" I said. "They're not using pesticides out there, no manure either. The site is Active Ground Cover certified. The soil purifies the air around the site. It's probably cleaner than this room."

Yagodo listened as he played with the model floating in front of him.

"No one knows what's going on out there. It doesn't hurt to

be prepared." His eyes were shining like a child's. "We know we're dealing with a mutation, not a natural plant. I checked Thep out. It looks like she knows her stuff, so I wouldn't bet on human error. Is there a bug in SR06 that triggered gene collapse? Also hard to believe. If it was gene collapse, we wouldn't see natural plant DNA in the data. Then there's the size of the intruder genome. Hopefully it's mostly meaningless junk, but..."

Yagodo fell silent. He poked a finger into his little cloud and took out a small red point of light. I thought it might be a clue, but his eyes were looking past it into a great distance. His hands dropped to his lap and his mouth opened slowly. Whoever he was talking to now, it wasn't us.

"Grasshoppers. Distilled site surrounded by DMZ. Can't allow grasshoppers near the crop."

DMZ: DEMILITARIZED ZONE floated briefly in front of Yagodo. I couldn't figure it out.

"Takashi, what's 'DMZ'? Is it a military term?"

"It's kind of a strange area that surrounds the site," said Kurokawa. "You'll see when you get there. Isamu, you seem to know everything. I almost wish you could come with us. You'd be a great help. But that would slow down the salvaging."

"Graft SR06 to the contaminant...no. Genetic distance from contaminant to MAFF standard genome. Start where? Niigata...no. Can't assume it's one of their cultivars. Three hundred million base pairs...A Fourier transform rainbow table might be faster...No, wait, maybe a superimposed deep search..."

"Um...sorry." Nguyen looked apologetic. "When he gets like this, he can't talk to anyone. I don't think he's going to be back for a while. You could wait, but why don't we go downtown? We can drop by Kim's shop. You might need to pick up some other things too."

"In that case, why don't you take Mamoru with you?" said Kurokawa. "I'll stay here and wait for Isamu. I have to plan our trip, and when he gets back—" He glanced at Yagodo, who was manipulating his molecular model like a Rubik's Cube—"I'll have him take me to get that gear fitted."

Just Nguyen and me, out and about in Ho Chi Minh City. Now that was an attractive plan.

"Going on a date?" Yagodo was still staring at his model. "Take the mobile stage. It should work fine through your phone. Use it as long as you like."

So he was still with us after all.

"Leave your data here, Mamoru. I'll look for matches on the Web."

7   Ho Chi Minh City

The breeze rippled the hem of Nguyen's ao dai.

"I'm sorry about everything back there." She dipped her head, embarrassed.

"No worries. It was fun, actually."

We were in a little market area not far from the office. I was stocking up on things I'd forgotten to bring in the rush to get out of Tokyo. Nguyen was in fine form, forgetting to take the change for purchases, catching her hem on goods piled on tables and sending them scattering to the ground...

We walked along Pasteur Street to where it bisected a large, rectangular park. The lush lawns were dappled with trees. Food stands lined the central promenade. Locals and tourists reclined on the grass in the shade.

Walking next to Nguyen, the heat didn't seem as oppressive as the day before. Maybe it was partly because we settled into a natural rhythm of walking from shade to shade and veering toward the doors of shops where the air conditioning flowed out onto the sidewalk, but the diaphanous flaps of her tunic and the hem of her sleeve fluttering as we walked along and brushing against my arm now and then might've also had something to do with it.

Like everyone in the park, we bought water at a drink stand and looked for a spot to sit. Nguyen used HMC to pay for my water. It was her compensation for Yagodo's odd behavior. I have to say, HMC did look convenient.

Just as I'd seen coming in from the airport, there was a conspicuous number of people in wheelchairs passing in both directions along the promenade, and many others on crutches with missing limbs. Nguyen noticed me staring at this strange parade of the disabled. Her face darkened. "There are so many of them. It's because of the herbicide the Americans used during the war."

I'd heard about Agent Orange, but I didn't realize it could still be a problem this long after the Vietnam War. Nguyen said that chemical residue from thousands of tons of defoliants dropped almost seventy years before was still leaching into the Saigon River, upstream from Ho Chi Minh City. The effects on people living near the river were actually getting worse.

"The company that manufactured that herbicide was famous for its GM crops too."

She meant Monsanto, which had been a powerhouse in pesticides as well as genetically modified crops. The company had gone under when distilled crops became the world's main source of food, since such crops required no pesticides at all. Now Monsanto was ancient history as far as the industry was concerned, but the people of Vietnam weren't likely to ever forget it.

As she was talking, a small red dot started blinking in my field of vision. Red meant Priority. I opened my workspace in the palm of my hand and checked the message. I could have read it heads up, but superimposing a text message on Nguyen's face would've been a waste of the scenery.

The message was from Kurokawa.

> MAMORU: I'M SURE YOU MUST BE ENJOYING YOUR
> SHOPPING WITH NGUYEN. SORRY TO BOTHER YOU, BUT
> COULD YOU PICK UP THREE DOZEN BARS OF CHOCOLATE?
> SOMETHING WITH ABOUT FIVE HUNDRED CALORIES
> A BAR. I'M NOT CRAZY ABOUT NUTS. TAKASHI

Three dozen? Was he going to eat them all himself? Chocolate bars didn't seem like a good way to break the ice with Mother Mekong's team.

"What is it?"

Takashi wants me to get him some chocolate bars. Three *dozen* chocolate bars."

"Wow, he must really like chocolate...Oh Mamoru, I just remembered. Could I leave you here for about half an hour? A friend of mine lives near here. I want to drop by. I'll get Takashi's chocolates on the way back."

"Why don't I just go with you?"

She paused. "No, that's okay. You can wait for me in the cathedral."

She pointed to a grove of trees on the other side of the park. A large red-brick building rose beyond the grove. I could see a row of latticework windows shaped like lotus petals set deep in the brick under a large white rosette filled in with stained glass. Two sharp white spires topped with tiny crosses thrust into the sky.

"That's the cathedral? It looks impressive."

Nguyen nodded happily and started telling me about Saigon Basilica—how it was modeled on Notre Dame de Paris, how it was a true example of Romanesque architecture, how the bricks were brought from Marseille and the stained glass made by local artisans under French guidance, and many other details she was enthusiastic about but not totally certain about either. Obviously it was a beloved landmark for the Vietnamese.

"In the visitor guidebook it says the name is Saigon Basilica, but in Vietnamese we call it the Basilica of Our Lady of the Immaculate Conception."

"Is there an image of Mary?"

"Of course." Nguyen pointed to a pathway through the grove. "Go through there and turn right. You'll see the statue in front. Go up to it. From there you can see the whole building. It's beautiful."

"Isn't the entrance under those windows?"

"That's the side transept. Could you wait for me inside? It's really nice. Cool too."

"All right. See you."

"I hate to do this to you. I'm supposed to be your guide. I'll be right back."

She got up and walked in the other direction, away from the church. I decided to follow her suggestion and get a look at the building from outside. As I stood up and took a swig of water, I got another message from Kurokawa.

> POSTCRIPT: WE LEAVE TOMORROW. MEET ME IN THE
> LOBBY AT SIX. WE'RE STAYING ONE NIGHT. YOU WON'T
> NEED ANY CLOTHES FOR THE FIELD WORK. I JUST FOUND
> OUT WE'LL BE SUITING UP NAKED. TAKASHI.

Tomorrow. Again. Go ahead, jerk me around. And why did we have to get into our suits naked? What kind of gear were we using anyway? I hoped Cambodia would be more temperate than Vietnam.

* * *

Nguyen was right about the basilica. The bone-white bell towers stabbing into the empty blue made a lovely contrast with the red-brick façade. The towering yellow sunflowers in the noon light around the plaza added a touch of quiet mystery. On the other hand, the statue of Mary struck me as a bit roughly hewn. The eyes seemed too large.

Maybe it was because Nguyen was gone, or maybe because I'd been sitting in the shade too long, but under the noonday sun facing the huge basilica, it seemed as hot as the day we arrived. I hurried toward the entrance.

The doors stood open. As I passed through the arch, I noticed Chinese characters engraved in the stone. I couldn't make out all the old-style characters, but I could see "basilica" and "holy mother." Kurokawa was right. Vietnam was full of Chinese characters.

I passed through the vestibule and almost stumbled into a camera crew with piles of equipment. The crew was busy setting up a shot. A multipoint camera with an eight by eight flash array was flanked by huge mesh panels studded with more cameras. I didn't have to look for the True Vision logo to recognize the equipment. This was a 3D RealVu shoot.

"Want a kick in the ass, moron? Move that light over there, now!"

A woman in sunglasses with a black bandanna on her head—the same woman who had called Takashi "kid" at the airport—was braying at a crewmember who was pushing one of the big flash arrays. Yagodo's translation engine was rendering the voices of the crew into Japanese with such smoothness and naturalness, it was hard to believe it was coming through a portable stage. I wished it wasn't translating the woman's barking so vividly. I decided to get as far away from her as I could.

A detour around the knot of people and equipment took me farther into the nave. As I was looking for a place to sit, my call light started flashing. Kurokawa, I thought. I accepted automatically.

Shit. As I was accepting, I realized the call was anonymous. An instant later, I was in Private Mode staring at an avatar I'd never seen before.

The man had straw-colored blond hair falling across his forehead, with eyes the blue of the sky outside. They drooped at the corners. He looked to be in his thirties, but the unnaturally deep lines around his mouth meant he was probably fifty or so and didn't want to be seen as faking too much.

"Mamoru Hayashida? I am Enrico Conti. L&B."

"Enrico? Is that really you?" This was the first time I'd "met" him. His appearance caught me off guard. Given his name, I wasn't expecting someone so Nordic.

"Thank you for accepting my invitation. This is the first time to meet, no?" He extended his hand. The AR feedback supplied a sensation of resistance as I shook it.

"What's going on, Enrico? Why did you invite me anonymously?"

"I apologize for that. There is something I have to tell you about the mutation at Mother Mekong. Can you give me a few minutes?"

He jerked a thumb over his shoulder in the direction of the pews behind him. The people in the church were now gray, featureless avatars, moving like phantoms in a dream.

"May I ask you, Mamoru? How far have you gotten with your investigation?"

"Not far. I heard you went AWOL from L&B. Are you in some kind of trouble?"

Enrico's avatar made his expression hard to read, but he sounded confident and determined.

"Don't worry about me. I could not be part of L&B's response to this problem. Listen, we are going to get pretty tired if we stand here talking. Shall we sit?"

He turned and walked toward the altar where there were fewer people and sat sideways in one of the pews with his legs stretched out in the aisle. I sat in the pew behind him. The bench was too shallow. My knees almost touched the seat in front of me. The wood was hard under my back and buttocks.

If you stand for too long in Private Mode, the feedback tends to leave you with an ache in your knees. On the other hand, I had a feeling this bench was going to do me in anyway if we sat here long enough. I had to fidget constantly to keep the blood flowing. Enrico leaned sideways against the back of the pew, his arm stretched out along the top.

"I left because I have given up on Lintz," he whispered. "I was the Mother Mekong PM only in name. Lintz gave me hardly any control. This was a project that wanted a firm hand keeping all vendors and subcontractors in line. But when the news from Mother Mekong comes to us, what does he do? He gives everything to Kurokawa, and I am sitting there doing nothing."

I wondered whether Enrico had called me just to whine. "I

heard L&B's team has its hands full dealing with customers and the government."

His expression seemed to harden for a moment, then a corner of his mouth lifted in a smile.

"Yes, there is a lot of that, but it is up to Barnhard and the sales guys to handle. They are the ones who wanted to do this. Is it my job to go around apologizing to everybody?"

I couldn't figure Enrico out. Was this why he dropped out of sight?

"Lintz makes everyone busy with silly administrative tasks. And then he gives the investigation—the only thing that matters—to a freelancer! Listen to me, Mamoru. I am sure you are a good specialist. The problem is that Lintz chose Kurokawa."

"Is that a problem?"

"Indeed, it is. Lintz is completely blind, you see. The real Kurokawa hates genetic engineering."

This was a new one on me and not believable at all. I'd worked with Takashi for three years, and his commitment to the job always came across loud and clear. Okay, so Enrico lost out in the corporate game. He would have to blame it on someone.

"I would not be surprised, even, if Kurokawa is behind this mutation. He had control of all the data and the specifications, everything going to the subcontractors. If he wanted to put in some malware along the way without L&B noticing, it was easy for him to do. Or just mess up the genome itself."

"Enrico, you're out of line. I was the last one to touch that blueprint, and it went directly from me to L&B. You approved it yourself."

His face hardened again. Now I knew what it was: an artifact. His avatar was covering his reaction. Maybe an expletive? We'd just met, but I was already starting to dislike him.

"Yes, that is true. It is a detail, okay? I am talking about Kurokawa. You met him in person. Don't you think there is something unnatural about his size?" Enrico gripped the back of the bench and brought his face closer. "He is a mutation himself. Distilled crop technology did that. And Lintz was involved."

He took a video file from his shirt pocket. "You are a gene mapper. All you can touch is the style sheet, so I am not surprised if you don't know that fourteen—no, fifteen years ago, L&B's first distilled rice caused genetic damage in the families of the people who ate it. Kurokawa is one of them. Take a look at this. It is from 2016."

He held the file out and pushed the play button with a long forefinger. I peered closer at the screen in the palm of his hand.

"Give me back my son!" The man in the video was Kurokawa, shouting in the voice I knew so well. Did he have a child?

He was sitting at a table before a clutch of microphones, glaring at someone out of the frame to his left. It was footage from a Japanese news show. I saw the same thick black-frame glasses, the same hairstyle, the same dark blue suit. But he looked like a mess—hair all over the place, dirty shirt, his suit shiny with wear around the sleeves. It looked like he hadn't had a bath in weeks. I'd never seen him so agitated.

The caption along the bottom read: ARE YOU AT RISK? SUPER RICE ZERO CAUSES GENE MUTATION!

A woman wearing a gray suit sat next to Kurokawa, gazing at him with concern. She looked like she might be his lawyer. But what was Kurokawa doing on a news program fifteen years ago?

"How dare you call it Super Rice? Why did you make something like that? Bring back Takashi! Give me back my son!"

Kurokawa looked like he was going to leap over the table. The woman gently restrained him. Enrico's finger overlapped the screen and touched the pause button.

"That is Kurokawa's father. It is strange, isn't it? How much they look alike. The video is genuine. It is from L&B's own archives. I will give you a bookmark. You can verify the date for yourself."

When I looked up, Enrico was standing between the pews, holding out a widget shaped like a bookmark.

"Okay, Enrico. I get that Takashi looks just like his father. What I don't get is, why are you showing me this?" I snatched the bookmark away and shoved it in my pocket irritably. Yagodo could confirm whether it was fake or not. I assumed that not all of it was, but Enrico had a prime motivation to enhance it since his job had been taken away.

"Watch the continuation and you will understand. Shall we?" He held up a forefinger and slowly lowered it to the file. I couldn't take my eyes off the tip of his finger as it moved in an arc to the playback button.

The video played. The camera pulled back and panned to the table facing Kurokawa. The image went out of focus and sharpened again. Barnhard. He was sitting there, far too large for his chair, looking suitably uncomfortable. He opened his mouth slowly before he spoke.

"Our product, Super Rice Zero, is specially formulated for brewing sake. It has not been certified safe for direct human consumption. Words cannot express my regret that Takashi Kurokawa and twenty-six other people were harmed by it." The Japanese interpreter's voice overlapped Barnhard's, the way they used to do it before machine translation.

"I won't even try to minimize what happened with fancy words. Our product put your son and twenty-six others in a coma. All those affected, as well as their families, will receive generous compensation from L&B. If you wish, we will see directly to the victims' care until a means of treatment is found."

Enrico tapped pause again.

"This goes on for a long time, but I think you get the point. Takashi Kurokawa eats Barnhard's Super Rice Zero and it puts him into a coma."

I shook my head. "Wait a minute. *Barnhard's* distilled rice, was it?"

"What do you mean?"

"The first distilled generation was SR01."

There was another facial artifact, then he shrugged his shoulders. "You should know."

Didn't this guy even know the terminology? I was glad they hadn't given him the investigation.

"Anyway, now you have seen it. Kurokawa's father feeds him L&B rice, Takashi falls into his coma. After he comes out, he goes to do freelance work for L&B. Doesn't that strike you as a little bizarre? Kissing everybody's ass in his Japanese English. But you never know what he's thinking, do you?"

Enrico rested his hands on the back of the bench and leaned toward me.

"Anyway, why would Lintz give him anything to do in the first place? It makes no sense. Would you give work to someone after robbing him of some of his life? I think Kurokawa knows something about Lintz, something Lintz is desperate to hide. I want to know what it is."

I glanced sharply at Enrico. There would be plenty of time to consider his warning about Kurokawa, but I could already see he was not a man to be trusted. I had lowered my Behavior Correction settings before I left Tokyo, and my distaste for him was probably easy to see.

And that was just fine.

"Come, you don't need to look at me that way. Just don't trust Kurokawa, okay? Take the investigation away from his hands, for your sake. Understand? You have been warned."

He logged off.

I shoved the pew backward to get some leg room. Sure enough, my butt was totally numb from sitting on the hard narrow bench. My joints kept popping as I stretched and tried to loosen up my neck.

I looked toward the entrance. Ms. Skinhead and her camera crew were gone too.

I turned back to the altar. My eyes were drawn to the image of the crucified Christ. The afternoon light pouring through the stained glass of the rosette windows on both ends of the transept threw multi-colored patterns on the floor and ceiling. As I gazed at Christ bathed in the shifting colors, Enrico's words started circling in my brain like vultures. Don't trust Kurokawa...Could he be right? Since this trip began, I had found myself liking him more and more. His refusal to let his size defeat him, his relentlessly cheerful and sincere approach to everything—was it all a deception?

"Takashi..."

I was letting my suspicions get the better of me when I caught sight of a white ao dai hurrying toward me like a small whirlwind.

"Mamoru! Sorry to keep you waiting. Oh, are you all right? Your face..."

"I'm fine, it's nothing. I felt a little unwell for a minute there."

"Well, I hope you feel better now. Oh, right, Isamu says he's not going back to the office today. You can take the rest of the day off. Would you like to have dinner with me?"

"I'm sorry, there's something I need to check at the office. Maybe next time."

*　　*　　*

I touched the brass door handle and let myself in. Two blinks to activate the augmented reality stage.

"Anyone here?"

The table was piled high with dirty Frisbees and tennis balls. John and Paul had been hard at work since I left.

I reached down to retrieve a ball from the floor. It changed into a folder before I touched it. The label read FAN FAN FARM: NIIGATA PREFECTURE, 2014.

What a mountain of work. I had a huge amount of matching to do, but at least I was looking at the beginnings of real progress. For the first time I felt like things were moving ahead.

"Maybe I can ask Isamu to match these while I'm gone..." Talking to myself again.

Something moved near the entrance. I turned and saw a golden retriever with a red bandanna peeking at me around the edge of the door.

"Hey, don't scare me, okay?"

John trotted over to the table, nails clicking on the floor, and deposited another tennis ball on the table. I put my hand out to pat his head. The feedback chip gave me a sensation of hand movement, and I could see the dog's fur move, but there was no sensation of touch. He was indistinguishable from a real dog, but the lack of sensation reminded me I was in augmented reality.

I patted him a bit more before he trotted reluctantly to the door, looking back at me a few times. He touched his nose to the handle and let himself out.

I sat down on the sofa. I thought I'd better take another look at Enrico's video after all. Not that I was eager to see it again, but I wanted to try his bookmark when he wasn't around. The image file that the bookmark pointed to played flawlessly. I watched to the end, but all I saw was more of the same: Takashi Kurokawa had gone into a coma after eating Super Rice Zero. The way Barnhard apologized made it sound like the coma was irreversible. How *did* Kurokawa finally recover, I wondered.

Something else bothered me. Kurokawa and his father looked far too much alike for father and son. The glasses, the hair, everything except the size was identical, so identical that it made the video look fake. I thought of having Yagodo do a forensic check, but then again, was this something I should even show him?

I looked closer at the video, thinking maybe I could figure it out myself, when a voice spoke from behind.

"So, you've seen it."

It was Yagodo. He was sitting at his desk in a cream-colored shirt. He hadn't been there when I walked in. He must have logged on from somewhere. He came over and sat on the couch.

"Isamu, do you know about this?"

"Yes. I did a background check on Takashi and there it was. It's an awful story. I found a few other articles that confirm it. Takashi is one of the Super Rice Zero victims. A lot of people in the industry still remember it, even this many years later. Hey, what's the matter? Is there something on your mind?"

What sort of expression did I have? Should I tell Isamu how I got this video?

"I know it's a shock, but why don't we wait and let Takashi tell us in his own time?" said Yagodo. "Right now we've got an intruder to identify."

He put his hands on his knees and stood up. "You'll be in Cambodia overnight. Don't worry. While you're gone I'll keep salvaging candidates off the Web. Today alone, John and Paul have already brought me about two thousand possibles. I'll take care of the matching work too."

"Hey, that's good of you, Isamu."

He logged off.

Tomorrow we were leaving for Cambodia. Yagodo was right. There would be time to consider Enrico's warning later. It was time to get back to work.

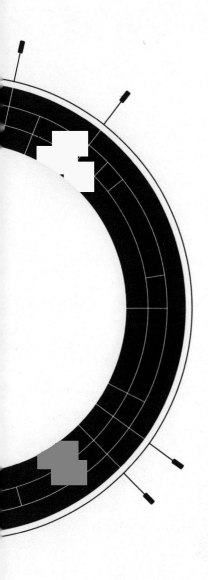

PART 3

KUROKAWA

8   Farm Manager

I was down to my boxers. I had my hands on them, ready to take them off, but I couldn't summon the nerve. The cold from the linoleum crept through the soles of my feet and up my legs. Shue Thep was putting us through Mother Mekong's standard security check.

"Shue, don't you have any guys who could cover this?" My hands were still frozen.

"We're short on people. Short on time too. Would you just get those off?"

Thep brushed a long strand of black hair from her face and leaned tiredly against the door. There were faint circles under her almond eyes. She was only a bit taller than Kurokawa, but with the top half of her too-large jumpsuit wrapped around her waist, she almost looked smaller. Her purple sports bra and tight-fitting T-shirt looked freshly laundered, but the jumpsuit and work boots were flecked with mud.

"It's just a formality. As soon as I see you're not hiding anything, I'll turn my back. Now get a move on." Her voice was as tired as she looked. Maybe her English was politer than it was coming across in Japanese, but Yagodo's translation engine favored mood over meaning. She certainly sounded more than a bit pissed off. I wished I knew how to change the engine's Mood Sensitivity setting.

Kurokawa stood with his back to Thep. He was out of his clothes and as close to the locker as possible, reading the warnings on a bottle of green gel.

Kurokawa and I had hardly spoken after I joined him in the

lobby that morning at six. We'd pushed the cart piled high with Kim's gear to the edge of the river near the hotel and loaded everything onto a waiting helicopter. Almost as soon as we buckled up, we were airborne and hard at work. Kurokawa conferenced with L&B over the noise of the rotors while I paged through the genomes that had started to come in from Yagodo. He had already salvaged over three thousand candidates, but he was coming up dry on matches.

The only words we exchanged during the flight came after Kurokawa unwrapped his fourth chocolate bar.

"You sure have a thing for chocolate."

"Yes. It's the calories."

*   *   *

"We're supposed to apply this to our genitals too. Very thorough."

The US Ground Forces biochemical warfare suits Yagodo had ordered for us were nothing like the "field gear" I had been picturing. The suits were assemblies of black carbon-fiber plates that encased the body in a suit of armor. The plates were joined with carbon-fiber ribbons that automatically adjusted for length, letting the user move freely.

When we opened the shipping container, a tutorial video started automatically on a monitor inside the lid. The suits came with mil-spec AR feedback. The green gel held millions of nanomachines that passed through the skin to stimulate the nervous system directly.

I'd never seen a tutorial like this, but I had to admire the care that went into it. The explanation of the suiting-up process, user features, and emergency escape procedure in case of injury were easy to understand the first time through. I was impressed by the narrator's guarantee of comfort in any environment, even in a sewer with one hundred percent humidity. The suit also protected the user from unpleasant sensory experiences, like the stench of rotting corpses on a battlefield.

Kurokawa started spreading on the goop. Thep took a long, thoughtful look at him.

"You're an SR Zero victim, aren't you? When did you come out of your coma?"

"Listen, Shue—"

She turned toward me, but her eyes were focused at a point in midair.

"Seven years ago," said Kurokawa matter-of-factly. "As you see, my growth stopped completely." His voice seemed to snap Thep back to reality. She blinked, shook her head, and straightened up.

"I'm sorry, Kurokawa-san. Maybe that was a little too personal."

"Don't give it a second thought. You look like you need some rest."

"Rest. Yes, rest would be nice. I've hardly slept since the mutation started. That was five days ago. I keep sending information to L&B, but they never get back to me. Instead I get two requests for samples from you, and you're not even L&B. Then I get a personal message from Barnhard telling me to let you tramp around collecting samples yourself. Isn't Enrico still the PM? What's going on with L&B anyway?"

"Enrico's disap—"

"Ms. Thep." Kurokawa cut me off. "From now on, please deal directly with me. The investigation on the ground will be conducted by me and Mamoru. I'll gather all the information you need and keep you in the loop."

Her dark mood seemed to lift immediately. The lack of response from L&B must have really been on her mind.

"You'll coordinate everything? I appreciate it, but what happened to Enrico?"

"He'll be on vacation for a while."

"On vacation? He's the PM. What happened? Did he have a breakdown?"

"Something like that." Kurokawa laughed regretfully.

"What a fool. Going mental at a time like this. I bet he ran back to Mama."

"Enrico is very good with the technology. I'm sure he'll be giving us valuable support as soon as he recovers."

"Is he really good with the technology?" I asked.

"Sure," said Thep. "But I don't need him. I'd rather work with you."

She leaned against the door, feet planted shoulder-width, arms folded. The muscles in her arms and shoulders flexed.

"Hayashida-san, your hands are frozen. Could you hurry up and get those shorts off?" Her voice had an edge to it, but a hint of kindness too. I sighed and dropped my drawers.

"Well, at least you weren't being shy about your size. Okay, I'll turn around. Get that gel on and suit up."

*   *   *

Thep walked ahead of us down a long corridor that led to the fields.

"I'm glad you brought this gear. Now we can do some night shooting." She was carrying a big tripod on one shoulder. An eight-by-eight True Vision multipoint camera array swung from her other hand. Both pieces of gear were from Kim's shop.

"Phnom Penh is two hours on the chopper. It's hard to get decent gear there, and since the mutation started we haven't let anyone on the site."

"Thank you," said Kurokawa. "We'd prefer to avoid panicking the public. I'm glad you secured the site."

"Yeah. Except for the squatters."

"Out here?" I was surprised.

"Sorry, we're all just country people here." Thep smiled. "Nature addicts. They've been living in tents around the perimeter since the site was constructed. They bring in all kinds of equipment and spy on us twenty-four/seven, trying to catch us using pesticides, chemical fertilizers, anything that could blow our certifications. At first I thought they might actually show the world what we're trying to do here. But their technique is sloppy and the data they're collecting is junk. Work that shoddy would never pass muster on *my* site." Thep threw her tank-topped chest out proudly.

"Now they're flying kites with cameras, shooting us at night. The glowing crops are perfect for their propaganda. Thanks to that we've had to spend extra on security. The detail you saw at the front gate is just the tip of the iceberg.

"They've been camping out for a year. I don't know where the money is coming from. I won't say genetic engineering and distilled agriculture are perfected, but what we're trying to do here is more sustainable, better for the environment, and safer than slash and burn or relying on natural mutation to produce better crops. I wish I could beat that into their heads." Thep was hardly breaking a sweat with the heavy tripod and camera array.

"Mother Mekong hires locally. That's Fair Trade. There aren't many people here that I can talk to on the same level. Kurokawa-san, after you guys finish, could you leave that with me?" Thep gestured toward me with her chin.

"What, me?"

"No, the suit. That's a Biochemical Command suit. The AR model, right?" She peered under my armpit, trying to read the spec plate. "I'm glad you came prepared. With things the way they are now, a suit like that would be good to have. All we've got for protective gear is this." She motioned to one of her wrists, which was sealed with an elastic band. The rubberized surface of her jumpsuit was dirty and the area around the knees was wearing thin. The tops of her boots were sealed to her suit legs with silver duct tape.

"It's not like we're dealing with a biochemical weapon," I said.

Thep stopped, put down the camera, and stared at me.

"I mean, there's no proof that it's anything like th—"

She gave me a hard shove in the chest. "Do we need proof?" Her eyes were almost wild-looking. "We've got *no* idea what this is! That's why it's frightening! Something is mutating on this farm. We checked everything—air, water, soil. And we still have no idea why this is happening."

Her hand was still on my chest. Her arm was trembling.

"We go out one morning. We find something that's not supposed to be there. It's not SR06. Something is very wrong. How do we know it isn't a threat? I can barely get my own people to come out here. They think Neak Ta, the spirit who owns this valley, is angry with us. And those grasshoppers—"

Kurokawa stepped between us. "Ms. Thep, we've received almost no information from you since the mutation started. Weren't you sending data to Enrico?"

The tension in her arm melted away. "That idiot. Didn't he send you my reports?"

"We can't reach him. L&B doesn't know where he is either. All we have is the data you sent me and the cultivation logs."

"Enrico didn't send you *anything*? I don't believe it." She stepped back and shook her head. "I'm sorry, Hayashida-san. You said 'weapon' and it set me off. It's just…it's so strange that we don't understand what's happening. I just pray that it's not some kind of weaponized genome." She picked up the camera. "Anyway, with this we can finally shoot the mutation as it happens. Sorry to get physical. I hope I didn't hurt you."

*   *   *

The UV in the sterilization chamber was intense even through the suit visor. I stood with arms straight out, blinking against the light. We had to cook off any contaminants before we went into the field.

"Those suits look new. They should be clean already, but my gear is not. This will just take a little longer."

Thep was encased in her dark yellow jumpsuit. I couldn't see her expression behind the eye slits in her clean mask. Not only was her rubberized jumpsuit from a different era, it was several sizes too big. She needed a web of silver duct tape to keep it in place.

"We're here to follow your procedures, Ms. Thep," said Kurokawa. "I don't want to complicate this investigation by bringing in some sort of contaminant."

Kurokawa opened his suit workspace and began inputting into the strange-looking interface. Thep peered over his shoulder.

"What is all that?"

"I'm inputting today's Operation into our control program. The three of us make up a platoon. The immediate goal of the Operation is to collect samples of the intruder, SR06, and the grasshoppers, along with any other relevant intelligence. The Operation comes under the Mission, which is to determine the nature of the anomaly threatening Mother Mekong."

"Do we really need a whole grasshopper?" I was hoping not.

"Of course!" Kurokawa and Thep answered in unison.

"How are we going to catch one? We didn't bring a net."

"Don't worry, the border between SR06 and the mutated plants is full of them. You can catch them with your hands." Thep sounded disgusted, though I still couldn't see her face. According to the tutorial, the AR that came with the suits let you "see" the expressions on your platoon mates' faces.

"Shall we go into AR?"

"Yes, it's time," said Kurokawa. "The video said to whisper 'activate' and gesture with the left hand over the face." He put the tips of his left thumb and little finger to his temples. "Activa—"

His head rolled back before he finished the command. He dropped to his knees and toppled over. His helmet thudded against the floor and he went into convulsions.

"Kurokawa-san!" Thep was on her knees beside him. His back was arched in a position that didn't seem anatomically possible. I could hear wet gurgling from inside the helmet. He was vomiting.

"We've got to get his helmet off!" Thep shouted.

"Wait!" I kneeled and pulled the release under his jaw. The visor popped off. Vomit flecked with tiny strands of fiber splattered onto the floor. His fingers were curled into claws. His eyes were locked open and jerked spastically.

"What's happening? What is it?" Thep was screaming now.

Kurokawa took a deep breath, tensed, and ejected another geyser of vomit from the pit of his stomach.

I cursed myself for not paying more attention to the tutorial. What was the emergency escape procedure? Kurokawa was fighting the convulsions, trying to reach behind his neck.

I remembered. The emergency release was at the base of the neck.

"Takashi, I'm getting you out of that suit!" I put my arms under his armpits and hugged him to my chest. He tried to say something but vomited onto my visor instead. I found the cable and jerked it.

The ribbons linking the suit plates loosened. Green gel oozed from the gaps. Thep grappled with the gel-smeared ribbons at the back of the suit and pulled the armor away.

"Turn on the shower!" I yelled at her. "We've got to get this stuff off."

"It's not sterile!"

"I don't care!"

She ran to a panel by the door and jammed her thumb on a blue button. Water came blasting out of nozzles on both sides with nearly enough force to knock me down. I lifted Kurokawa into the stream. The water pummeled his skin as it flushed off the gel.

"I called for help!" Thep yelled in my ear. The door was already open and several of her people were coming in with a wheeled stretcher.

"Clean him off!"

Multiple hands held Kurokawa and wiped off the last bits of gel with towels. They picked him up and put him on the stretcher. While they kept wiping him down, I noticed something odd on his right shoulder.

It was a three-line bar code. Not a tattoo—it was different somehow. I looked closer. The bar code glowed softly and faded, with a rhythm like a heartbeat.

"Don't put him on his back! He'll choke," Thep shouted. "Hayashida-san, what are you doing?" She was leaning over Kurokawa, shouting in my ear, but her voice seemed far away.

A luminous bar code?

Thep and the others pushed the stretcher outside. For a moment I was too stunned to move. Then I ran into the corridor after them.

I wasn't used to running in the suit. The tutorial said it would feel as natural as the user's own skin once AR was activated, but I wasn't about to do that after what I'd just seen.

They had just wheeled Kurokawa into another room off the corridor when I heard Thep scream. Two staff members with AR glasses backed hastily into the corridor. Their faces were pale with fear.

"Neak Ta! Neak Ta!"

I pushed past them into the room. Kurokawa was sitting on the stretcher in a dark blue suit. He bowed. Thep stared at him, dazed.

How had he gotten a suit on? And why were the two people behind him doing manual CPR into empty space over the stretcher?

"Ms. Thep, Mamoru, I'm sorry this happened." He hopped down from the stretcher, buttoned his suit coat and bowed again.

"I'm a mess right now. The feedback was too strong. I couldn't handle it."

One of Thep's people laboring away at the empty stretcher turned pale and yelled, "He's got no pulse! Khun Thep, what are you doing? Get the defibrillator!" He pointed at the orange AED box near the door. I reached for the latch, but Kurokawa stopped me.

"No AED!" His tone was commanding. "I don't need it, Mamoru. I can communicate with you through my avatar. They're not in AR." He pointed to the people hovering over the stretcher. "They can't see me or hear me. Tell them exactly what I tell you. No matter what, don't use the defibrillator. It'll fry my feedback chips."

Something was wrong. How could he control his avatar with his heart stopped?

"I have to empty my stomach completely. Turn me on one side and keep my airway free. Ms. Thep, I need intravenous glucose. Can you do that?"

Thep shook her head.

"No? Digestion is inefficient…Oh well, tell your people to break a chocolate bar in quarters and put one in my mouth every fifteen minutes."

"What are you guys standing there for? We're losing him. He's got no pulse." One of the staff grabbed my shoulder and shook it. I didn't know how to explain what was happening.

"Khun Nimol, he's going to be okay," said Thep. "Clean him up and get him into bed. No AED. And get someone in here who can use AR. Glasses are fine."

"But his heart—"

"Just do it!"

"Thank you," said Kurokawa. "Don't worry, I'll be all right." Kurokawa's avatar glanced at his wrist, as if checking a watch.

"Mamoru, I need both of you to get to the mutation site right away. The feedback was too strong for me, that's all. Disable your own stage and activate your suit. All the Operation parameters are set."

He took a step toward me. He looked more serious than I'd ever seen him. The avatar's forehead glistened with tiny beads of sweat.

"The Operation is in your hands now."

"But shouldn't we wait until you stabilize?"

"There's no time. Two days from now, TerraVu will photograph the site in daylight. We've got to get some kind of explanation in place before that happens."

"What's so important about TerraVu?" said Thep. Kurokawa checked his wrist again.

"I'm sorry, but I've got to get back to my body. My brain needs oxygen. I'll tell you about TerraVu later."

He gave us a sweeping bow. "I hate to ask you to carry on without me, but it's the only way. I have to get my body under control."

Kurokawa's avatar got onto the stretcher and lay back. The next instant it was gone, replaced by the real, naked Kurokawa. He lifted his head.

"Mamoru...please..."

"Don't try to talk. We'll handle it."

He gave us a gentle look, then turned onto his side and started vomiting again.

*   *   *

I was back under the UV with Thep.

"Are you really going to risk it?"

After we left Kurokawa I had checked the suit manual, hoping I could use it without activating AR. The answer was negative. The life-support system would not function without nanomachine-enabled neural feedback.

The image of a convulsing, vomiting Kurokawa was still fresh in my mind. I couldn't quite summon the courage to use the activation command.

I was afraid.

"Hayashida-san, I know your friend is desperate to get us out there, but can't this wait until tomorrow?"

Thep's voice was muffled by the clean mask, but she sounded as scared as I was.

"No, we've got to do what he asked. Otherwise how can I face him?" I checked my courage for the umpteenth time. Taking samples before TerraVu photographed the site in daylight was important, but was it urgent? Yet Kurokawa had begged us to go, even as he fought for his life.

I blinked twice to deactivate my stage.

"Hayashida-san, take care well." I heard Thep's unfiltered English. Her pure, singsong intonation was like a tiny silver bell.

"Thank you, Shue."

I flashed back to Kurokawa vomiting again. Still, he was probably right. The tutorial said that the risk of unexpected side effects from the suit's feedback was extremely low for the average user.

I lifted my left hand, encased in the black carbon fiber glove, to my face. I placed the tips of my thumb and little finger at the level of my temples and whispered "Activate."

A million tiny feathers swirled over my body. The sensation was so arresting that for a moment I had to close my eyes.

Something was touching my temples. I could feel the warmth of my fingertips against my skin. I opened my eyes and saw my hand. The glove was gone. As I lowered my hand, I could feel the current of air it made against my face. The carbon-fiber armor was gone. I was wearing a crisp new rubberized jumpsuit. I could feel its sleeves touching my wrists.

Every sensation—the touch and warmth of my fingertips, the movement of air against my skin—was artificial, mediated through the nanomachines that penetrated my skin to stimulate my nerves, yet everything was completely indistinguishable from reality.

"Mamoru, are you all right?"

Thep was wearing the same-style jumpsuit. Her silky black hair was tied in a pony tail. It swayed gently as she cocked her head.

"Ah...yes," I answered. "Yes, I think I'm okay."

OPERATION MOTHER MEKONG FIELD RESEARCH
INITIATED 15 JUNE 10:45:22
RECORDING ALL ACTIVITIES
EMOTION CONTROL ACTIVATED

The suit readout scrolled across my field of vision. Again I felt a million tiny feathers stroking my skin. I was filled with an emotion stronger than anything I had ever known.

I had to move out now.

"Shue, are you ready? Suit sterilized? Then let's get to it."

"You're acting strange. Are you really all right?"

Thep's words betrayed anxiety, but her expression was gentle. Her eyes were filled with trust. Thep was my buddy. We were part of a Mission to investigate the anomaly threatening Mother Mekong.

We had another buddy, Kurokawa. He was injured and had to stay at the base. It was up to us to reach the site, collect samples of the intruder, SR06, and the grasshoppers, and return to base safely.

Grasshoppers? Something far back in my mind protested. Was catching a few grasshoppers such a big deal?

A profound sense of the Mission's importance welled up in my chest.

Yes. I will capture the grasshoppers.

"Come on, Shue. Let's move out."

9   Field Research

A fluorescent green carpet spread left and right as far as I could see.

This was my color setting for SR06. I could see white streaks across the tips of the tall rice plants extending out of sight. These were probably the L&B and Mother Mekong logos.

Thep was walking point. We were about ten yards apart. It was slow going because even here on the "road," we had to push our way through chest-high grass and shrubs. It wasn't much different from virgin jungle.

I had never given a lot of thought to how these five-star sites operated. To cut emissions to zero, no internal combustion engines were allowed. Active Ground Cover certification meant no paved roads. The "road" we were on was about five yards wide. The only difference between it and the surrounding forest was the height of the undergrowth. The grass was full of insects—no defoliants or pesticides were allowed here. Naturally all the insects were theoretically harmless to SR06, but the sight of them buzzing around didn't make me feel as if we were on a road.

"I wasn't expecting it to be like this," I called to Thep.

"Like what? Are you disappointed?" Her ponytail flipped as she looked back at me. Her flawless teeth flashed in the tropical sun. She looked strong and full of energy. Her lips had an attractive sheen. The big tripod on her shoulder and the heavy camera array in her hand looked practically weightless.

"I mean, couldn't you at least cut the weeds?"

"You must be joking. You know the Active Ground Cover specs."

The undergrowth crunched under her boots as she moved forward, opening a path for me to follow.

It hit me that I was starting to forget what Thep looked like. What I was seeing now was a platoon buddy in the same light field gear as my own. An avatar.

The real Thep was encased in her ill-fitting protective gear, sweating like a pig as she trudged through the foliage. I was starting to wonder if my suit's augmented reality might not be a touch too realistic. The physical environment was indistinguishable from reality, even though the images were thoroughly processed before they hit my retinas, but the suit enhanced my "buddy's" appearance with such realism that I was starting to forget the real person.

The feel of foliage brushing against my trousers, the smell of grass, the sweet, humid breeze that tousled my hair—everything was augmented reality. Everything reaching my senses was mediated by the suit and the gel covering my body. I had the sensation of bugs colliding with the jumpsuit, sometimes even against my cheeks—modulated, of course, so as not to be actually irritating. But why go to the trouble, when I knew I was wearing protective armor?

"Shue, how far is it?"

"At this pace? Twenty minutes. Your gear is better than mine, so try to keep up."

I breathed harder as we climbed the slope. As I stepped over a branch, I took a deep breath and had the sensation of an insect flying up my nose. My visor was down, though of course I couldn't see it. What was the point of all this extra detail?

I was rubbing my nose frantically, trying to get the bug out, when Thep stopped ahead of me. She put the tripod down, opened her workspace in the palm of her hand and stared at it.

"Takashi's convulsions have stopped. Nimol just sent a message. He's still unconscious, but his pulse is stable. Sometimes his avatar gives instructions about treatment."

"That's good to hear. I was worried about him."

"How about you? You don't feel strange at all?"

"No, but this AR is a bit over the top."

EMOTION CONTROL ACTIVATED
FEAR PHASE 1A: DOUBT

The readout again. I felt a light constriction in my chest. Was the suit adjusting for fit?

"What do you mean, over the top?"

"Kind of like sensory overload. I feel like I'm wearing a woven jumpsuit, and you're—"

Looking very beautiful. Right. Better not say that. Thep cocked her head at my sudden silence.

"Anyway, with full-body feedback, it's impossible to tell what's real and what isn't. I'm not surprised it made Takashi sick. Total sensory overlo—"

EMOTION CONTROL PROGRESS
FEAR PHASE 2: PLAYBACK
DURATION: 0.2 SEC

I felt a stronger constriction in my chest. Thep's face blurred. The edges of my visual field disappeared in a blazing white light.

Kurokawa lifts his left hand to touch his temples.

No! Don't activate!

His visor goes dark. His head drops. Thep springs to his side.

I open his visor. Vomit spills out.

Get his suit off!

Kurokawa's wildly gyrating eyeballs lock on mine for a split second.

Someone is gurgling. I can't see! There's too much vomit.

EMOTION CONTROL PROGRESS
FEAR PHASE 3: PERSPECTIVE CHANGE

I feel the vomit rising in my throat. The stench makes me vomit harder. The puke fills the narrow space inside the visor.

Pull the release cable! I'm yelling, but it's Kurokawa's voice.

Thep is holding me close as one arm gropes for the release cable.

Please, please get this off me! I can't— The suit—

EMOTION CONTROL PROGRESS
FEAR PHASE 4: RECOVERY SEQUENCE
DURATION: 0.2 SEC

As disoriented as I am, I can still see the readout clearly. I feel the warmth of Thep's arms around me. Our hearts beat with the same rhythm. The heat from her body spreads through my chest and fills me with courage. I have a mission.

Thep clings to me. Her face is inches from mine, eyes glowing with trust and affection.

"Mamoru?" I hear Thep's voice across a great distance.

EMOTION CONTROL PROGRESS
FEAR PHASE 5: SEQUENCE COMPLETE

"What's wrong? Is it the suit?"

Thep is clinging to me, but her voice is far away.

What just happened? What did the status messages mean?

I lifted my leg and took a step forward. The foliage snapped under my boots and brushed the legs of my jumpsuit. I could still feel a tiny flame of resolve in my chest, but the sense of elation was ebbing away rapidly.

"Come on," called Thep. "We're wasting time."

*   *   *

"Take a look. There's your masterpiece."

We were midway up the slope that ended at the edge of the site.

Thep put a hand against the side of a white messenger tower that looked as new as the day it was installed. With the other she pointed to the fields dropping away in the distance, terrace upon terrace of green.

I had never seen my work from this perspective. Irrigation canals snaked around the terraces and followed the contours of the undulating terrain. The huge logos filled my field of vision, splashed across the landscape four miles across. The Mother Mekong logo was slightly smaller. Kurokawa once told me that the size of the logos precisely reflected the ownership share of each partner.

The terrain, the irrigation canals, the location of the buildings far below us—everything was exactly as I had seen it in the three-dimensional model that had burned itself into my brain as I was designing dispersion algorithms for the towers. Thep had followed my specifications to the letter when she built the site. The hundreds of messenger towers were exactly as I remembered placing them. The signals transmitted by the chemical messengers activated the style sheet mapped into SR06 to trigger color change precisely as specified.

"Sorry, Mr. Designer, but that color is awful. And the nocturnal glow is so bizarre. It really complicated our recruiting. At first even I thought it was the work of Teak Na."

As the sun dipped behind the mountains, the jellyfish protein in the rice plants would glow faintly blue-white. Barnhard had convinced Mother Mekong to add this feature to the plants. I couldn't picture how such a huge expanse of glowing vegetation would look at night.

Getting the protein to actually work with SR06 was an achievement, but I felt a surge of regret that I hadn't at least tried to propose an alternative.

EMOTION DETECTED: REGRET

EMOTION CONTROL PROGRESS: RECOVERY PHASE

CONFIRMING EMOTIONAL ISSUE

Again the tightening in the chest. Now the edges of my field of vision darkened and blurred.

Why did I give in so easily to that insane idea?

EMOTION CONTROL PROGRESS: RECOVERY PHASE 2
RECONFIRMATION

*   *   *

The sun falls rapidly behind the mountains. A moonless night comes on in seconds. With no light pollution this far out in the countryside, the stars look close enough to touch. SR06 glows and turns my chest and face blue-white.

Thep huddles at the base of the messenger tower, hands over her mouth in terror. Her body is shaking with fear.

"It was you, wasn't it? Why did you have to make them glow?"

"Shue, I was just—"

"Stay away from me. It's too late to apologize." She starts sobbing. My chest tightens even more. Why did I do this?

Now I'm crying too.

EMOTION CONTROL PROGRESS: RECOVERY PHASE 3
GAINING CONFIDENCE
DURATION 0.2 SEC

My eyes are blurred with tears, yet the readout is sharp and clear.

"I'm sorry. I was too hard on you. Everything's going to be fine, Mamoru. You know what? Your plants are beautiful. You're a master of your craft, to be able to do this."

She unzips her jumpsuit to her waist and walks slowly toward me, giving her hips full play. Even in the dimness I can see her half smile and parted lips. I ignore the faint warning in my head as she bares her breasts and extends her arms invitingly.

"Have faith in yourself, Mamoru."

Her fingers play over the back of my neck. The scent of her sweat-bedewed skin reaches me, penetrates me, and kindles a fire. I raise my arms to embrace her. My knees are trembling. I feel the blood flowing to my crotch. I inhale her breath and part my lips. Every nerve in my body is on fire.

Reason is down, but not out. I just manage to say it.

"Cancel emotion control."

EMOTION CONTROL TERMINATED

Emotion control has been terminated. It will not be reactivated unless required for the completion of this operation. Your orders remain in effect.

It was the voice of the tutorial. I was back in daylight, looking out over thousands of acres of rice.

Emotion control. The gel I applied before suiting up not only was creating the world I saw, it was manipulating what I felt. If the system message was to be believed, the whole experience took a fifth of a second.

Showing me an idealized buddy was supposed to bolster my fighting spirit. The tutorial had promised boundless courage even on a battlefield littered with corpses. The flashback to Kurokawa was another "treatment." The system had amped up my negative emotions to the point where I was able to see them as absurd and discharge them.

That feeling I had, of something rising in my throat—was that real, or another hallucination?

"Mamoru? Did something happen to you?" Thep was standing at the base of the messenger tower.

"No, I'm okay." I felt something rising in my throat again. I swallowed and got a bitter aftertaste. This was real. There was no gel in my mouth.

"You're not acting okay."

She stepped toward me. I remembered how she looked in the vision: the gloss of her lips, her satiny skin, the sweetness of her sweat still in my nostrils. My cheeks burned.

"You've been acting strange since we left the facility. Haven't you noticed? It's time for a break. Sit." She pointed to the base of the tower.

"Good idea." I looked up at the tower. "This is the first artificial structure I've seen since we got out here."

"Not completely artificial. It's sustainable cement, from terrestrial coral." She sat next to me. "Or maybe I should say, 'carnivorous coral.'"

I actually stood up in surprise. Thep laughed. Her flashing white teeth reminded me again of how she'd looked in the vision—her lips and the smell of her body. What the hell were the people who came up with Emotion Control thinking anyway? Was the US military that stupid? There was something fundamentally gross about giving people confidence by putting artificial emotions in their heads.

"I never thought I'd hear you say that." I sat down again.

"It's what I hear every day. Man-eating cement, vampire soil, killer crops. I know all the insults. In multiple languages." She started counting terms on her fingers.

"Is that what your staff says?"

"Those guys? You're joking. No, it's what *they* say." She pointed to the tree line beyond the fields. I could see a small black dot hanging above the ridge. As I squinted to bring it into focus, a circle appeared around the object and the image zoomed in. The suit's high-resolution camera was synced to my attention.

"It's a kite. There's a camera array hanging off it."

"Nature addicts. They're into aerial photography these days, trying to shoot the progress of the mutation. I told my people to shoot down anything that comes over the fields, but our friends are careful about keeping their kites over the DMZ."

"All I know about 'DMZ' is that it's a military term. What's it all about?"

"The DMZ is a buffer zone to protect the crops from insects and weeds. You can just see it there, at the base of the hills." She pointed. Between the edge of the site and the dense forest beyond was a ribbon of a different green. It looked like only one species of plant was growing there.

"They came up with the concept in the 2010s. It was supposed to make large-scale organic farming possible. Farms were surrounded by barren belts of land that were heavily sprayed with pesticides and defoliants. It was a kill zone for whatever you didn't want in your fields. Some of the zones were ten clicks wide.

"A DMZ is supposed to maintain peace by keeping combatants apart. I guess the farmers needed a catchy acronym. The thing is, most 'organic' farmers still use all kinds of chemicals in the DMZs around their farms."

"Even around Full Organic distilled crops?"

"Yeah, it's our dirty little secret. As long as the DMZ is owned and operated by someone else, you can get certified Full Organic without much hassle."

"I had no idea."

"It's kind of a scam, really. You buy a farm with its DMZ. Then you sell the DMZ to a company that specializes in that kind of thing, so it's not part of your farm anymore. Things have changed, of course. Now there are designed grasses you can plant in your DMZ. They keep out most insects and weeds, so you don't need to go around blasting chemicals. Even if you do, pesticides these days are safer than they used to be, but a Full Organic zone completely surrounded by a chemical kill zone doesn't make a lot of sense on its face.

"The point is, we didn't do that here. Our DMZ is also Full Organic. It gets the same five certs as the rest of the site. It was tough getting those certifications, let me tell you." Thep put her arms around her knees and stared off toward the tree line. "We planted ours with designed mustard greens."

"Was that your job? To get the certifications?"

"The whole idea was mine."

I looked at Thep with new respect.

"Sure, I had help. Takashi took the proposal to L&B and got them to approve it. He also got Enrico and Lintz to give me a research budget. I'm really grateful for all the support."

The wind was blowing Thep's hair into her eyes. She made no move to brush it aside—it was just my suit's projection—as she gazed at the terraces falling away toward the valley floor, lush with the fluorescent green of SR06.

"The nocturnal glow is a downer, but at least we have a DMZ free of chemicals. The next time we build one of these sites, I may have to toss out the whole DMZ concept."

Even with Emotion Control disabled, the suit's projection of my "buddy" was very easy on the eyes. Still, just then I was feeling drawn to Thep in a way that had nothing to do with the suit.

"Well, are you rested up? We better get going. My gear is so shitty, I can only stay out here for a few hours."

Thep stood and massaged the base of her spine. At least that was what the suit showed me. She was probably checking to make sure the replacement filter for her gas mask was still hanging off her belt.

*   *   *

Thep planted the tripod at the edge of the road next to the field and hoisted the camera array into place.

"This is today's border between SR06 and the advancing intruder. SR06 to the left of the line, intruder to the right. By tomorrow we should have footage of actual mutation."

"The grain heads are forming. Hey, what's that?"

The line between SR06 and the mutated plants was blurry, as if something was swarming over the leaves.

"We harvest in thirty days if everything stays on track. If we can't ship because of the mutation, we won't even bother to harvest." Thep noticed my gaze. "What's wrong?"

Tiny green dots were moving all over the SR06 leaves. Was it the suit again?

"I'm seeing some kind of visual noise, like a moire pattern. It's starting to make me nervous."

"Disable AR and check it out."

I touched the thumb and little finger of my left hand to my temples. "Deactivate."

The millions of feathers vanished. My suit was back. The gel was warm and slippery.

My visor was clear now, but what I was seeing was unchanged. It looked just like the suit's AR mode.

"There's no change."

"Pardon, what did you say?" Thep's English was back.

"What I'm seeing has not changed."

"Must be grasshoppers."

I walked to the edge of the road for a closer look. Now I could see that the green dots were insects—thousands or millions of them. Every SR06 leaf had a little colony. I was getting dizzy trying to take in the whole scene. That, and the warmth of the goopy gel, gave me that feeling of something rising in my throat again.

I made the gesture, reactivated the suit, and pointed to the swarming grasshoppers.

"This makes no sense. I thought insects wouldn't touch SR06."

"That's why I tried to warn L&B. Many times. Enrico's not there, you said. I guess that's why my messages didn't get through."

"Did you take samples?"

"Of course. I was going to sequence them and find out what they were. But our sequencer and the PC with Gene Analytics crashed the same day. Shit, I should've asked you guys to bring me replacements. That's why we couldn't do the second round of samples."

"Don't worry. We'll take care of that today."

"The first grasshopper samples I took disappeared, you know. I shouldn't have left them lying around. I forgot that the staff here are pretty superstitious."

Teak Na again. Fair Trade local hiring had a downside. The sight of all these insects busily chewing away at L&B's "insect-proof" rice plants must have looked like divine retribution.

I squatted to get a closer look. The suit zoomed in on one of the bugs. It had sturdy, tiger-stripe wings and was motionless, except for the constant movement of its mandibles chewing away at the leaf. Thep was right. It looked like you could just pick them up.

I heard a beep close to my ear. A suit alarm? A message appeared beside the enlarged image of the grasshopper.

IFF RESPONSE: NEGATIVE
FOUND OBJECT: GRASSHOPPER TYPE
THREAT LEVEL: UNKNOWN

"What the hell?"

"What's wrong?"

"My suit is telling me the grasshopper isn't responding to Identify Friend or Foe. Says it doesn't know how much of a threat it is."

"Maybe there's something wrong with your suit. Grasshoppers are grasshoppers."

If a grasshopper was all it took to set off the suit's IFF, how would it detect real threats? The suits we got from Kim were military surplus. Maybe they needed adjusting.

"Yeah, I think you're right. Anyway, I'll take a sample."

I took a jar from my backpack. Leave it to the Americans to use love as a motivational tool for soldiers while challenging insects to declare whether they are with you or against you.

10   Dong Duong Express

I sat in our private compartment waiting for the Dong Duong Express to get underway for Ho Chi Minh City. Kurokawa was lying on the seat across from me, wrapped in a blue blanket. The sun was just starting to lighten the horizon, but the curtains were closed so he could sleep.

"You've got chocolate on your face."

Thep, sitting next to me, pointed to my mouth. I wiped the chocolate off, leaving a brown streak on my thumb. The candy smelled cheap.

"Sorry about that. I told Nimol it was Kurokawa-san who needed the chocolate, not you."

"Don't worry about it. Give everyone my thanks for their help."

When I ended up collapsing like Kurokawa, Thep's people figured they should be shoving chocolate in my mouth every fifteen minutes too. When we got back from the field and I deactivated the suit, I'd been hit with some major side effects.

It happened in the sterilization chamber. They told me afterward that I let out a long howl and clung to Thep for support. Suddenly shutting down the suit's continuous feedback was too much for my nervous system, and I panicked. Thep's staff were used to the drill by now and got me out of the suit, flushed away the gel, and tied me to a bed in the infirmary where they pumped me full of tranquilizers. I remembered that much, then woke up in the van taking me and Kurokawa to Phnom Penh. That had only been an hour ago.

At Kurokawa's insistence, Thep and Nimol had loaded us into

the van late the night before and headed for Phnom Penh, racing to get us on the first express for Ho Chi Minh. Their chopper pilot wasn't certified for night flight.

"I suggested to Kurokawa-san that you stay an extra day to rest up, but..."

While I was sleeping off my reaction to the suit, Kurokawa had been "awake," using his avatar to interview Thep's employees and wrap up the other parts of the investigation. He insisted that we return to Ho Chi Minh City today and send some findings to L&B before the TerraVu satellite passed over the site. Yagodo had discovered the mutation from TerraVu's last batch of images, but those were taken at night. This time, the satellite would be shooting Mother Mekong in daylight. The images would be higher resolution and more damaging.

"I still don't understand how he can sleep and still control his avatar," said Thep.

"Yes, I've been wondering about that myself."

Feedback chips in each major joint control the user's avatar in augmented reality. The chips monitor actual movement and nerve impulses. Finer movements are filled in with simulation software, though the results are not very precise. I had never heard of people controlling a moving avatar while their body was immobilized.

"You don't move in Private Mode, but this isn't the same. He was controlling his avatar even while he was lying on his side, vomiting."

"Vomiting? That's nothing. His heart was stopped. How does he do it?"

The warning buzzer sounded. It was time to go.

"I'd like to tag along as far as the border, but I have to get back to Mother. I'll ping you if something comes up. Let me know as soon as you have positive IDs."

Thep thrust out a hand that was scored and scratched from working in the fields. "Well, see you."

I shook her hand and felt the warmth of her body. Her hand

wasn't as warm, or as soft and unmarked, as in the vision. But at least it was real.

"Hope to see you again."

In reality, if possible.

*   *   *

The train started moving. I blinked twice to deactivate my stage. If I maxed out on roaming in Cambodia, it would run me fifty bucks. In two hours we'd be across the border and the cost would drop to twenty. I'd just have to put up with the real world until then. I didn't need Yagodo's translation engine anyway.

Across from me, Kurokawa moved under his blanket. He was so small that a seat for two was big enough for him to lie down, as long as he curled up. Still, the cushions couldn't have been all that comfortable.

"Takashi, we're on our way. We'll be in Ho Chi Minh in five hours."

Kurokawa's jaw moved. I could hear him exhale.

"Try to get some rest now."

His head inclined slightly and he blinked twice. Was he inviting me into AR? I blinked twice and reactivated my stage. On the second blink, he was sitting upright, dressed in his suit.

I was rarely this close to his avatar. The sense of realism was astonishing. Morning sunlight through the gap in the curtains picked out vividly real details in his hair and the fabric of his suit. If I hadn't known he was curled up under a blanket, I would have sworn he was actually sitting there, using RealVu. Or maybe I had it backward—what I'd always thought was RealVu in our meetings was actually this avatar.

"Mamoru, I want to thank you for taking the samples. Ms. Thep told me that your suit knocked you out too. How are you feeling?"

"No worries, I'm all right. It didn't hit me that hard. I panicked a bit when I deactivated, that's all. I had a good long sleep. But what about you? Is it okay for you to be up like this?"

"Yes, as long as you keep feeding me chocolate every fifteen minutes. The calories will help me recover while I apply homeostasis behavior. I should be up and around by the time we get to Ho Chi Minh."

"Homeostasis behavior? What's that?"

A corner of his mouth twitched. He scratched the tip of his nose. It was as good as RealVu, and he was doing it while he slept.

"I guess it's about time I told you. You've seen what I can do. I appreciate your help, Mamoru. I want you to know that it wasn't my intention to hide this from you." He leaned forward with his elbows on his knees, hands clasped.

"During the East Asian Famine, I ate Super Rice Zero. It put me in a coma. Were you aware of this?"

"Well, that's what...Thep said when we were in her locker room." I almost said "Enrico." I was glad I hadn't, because it would have taken the conversation in a nasty direction.

"Oh, yes. I remember. I was fourteen. Everyone was hungry all the time. My father got hold of some rice for brewing sake. Super Rice Zero. I ate it. It caused brain damage. Polyglutamic acid isomers in the rice triggered excessive levels of mutated ataxin-l in my brain. Ataxin-1 is a protein that causes neuron death."

Kurokawa reached into his jacket pocket and brought out a model of a highly folded protein molecule. He held it in the palm of his hand. It looked like two tangled protein circles linked by a few strands.

"Take a look. This is a mutated ataxin-1 protein. The two circles are supposed to be side by side, but—" He pointed to a blue strand crossing the bottom of the gap. "As you can see, the polyglutamic acid isomers cause this strand to bend. The protein circles become entangled with each other. Some of you may find this hard to follow because it involves both isomers and mutation."

Kurokawa seemed to be looking right through me, as if he was talking to a room full of people.

"Takashi?"

"I realize that some of you here— Sorry. I was replaying a lecture I gave last year at L&B. It's in their archive."

Replaying a lecture? From an archive?

"Simply put, after I ate Super Rice Zero, I lost most of my cerebellum and brain stem." He turned his head and pointed behind his right ear. "I think you know what functions those parts of the brain handle."

"That's impossible. You wouldn't be able to move at all without function in those areas." The cerebellum maintains motor coordination; the brain stem regulates the central nervous system. Both are critical for survival in vertebrates. If the brain stem stops functioning, the result is brain death. Kurokawa was saying he had lost most of those areas, but that was impossible. He was alive.

"I don't blame you for being surprised. I use my avatar and precisely configured homeostasis behavior to compensate for the lost brain function. The behavior mostly makes up for the brain stem—"

"Hold it, Takashi. Conscious behavior as a replacement for autonomic brain function? How is that possible?"

"You saw the bar code on my shoulder yesterday?"

"Yes. I glanced at it."

He took a photo from his pocket and held it out. It showed a young man in a hospital bed. His right shoulder was visible. A bar code peeked from under the sheets. It looked like the one I had seen yesterday.

The photo had a caption.

TAKASHI KUROKAWA, L&B CORP. SINGAPORE CENTRAL LAB

L&B's Singapore facility was known to everyone in the industry. The first distilled crop plant, SR01, was engineered there. Along with his other work, Barnhard had been the lab's managing director for more than twenty years.

Kurokawa drew his right index finger horizontally over his lips in the NDA gesture. I blinked once to agree and register the conversation in my NDA database. If I ever discussed this conversation with someone else, my avatar would keep me from disclosing anything confidential.

"They used me as a guinea pig. The bar code is my patient number and experimental subject code. I got it at L&B's Central Research Lab. They didn't ask for permission, they just did it. When Barnhard found out what was going on, he fired the director and took over himself. He had to get my consent after I woke up."

Kurokawa lowered his index finger.

"It wasn't as if I had a choice. I was in a persistent vegetative state. My parents could've pulled the plug, but by the time I was shipped off to Singapore, they weren't in a position to make rational decisions. Barnhard was offering me a new life. I would be able to control my body with homeostasis behavior and an avatar. If my parents had refused to subject me to the experiment, I probably would've spent the rest of my life in a bed in Singapore.

"It was strange when they connected my body and brain again. When they started streaming tactile sensations to my cortex with AR feedback, I regained my sense of time passing. For me, time stopped soon after I started feeling nauseous and crawled into bed after eating SR Zero. I have a sense that I was dreaming while I was in the coma, but I have no specific memories of those dreams. Without my hippocampus, I was unable to form them."

The feeling of being controlled by the biochem suit came back to me. Everything I had experienced was as vivid as reality itself, yet it only took a fifth of a second to go from the pit of despair to the summit of bliss. My emotional state was controlled by a machine. Machine reality was my reality.

And that was Kurokawa's world, right here, right now. His peripheral nervous system was communicating with his brain through AR feedback. His avatar was the gateway to controlling his physical body. An avatar, alive in the real world.

"Don't get me wrong, I'm grateful to L&B. They gave me a university education—online of course—and a start in the industry as a 'ghost' employee." Kurokawa smiled. "Naturally I felt a certain amount of resentment. My face and body..." He touched his jaw.

"I asked them to do this. Make me identical to my father. I stopped growing at fourteen, and I didn't want to look like a child for the rest of my life. So I asked them to give me the face, body, and voice of my father. That way L&B would never forget what it did to me. Even now, Barnhard sometimes finds it hard to look at me. So I got what I wanted, I suppose. If I had to do it over again, I'd have them make me handsome. Maybe make me look something like you. But with my height, it wouldn't count for much." He smiled again, that gentle smile.

"It's not a bad way to live, all in all. Meeting people in augmented reality and in the real world is the same to me. Instead of my body controlling my avatar, my avatar controls my body. If I do a presentation, it goes into the archive and I can play back any part of it, down to the gestures and tone of voice. If I don't want to experience a particular sensation, I can block it. How do you think I can stand eating chocolate all day?

"Unfortunately, the solution to my coma was what caused that reaction to the suit. I have more than two hundred feedback implants. You have, what, seven?"

I nodded vacantly. I could only wonder what sort of look I had on my face.

Seven chips: one in each wrist and ankle, one in each ear, and one in my throat. Some people have many more for professional reasons. Actors, say, or people in the military—anyone who needs extra AR support functions. People have implants in other joints, like the elbows and knees, but two hundred? I couldn't begin to imagine where Kurokawa's implants were.

"I can't deactivate my internal AR stage, and the conflict with the suit's AR made me go haywire. To let me use AR feedback to control my body, they had to sever the corpus callosum that links the two hemispheres of my brain. This came with an advantage, though. Whenever I need to, I can deploy two avatars at once, one from each hemisphere. Still, the information overload from the suit disabled both of them.

"I'm getting better now. I should be fully functional by the time we reach the border. Until then, please don't forget the chocolate." He put his hands on his knees and bowed. "I just need a little more time. If you need to talk to me, open your stage and let me know.

"Oh, one more thing. I just made a reservation with Kim to handle the sample analysis. When we get to Ho Chi Minh, could you take the samples over to him?"

"Okay, but . . . you just made a reservation?"

"Yes, while we were talking. I told you, I can use two avatars at once. That's why I need so many calories. My brain burns a lot of glucose. Well, time to sleep."

He bowed again and disappeared.

*   *   *

I unwrapped a chocolate bar, broke it in four pieces and put them on the tray under the window.

"Takashi, time for your chocolate."

I lifted his blanket and looked closer at the bar code on his right shoulder, proof that he had been a guinea pig. I froze.

The bar code was surrounded by hundreds of tiny scars I hadn't noticed at Mother Mekong. A lot of them looked like razor scars. There were also welts that looked like nail scratches, even a few burn marks. Some of the scars meandered, as if the cuts were inflicted in a frenzy.

The image of Kurokawa at the Central Research Lab didn't show anything like this. He must have done it to himself after he regained control of his body.

But it wasn't the scars that stopped me in my tracks. There were three fresh welts over the bar code itself. The raised flesh was spotted with dried blood. He must have tried to rip the bar code off yesterday, after the suit sent him into a tailspin.

The words seemed to echo in my head. Central Research Lab. Plastic surgery to make him look like his father. Biological experiments. A brain that used implants and avatars to control the body...

I replaced the blanket and tucked it around him so only his head was uncovered. His face was utterly peaceful in sleep. I brought the chocolate close to his mouth. He opened it, put out his tongue, and took the candy. The movements of his jaw and tongue were unnaturally smooth, almost mechanical. They were not the movements of a body under direct physical control of a brain.

As I watched him chewing the chocolate, his words were replaced in my mind by Enrico's, words I had been trying to forget.

"Don't trust him, okay? He hates genetic engineering."

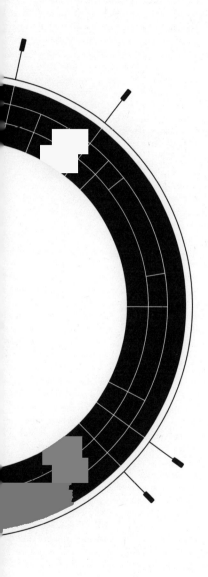

PART 4

THE FACE OF TOMORROW

11   Kim's Bio Solution

The Dong Duong Express pulled into Saigon Station at noon. The area around the taxi stand was clogged with electric bikes. There was a constant beeping of horns, like cicadas chirping. The afternoon traffic jam was in full swing, but I bundled a hesitating Kurokawa into a cab by himself.

"All right then, I'll wait for you at Yagodo's office," he said.

As I watched the cab pull away, I remembered his transformation that morning. Soon after we crossed the border, he had suddenly sat up, said "Excuse me" and changed into his suit. He used gel and a comb to restore his hair to its trademark condition.

I wanted to ask why he was so anxious to beat the TerraVu satellite, but there was no time. I was glued to my workspace, reading the latest from Yagodo. Yesterday's haul alone was six thousand-some genomes, and he was hurrying to find a match. Most of the salvaged data was for cross-bred cultivars or random mutations. It astonished me that Japan had once been home to so many different rice cultivars. It was unbelievable.

Yagodo wanted to know about the grasshopper. He wasn't sure whether or not it had anything to do with the mutation, but he wanted to look into it anyway. I sent him footage of the insects munching on SR06 along with a shot of our sample specimen lying motionless in its jar.

I spent the three hours from the border to Ho Chi Minh reviewing Yagodo's reports and sending him comments and visuals. By the time we reached Saigon Station, it was time for the afternoon traffic jam.

I watched Kurokawa's taxi disappear into a sea of electric motor-bikes before turning away and setting off on foot for Kim's shop in the Old Market, which was spread out on the west side of the vast shopping area that lay south of the station.

The Old Market was hot, and it smelled. The ground around the food stalls lining the narrow lanes was littered with vegetable scraps, egg shells, and other kinds of raw garbage. The sewage system consisted of open gutters brimming with household waste. Though the area was densely inhabited, judging from the smell, foot traffic was light. As I walked deeper into the maze of streets, the constant honking from the big avenue faded.

What kind of location was this for a bio lab? Just when I was about to decide I was lost, I arrived at my destination. It was a very strange building. No way was anyone going to miss this one.

The structure itself was more or less like the souvenir shops on either side, but with rectangles of four-inch angle iron, painted orange and set in the wall where the window frames used to be. The windows were caulked all around with fresh silicon sealant. The walls and door were plastered with so many biohazard stickers it almost looked like a horror movie set. The average passerby would be certain to give it a wide berth.

Below the black-lettered KIM'S BIO SOLUTION sign was a menu of services in spidery script. He offered a full range of DNA profiling and analysis and even leased and sold lab equipment. I assumed that the name meant he was Korean. In these surroundings, which time seemed to have forgotten, his shop looked like it meant business. I pressed the intercom next to the door. A male voice answered.

"Hello? Do you have an appointment?"

"Yes, Mr. Kurokawa reserved. He told me to come here."

The response came back in fluent Japanese. "Oh, it's you. Let me open up."

The rattling of heavy bolts went on for several seconds. Air seemed to be squeezing past the door frame into the interior, making a high-pitched whine. The ventilation fan on the wall started blowing outward, the cool air from inside carrying the smell of ozone. Kim was keeping the inside atmospheric pressure below ambient to keep any microorganisms he was dealing with from escaping. These sorts of arrangements were not easy to make. I decided I could trust his technical chops.

I put my hand on the knob and turned it. When the door opened inward, I was caught off guard and sucked inside so fast that I nearly stumbled.

"Whoa, watch your step!"

A huge man in a white lab coat caught me as I came stumbling into the room. His voice was gruff but cheerful. He steadied me with one hand, put the other on the heavy door, and closed it easily.

"The damn door opens the wrong way. Should've used a decent contractor."

He let me go and took a step back. My eyes were at the level of his throat. His bulging chest muscles strained at the fabric of his silk shirt.

"I am Kaneda." He extended a hand that was twice as beefy as mine. Its deeply tanned skin was crisscrossed with white scars. The ball of muscle at the base of his thumb looked like stone.

"Mamoru Hayashida."

"Sit. Yagodo told me a little about your project." He gestured to a white plastic table and some chairs of the same cheap material, the type the food stands used. The table was surrounded by strange equipment of all kinds and sizes, stacked nearly to the ceiling.

"Thanks. So you're Japanese."

"Oh? Did you think I was Korean? Good, that's the whole point. But as you see, I'm Japanese."

I wondered if I was supposed to laugh. He didn't look Japanese at all. He was as tall as Barnhard and must have been twice my weight. His loose-fitting lab coat could not hide the thick musculature of his torso. His face was sunburned and deeply lined, and his white hair was cropped short. He looked more like a soldier than a biochemist.

But it was the eyes that made his ethnicity iffy. The strange color was not a trick of the light. His right eye was light brown, like Yagodo's, but the left, the lid of which was crossed by a deep scar, was inky black.

"Yagodo told me you needed DNA profiles for two plants and one insect. Do I have that right? I'd like to do a separate contract for this, not an attachment to the one I did with Yagodo for the helicopter and the suits."

"Sure, that's what I was planning. L&B will be subcontracting you directly. There'll be some confidentiality clauses."

"In AR, right? We can do that now. Gotta warn you, my stage is pretty basic." He put an index finger to the temple of an imaginary pair of glasses in the invitation gesture. I blinked twice to activate. He opened his left hand, put his thumb and little finger to his temples and whispered "Activate," the same protocol as the biochem suits.

The stage was generic. Nothing was altered or enhanced. The table was the same. Kaneda had put all of his computing power into his avatar; it was only just recognizable as one.

"Well, this is fine," I said. "I'd like to keep the whole agreement confidential, if you don't mind." I zipped my index finger across my lips in the NDA gesture. Kaneda nodded and I unlocked my NDA filter. Avatars are useful for transactions like this.

"The work is for one sample of SR06, one sample of an unknown rice plant, and one insect specimen, all from Mother Mekong. You will extract the genome to a gXML file."

"The insect is from Mother Mekong?"

"Yes, a grasshopper. The site is crawling with them."

"But SR06 is supposed to be *the* sustainable crop. No insects, no pesticides. What are grasshoppers doing out there?"

"We don't know. That's why we need an ID first."

"Do you have a photo?"

I handed him an image of a grasshopper chewing on an SR06 leaf, taken with the suit camera.

Kaneda studied the photo. "This looks like a locust." A subtitle appeared in the air in front of him.

LOCUST: SWARMING PHASE OF CERTAIN SPECIES
OF SHORT-HORNED GRASSHOPPERS

"Maybe a desert locust. It's just like something I saw in Somalia years ago. I can't say for certain until I have the genome, but this is no Asian pest. This sick green color is the distilled plants, right? Wait a minute, this could..." He stroked his chin and raised an eyebrow. "This could be worth a fortune."

"Say what?"

"Can I have commercial rights to my findings? L&B and other distilled engineers would love to get their hands on the genome of an insect species that actually feeds on distilled crop plants. We could split it fifty-fifty—"

"You're not serious, are you?"

"No? Too bad. Okay, how about a thousand US to do the work and keep my mouth shut?" He held up a finger and winked. His eyes were smiling. A thousand dollars was not much at all. That stuff about selling the genome and hush money had been a joke.

"The price is right, but I need it now." I was too anxious about getting the work done to laugh at the jest.

"I'll be running these through the serial sequencer. I assume that's okay. Is tonight soon enough?"

"That would be great. Let's do that agreement—" I reached for the template.

"This is great. You're just like your pal."

"Who? You mean Kurokawa?"

"Yeah. Your way of doing business is the same. That's what Yagodo told me. 'Two good guys brought us an interesting job.'"

I wasn't sure how to answer. "Well, thanks for that," I said finally.

Kaneda guessed right. My contract template was cribbed from

something I got from Kurokawa. His jobs were not always interesting, but the arrangements were always fair and speedy.

"How about a cup of tea while you get that ready? You need a break from the heat."

I looked up from the contract and saw an artifact I'd never seen before. A clear liquid was pouring from a point in midair into a glass with ice at my elbow. At first I thought it was an AR widget, but I could feel a few drops of liquid splash onto my arm. The cup and the tea, at least, were real.

"Don't be startled. It's just iced tea."

"But it was coming out of nowhere..." I pointed to a point above the glass.

"Out of this, you mean." A bottle appeared suddenly on the table next to the glass. "Like it? This is Physical Mixed Activity. PMA. It's a method for doing things with your avatar while you do something else with your body. With practice, you could even strangle someone in Private Mode."

Kaneda showed me how he could sit with arms folded and move the bottle on the table. "This is the simplest kind of PMA. You fold your avatar's arms and then slowly unfold your own arms. You have to ignore what the feedback chip is telling you. Your avatar is programmed to show natural movement only, so if you unfold your arms from a slightly unnatural angle, the chip can't read what you're doing."

"I get the basic principle. But you were pouring tea into a glass. How could you see the real cup in AR?"

"Didn't you notice my eyes? I can use augmented and nonaugmented vision simultaneously. I have one corneal implant. Simple, no? That's all you need to do all kinds of things." He grinned. "If you want to learn, you have a good teacher."

"Kurokawa, you mean?"

"Yeah. He's the only person I know who can use PMA to make himself look taller. I can only do PMA with simple movements and my dominant hand, but I bet he can use it to control his expression."

Kaneda's avatar sat with arms folded while the bottle levitated again and poured tea into his glass.

"Anyway, let's do that contract. Not ready? You do it like Kurokawa, but you sure are slower. His contracts are finished as soon as he pulls them out."

I wasn't sure I could compete with a man who had two avatars.

After tea, I followed Kaneda into his lab. The intensity of the lighting made me blink. Every inch of the room was bathed in light. A bewildering array of cutting-edge and vintage equipment was neatly arranged. The room was small, but everything looked organized and efficient.

A cell-processing workstation with a manipulator stood in the center of the space, along with a blacklight-illuminated work table.

"Mamoru, can I ask you to put the insect in the chamber yourself?" Kaneda opened the hatch and inserted the serial DNA sequencer read head.

"Sure, but why?"

"I don't need the headache. Sometimes I get idiots in here with containers that aren't properly sealed."

"All right, no problem." I pulled the sample jar with the grasshopper out of my shoulder bag.

The jar was empty.

"What the fuck?" I was so shocked, I started twisting the lid.

"What are you doing? Don't open it!" Kaneda put a huge hand over mine.

The jar contained a small, dry clod of dirt, and that was all. I turned it upside down and peered at the inside of the lid. The dirt made a tinkling sound. The lid was empty.

I knew I had placed a grasshopper in the jar yesterday. The sensation came through the suit's AR, but I could still feel the dry carapace of the insect with my fingertips as I interrupted its single-minded munching and plucked it off the leaf. I even felt a slight letdown when the bug made no move to escape.

The lettering on the label was my own. Kaneda took a closer look at the jar and snatched it away from me.

"Give it here. We're in business." He tossed the jar into the chamber.

"What are you doing?" I was dumbfounded.

"I saw some grasshopper parts in there. It looked like the dirt was eating them—they're disappearing right now. Get back to the office. I've got to grab some viable cells before they disappear."

Kaneda hunched over the manipulator and went to work.

*   *   *

I sat at the plastic table with my head in my hands. The other two sample jars were in front of me.

I had returned from Mother Mekong with three sample jars— one grasshopper, one SR06, and one intruder sample. Kaneda had the jar with the grasshopper. The problem was the two jars in front of me. Both contained the intruder. There was no mistaking that dull green hue and the red-tinged grain head. I thought I was losing my mind.

"Well, Mamoru, we lucked out." The vinyl curtain parted and Kaneda came through. "I managed to isolate muscle and intestinal cells. The sequencer is reading the DNA. It's working very slowly for some reason, but we're home free. We'll ID that bug—hey, what's the problem?"

I handed him the sample jars and explained what had happened.

"I don't get it. Well, we'll read both of them. We can get to the bottom of this later. Maybe your SR06 and the intruder are the same plant."

I couldn't think of anything to say. Everything I had seen at Mother Mekong was mediated by the suit's AR stage. How and why it presented things to me the way it did was something I wasn't in a position to know.

"Don't worry, Mamoru. I've never seen it before either." Kaneda sat down heavily in the chair across from me. The plastic legs squeaked under the weight.

"Seen what?"

"Seen something degrade like that while I watched. Mother Mekong's soil can break down waste products, I heard. If it's that aggressive, it's practically carnivorous."

Was he right? Was the ground cover really that aggressive? I hadn't touched it. I grabbed the bug right off the leaf. It didn't have a speck of soil on it. And—

I had a photograph.

"Wait, I took a photo of the specimen this morning. Here, take a look." I handed him the same image I'd sent Yagodo earlier. The grasshopper was motionless. It was impossible to tell if it was alive, but the brilliant green body and the tiger-striped, semitransparent wings were not degraded at all.

"This is it, huh? Very pretty."

"It didn't look alive when I took the photo, but I didn't see any decomposition. This was only five hours ago."

"Then someone poisoned it."

Kaneda had given voice to a suspicion that had been quietly trying to break through into my consciousness, a suspicion I had been ignoring.

"Sorry, just joking. Mother Mekong doesn't use pesticides."

He was right. If someone had put something else in that jar along with the grasshopper—such as a bit of sustainable ground cover—then the rapid disintegration would be explained. And only one other person had had access to the jar after I took the picture. Someone who was adept at PMA.

Kurokawa.

12   Terrorism

I left Kaneda's lab and set out for the office. Traffic was finally moving again, but there were no taxis to be had in the Old Market.

I climbed the steps to the second floor and touched the brass door handle. The access tone sounded softly, and the door swung open. After only two days in this office, it already felt good to be back. I blinked twice and stepped inside.

"I'm sorry, Mamoru." Kurokawa was sitting on the couch. He bowed apologetically.

"About the grasshopper?"

"What about it? Did something happen?" He looked up at me wide-eyed.

"When I got to the lab— Wait, what's going on?"

Yagodo sat across from Kurokawa, wearing a bright red shirt. He had one arm stretched out on the sofa back and stared at me quizzically. Nguyen was at her desk in her ao dai and AR glasses. She sat with arms straight, her hands on her knees, and peered at me with the same odd expression. All three of them looked slightly grim.

I stroked my jaw in puzzlement. The sweat on my face ran down my wrist.

"He hasn't seen it yet." Nguyen raised a shapely eyebrow. Yagodo nodded.

"What is it? What happened?" I sat next to Kurokawa. Yagodo pointed at two news widgets on the table. Each bore a little banner with a countdown to January 19—the 2038 Problem.

"Have you seen today's *Times of the World*? Or Common News Network?"

I shook my head. I never watched either of them regularly, and I had enough to think about, with carnivorous ground cover devouring our grasshopper and the possibility that Kurokawa was somehow connected to our problem.

"Listen, Mamoru. These segments are airing tomorrow. Both of them will report the mutation at Mother Mekong. Other news shows may carry the same story, but the previews for these two are already out."

Kurokawa furrowed his brows in concern, though I couldn't see why. We knew the media was going to catch on sooner rather than later. If they found out about the mutation before the investigation had a chance to show results, so much the worse, but we couldn't hide it forever. Yagodo had discovered the mutation on his own from the TerraVu photos, and the nature addicts at Mother Mekong were photographing and taking instrument readings every day, even if their technique was sloppy. Obviously they would be happy to give their data to the media.

"Mamoru, you need to see this," said Yagodo. "It may come as a shock, but before we play it, please understand: I'm on your side. So is Takashi. Ready?"

"Wait a minute, what the hell—"

Yagodo pointed to the wall. A video frame appeared with a red, wire-frame globe over a banner reading, "World Reporting: Truth They Don't Want You to Know." It was the opening for the same program I'd seen at Café Zucca.

The banner and globe pulled back into the frame and were replaced by a studio set. Sascha Leifens stood center stage, hands behind her back, blue eyes leveled at the camera. She was illuminated by a spotlight.

"Sascha Leifens for World Reporting. Tomorrow, we unmask the gross negligence of an agricultural industry completely warped by genetic engineering." Footage of Barnhard at his distilled crop presentation to the FAO faded in behind her.

"We know every base pair in this genome. Every trait is under our control. SR01 is just the first drop from the distiller's pot—"

"This is Lintz Barnhard, vice president of L&B Corporation, a producer of distilled seedlings. For the past twenty years, this man has been hawking his genetically engineered plants to farmers all over the world. In the process, his company has ravaged the planet with its corporate greed. Look at this."

Three-dimensional images of SR06 sites started rising from the floor around Sascha. She strolled between the miniature landscapes and continued her denunciation of distilled crops. She used all the clichés I'd heard a million times, but her words barely penetrated my awareness.

I couldn't believe it. I had worked on every one of these sites: Hop Inn Farm in Adelaide, Heaven's Farm in Borneo, Barmy Plantation in the Gobi Desert ... With several thousand SR06 sites around the world, why were they only showing my work?

Sascha strolled slowly back to center stage. "World Reporting has discovered a site where the L&B logo is disintegrating—proof that SR06 is out of control. We've also identified the reckless gene mapper behind this fatal flaw."

The floor of the set morphed into a checkerboard pattern. Bone-white stucco walls rose on either side. A cathedral. There was an image of Christ in the alcove behind the altar.

"This is Saigon Cathedral in Vietnam's Ho Chi Minh City."

Sascha turned and walked deeper into the set, toward a man in one of the pews. He seemed to be staring at his lap.

"That's me. How...?"

"His name is Mamoru Hayashida. He is a freelance gene mapper working for L&B Corporation. As you can see, he's praying."

She turned to face the camera and pretended to put her hand on my shoulder. Sitting in the pew, I raised my face to the image of Christ, then hung my head again.

"A deadly mutation is rampaging through the Mother Mekong

Project—his project. Did guilt bring him here? Guilt for meddling with life itself? For the damage he's helping L&B wreak on the environment? Or is it sorrow over what this blunder will do to his comfortable lifestyle?"

"It was her..." The skinhead in the cathedral. She had turned her cameras on me.

"After a year of careful investigation, World Reporting will unmask the dark world of genetic engineering and the negligence and arrogance of those responsible for this project."

The video clicked off.

"We didn't know the target would be you." Kurokawa frowned. "We assumed it would be Barnhard or Mother Mekong. We were getting ready to rebut whatever they came up with. World Reporting got the drop on us, but we're going to do everything we can to protect you. I just talked to Barnhard. He's committed to giving you all the legal support you need."

Kurokawa leaned forward to look me square in the face. "Since your name is public knowledge now, the media will do whatever they can to find you. I can ask L&B's corporate communications department to represent you—"

"Not a good idea." Yagodo shook his head. "Running questions through L&B would add fuel to the fire. It would look like Barnhard was trying to muzzle him. All he can do is ask the media to leave his contractors alone."

Kurokawa bit his lip. I couldn't think of a better plan.

"World Reporting needs a scapegoat," said Yagodo. "Their reporting is hate speech against distilled crops and genetic engineering. They'll ignore L&B's side of the story, and whatever L&B says, they'll use it against you."

"You're right. We're not ready to rebut their story. I wonder how they knew Mamoru would be there?" Kurokawa peered at me curiously.

"...Enrico."

"The project manager no one can get ahold of?" Yagodo smiled.

"He called me. I was in the cathedral. He wanted to meet. I didn't know it was a setup."

"I'm sorry," said Nguyen. "If I hadn't asked him to wait for me—"

Yagodo cut her off. "They were tracking him. They would've gotten their footage somehow. It could just as easily have been Takashi."

"I wouldn't have minded at all," said Kurokawa. "But this body of mine disqualifies me. Using a victim of Super Rice Zero as an example of people who benefit from the distilled crop industry would've been slightly bizarre."

"In any case," said Yagodo, "there's nothing we can do to stop the presses. Getting to the bottom of this mystery is the only way we can fight back." He spread the SR06 and intruder images—the photos I sent him from the train—across the table. "We've got to focus on identifying your intruder."

I nodded, but I couldn't get Enrico's words out of my head. Was Kurokawa pulling the strings in the shadows? And if that was true, why help the media frame me?

*   *   *

The office was filled with the aroma of sweetened coffee. When I came out of my reverie I found Nguyen sitting next to me, stirring sugar into a freshly brewed cup.

"Just sugar, right?" She poured the coffee over ice and set the glass in front of me. I nodded thanks but didn't feel like drinking it. Yagodo had our priorities right, but after salvaging nearly ten thousand candidate genomes, we still didn't have a candidate, much less a confirmed match.

Yagodo was studying the three-dimensional images of full-grown SR06, searching for something in their physical appearance that could speed up the search. I was skeptical. If it were that easy, we would have found our match already. I didn't believe a visual inspection would show much of interest.

"You know, there's something odd here," said Yagodo. "The seed heads on both plants are more or less identical. If this was a legacy cultivar with vulnerability to red rust, there ought to be more variation."

He zoomed in on the seed heads of each plant, marked the base of the husks and counted on his fingers. "Distilled crops are designed down to the number of seeds on each stalk. It's amazing. The vascular bundle branching is different from natural grasses, so you designed it as a spiral . . . Hold it, we might be on to something here."

He took a long drink of coffee and condensed milk. "Mamoru, each SR06 stalk is designed to yield a thousand grains, correct?"

"Under optimal growing conditions. L&B designed the vascular bundle to respond dynamically to the weight of a thousand-grain seed head by boosting the hydraulic pressure. They got a patent for it."

"Then we've found something interesting. The intruder is supposed to be a legacy plant, but it has roughly the same number of grains. The way the grains are setting looks the same too."

I took a closer look at the grains Yagodo had marked. They were arranged in more or less the same way.

"You're probably too young to have seen an ear of legacy rice. A yield of two hundred grains would be very high for a natural cultivar. But the intruder has more like a thousand grains. It's as if someone took an SR06 plant and painted it with the old rice color."

Yagodo enlarged a grain from the intruder. "Up close, though, the rice is different in certain ways. These intruder grains look slightly withered too."

If the intruder and SR06 had the same yield, that was an important discovery, but all it did was deepen the mystery. No legacy cultivar could boast that kind of yield.

"Mother Mekong's ground cover doesn't offer enough nutrients or moisture for most natural plants. I'm not surprised the grains are drying out." I looked at the tip of the grain Yagodo had enlarged. It was slightly red. "Wait, what's going on here?" I stood and held the image up to the light.

"This isn't dying. It's naturally red. The color has gradations from red to purple." I swept a finger from the tip of the grain to the base. Held against the light, it was clear that the color was transparent toward the middle. Grains on a dying plant would have been opaque.

Yagodo looked at me with open-mouthed surprise. "You found it! Why didn't we notice?" He gave me a playful shove. "This is a heritage rice. It's close to wild rice. Heritage grains are the color you see there. What gives it that color? Like with eggplants. One of the anthocyanins...Right, cyanidin."

Yagodo suddenly had a soiled rag in his hand. "John! Paul! You've got work to do!" The door opened, and the two golden retrievers came running in.

"Fetch me the genome for black rice! The ones with lots of $C_{15}H_{11}O_6+$ cyanidin." He held the rag out for them to sniff. "It's urgent!" The dogs gave a short, excited bark and ran out the door.

"What's that rag?" I asked.

"The search query. It's a matter of time now. There aren't that many varieties of heirloom rice. I think we'll have your intruder identified by the end of the day."

Yagodo reached for his iced coffee, but Nguyen was already picking the glass up off the table. She took mine too, though I'd only had a sip or two.

"You can't let the ice melt. It's made from raw tap water."

Kurokawa was about to take a drink of coffee but handed his glass to Nguyen.

"This is perfect," he said to Yagodo. "By the end of today! It won't give us enough ammunition to shut down World Reporting, but at least we'll have something—sorry, someone's calling me. Hello?"

He stood up and took the call on a "receiver" formed from his extended thumb and little finger, like something out of an old movie.

He took the "receiver" from his ear and put his other hand over his little finger.

"It's Thep. I'd like to invite her here. I think you should all hear this."

"Fine with me," said Yagodo. "Mamoru?"

"Why not? Tell her yes."

Kurokawa made the gesture of invitation and pointed to the sofa. Thep's avatar popped in, sitting next to me. She was wearing cargo pants and a windbreaker with the Mother Mekong logo emblazoned on the back. This must be her work avatar.

"It's the grasshoppers."

"What happened?"

She just shook her head. Her avatar was pink-cheeked and healthy looking, but her voice trembled.

"I don't know where to start. Everything is so strange, so confusing..." She balled her fists on her knees and stared at her lap.

As we waited for her to say something, the door opened noiselessly and John came trotting in with a tennis ball. He noticed Thep immediately and kept his eyes on her as he approached the table. He dropped the ball and rubbed his muzzle on her knee. The muzzle of a real dog would have passed right through her, but one avatar can interact physically with another.

Thep gasped and looked up. Yagodo grinned and touched the ball, changing it to a folder. He held it up to Thep.

"Nice to finally meet you, Ms. Thep. My name is Isamu Yagodo. The dog is John. He's brought us a file salvaged from the Internet—a candidate genome for the intruder at Mother Mekong."

John continued rubbing his head affectionately against Thep's knee. "Do you like dogs?" asked Yagodo.

"Of course." She stroked John's head and looked over my shoulder toward the door. "Wait—how many do you have?"

The door was standing open. Paul ran in, a red bandanna around his neck, followed by another John. Each dog left a file on the table and scampered out again, but before they reached the door more Johns and Pauls came trotting in with more balls and Frisbees. The table was quickly piled high with their booty.

"Sixteen all together. I'll be at my desk searching for matches. Please continue."

"Your dogs made me feel better," said Thep. "I have two things to report. First, look at this video from the camera array. We captured the moment of mutation."

Thep put a video file on the table. The thumbnail showed a group of grasshoppers clinging to an SR06 plant. I recognized the hills in the background.

"I'm going to play this. Pay attention to the spot where their legs touch the leaf."

Thep set playback at 3,000X and touched PLAY. The sun shot into the sky, peaked, and dropped behind the hills. The fields in the background started glowing faintly blue. The grasshoppers moved slowly and jerkily across the surface of the leaf. It looked like their legs were leaving a stain on its surface.

"See how the color changes? Look again, closer this time."

She zoomed in on a single grasshopper and set playback at 100X. "Look at the mandibles. It's not eating the leaves."

I almost doubted my eyes. Wherever the grasshopper bit the leaf, it turned a dull green. The color change spread out as if a drop of ink had fallen on the leaf and was wicking along its veins.

"I couldn't believe it at first," said Thep, "but the grasshoppers are changing the color of the living plants. Wherever they bite, the leaves start mutating."

Now I knew why the grains in SR06 and the intruder were setting in the same pattern. SR06 was mutating directly into the intruder. But could a living plant mutate into another living plant?

Thep put two new photos on the table side by side. "These are microscope studies of SR06 cells before and after mutation. Can you tell which is which?"

The photos showed cells in cross-section, surrounded by thin membranes. Tiny fluorescent-green granules surrounded the nuclei of the cells in both images, but the cell on the left had objects like small, black strands scattered among the green granules. The strands were roughly the same size as the nucleus.

"The image on the right shows normal SR06 cells. The cells on the left have something new. They look like organelles, but no organelle is large enough to see at this magnification without staining."

"What are they?"

"Don't know, and I don't have the gear to investigate further. I never thought I'd be doing detailed cell studies out at the site."

"Ms. Thep, could you send samples of the intruder cells to the Central Research Lab?" said Kurokawa.

"It's taken care of. They'll arrive the day after tomorrow." She pulled out another folder. "The cell studies were one thing. Now for the main problem."

Yagodo looked up from his search for matches. "Shall I guess? The grasshoppers aren't only going after SR06. They're attacking plant species all around the site. Am I right?"

Thep's expression hardened, then changed slowly to a smile. Her avatar's Behavior Correction was searching for a straightforward way to reproduce her expression. A smile is the system default for anything too subtle—or inappropriate—to reproduce.

"I wish I could say you're wrong."

Yagodo shook his head and sighed. Kurokawa leaned forward, body tensed. "Ms. Thep, are you telling us that the vegetation beyond the perimeter is also mutating?"

She nodded, took several more images from the folder and laid them on the table. The photos showed a strange change coming over the vegetation.

The rice plants and the forest beyond the perimeter were a monotone green. Neither the deep green of mature foliage nor the yellowish hue of newer leaves was visible. Everything was the same dull green as the intruder. Even the red bark of the gum trees was dyed a dull green. It looked like an image processing error.

A closeup of the mutated foliage showed an even more ominous development. The plants were sprouting rice stalks with tendrils—genetic chimeras.

"The smaller the genetic distance between rice and the affected plant, the faster the mutation," said Thep. "The angiosperms are changing too, though not as fast. Ferns and lichens are unaffected. As to the effect on non-plant life, we can only pray..." Her expression defaulted to a smile again as her voice faltered.

"You've got a biohazard."

At Yagodo's words, everyone froze. Kurokawa's eyes widened with fear. His jaw trembled. Nguyen swallowed hard and stared at Yagodo.

"Who do you contact about biohazards, the World Health Organization?" I wondered out loud. "Takashi?"

"Can't we... eradicate the grasshoppers? If we send a sample... to the research lab..."

He hadn't even heard me.

"We've got to notify the WHO!" I heard myself shouting. If we were dealing with a biohazard, it wasn't just a problem for L&B and Mother Mekong. We had to alert the Cambodian government and the international community.

"I just notified L&B and Mother Mekong headquarters," said Kurokawa. "We'll let them handle the notifications. I want to get a clear handle on the situation and find a way to keep this from spreading further."

"Shouldn't we alert the WHO directly?"

"The first thing they'll do is shut us out of the process. We should let people like Barnhard handle them while we stay close to the problem on the ground."

"But—"

"Listen, Mamoru. We have Ms. Thep. She can get us front-line data. We have Isamu's experience and knowledge and your talents as a distilled crop engineer. We could tell the world right now, but the only thing anyone can do immediately is quarantine the site. Until agencies like the WHO are ready to take over, we should collect all the information we can."

"I agree." Yagodo was paging through a red folder as he walked over from his desk.

"This is it. We have a confirmed match—an heirloom rice species. It's called Purple Dusk. The cultivar was typed at an agricultural testing station in Niigata in 2003. This mutation didn't come from mishandling genetic material. Purple Dusk itself is unremarkable. The grasshoppers...the grasshoppers are no accident, I think."

We stared at Yagodo, half knowing what he was about to say.

"This is terrorism." He sat down and tossed the folder on the table. "Purple Dusk was discontinued twenty years ago for its lack of resistance to red rust. It never had much of a following anyway. The idea of a grasshopper chewing on an heirloom cultivar and triggering a mutation has no basis in science." He pointed to Thep's cell studies. "This is no accident of nature.

"I'll need more time for analysis, but I bet those large black structures are nanomachines with one function: embryo printing. Two hundred gigabytes of information would be more than enough to include all the design data for a nanomachine in the genome itself, and who knows what else. The grasshoppers propagate the nanomachines. Their role is to act as a pathogen vector for the intruder, like mosquitoes for malaria."

I remembered Yagodo's huge molecular model. He described it as virtual nanomachines with code-breaking functions, but it was basically a thought experiment. Nanomachines that could insert DNA data into embryonic cells and "print" them with new characteristics were something different. If machines capable of rewriting the DNA of living organisms were loose in the environment with a dedicated vector...

My mind wanted to deny the possibility, but Yagodo's hypothesis was the best fit to what we were seeing. Someone—acting on some unknown motive—had created nanomachines to convert plant species into heirloom rice plants and was somehow propagating them with grasshoppers.

"Do you have any pesticides on-site?" Yagodo asked Thep.

"No. For Full Organic certification, we're not even supposed to poison the cockroaches in the offices. One of my people brought a can of insecticide from home and tried it on one of the grasshoppers. It didn't even seem to notice. Yet when we brought one back from the field, it died almost immediately."

"Pesticide resistance. I'm not surprised. An insect vector for nanomachines would not be an ordinary insect."

I had seen the infestation with my own eyes. Any plant bitten by the grasshoppers would become a chimera with two sets of DNA, one shared in common with other chimeras. If we couldn't kill them, they could transform all the vegetation in Southeast Asia into heirloom rice.

"Mamoru, when did Kaneda say he'd have the DNA data for us?" Yagodo asked.

"Tonight. Wait—he sent me a message." I opened the message in my workspace. It was marked Normal Priority, which was why there hadn't been an alert.

> MAMORU: I'M SORRY. THE CELLS FROM YOUR
> GRASSHOPPER CRASHED MY SEQUENCER AND
> WORKSPACE. I DON'T THINK I CAN GET THE DATA OUT
> TODAY. I'LL PING YOU AS SOON AS I KNOW MORE.

"Nothing tonight? If we at least knew the species, we might be able to order an effective pesticide. Bad luck." Yagodo's look was dark.

"He also says the cells took down his sequencer and workspace."

"That's what happened to us." Thep shook her head in surprise. "We put grasshopper cells in our sequencer and it malfunctioned."

Every attempt to identify the grasshoppers led to a dead end.

Even Kaneda had been defeated. Things were starting to feel less like a run of bad luck and more like someone's plan.

"Then we'll have to spend the rest of the day working on what we can." Yagodo stared at the ceiling and sighed. "I'll search for Purple Dusk farmers. They might lead us to the person who turned the grasshoppers into a vector. Ms. Thep, I think it would be helpful if you could find out how far the grasshoppers have spread and how fast the vegetation is mutating."

"I'll get on it. The sun won't be up much longer. I hate to do it, but I'll see if the nature addicts have anything useful." She stood up. "I just hope the grasshoppers don't bite *me*," she said and logged off.

Kurokawa got up and shouldered his briefcase. "I'll get the word out and work on a media strategy for Mamoru. L&B's legal team is at our disposal, but they won't be at work until the middle of the night our time, so I think I'll get some rest. Be sure to wake me if there are any developments." He performed his trademark flawless bow. "See you tomorrow, then."

Kurokawa logged off the stage as he turned toward the door. Suddenly there he was, normal size. I hadn't noticed it from his avatar, but his slumping shoulders bespoke a deep weariness. I wasn't surprised. Only the day before he had been vomiting and convulsing.

Yagodo rose and picked up the red folder. "I'll let Kaneda know things are urgent."

"Thanks. I'll reconfirm your ID of Purple Dusk as the intruder."

"You're going to be busier than any of us when we get that grasshopper DNA. You should probably get some rest."

"Would you like to have dinner with me, Hayashida-san?" Nguyen was picking folders off the table and sorting them into some kind of order.

"Love to, but I better not. Who knows where World Reporting is lurking. I'd better eat at the hotel."

Another missed opportunity, but I'd had enough of Sascha's games.

13 Bioweapon

The stubble under my jaw snagged on the collar of my terrycloth bathrobe. I was starting to think I'd never get used to hotel razors.

I stepped out of the bathroom, still rubbing my jaw, and reached for the closet door when I noticed something different in the air—a humidity that wasn't from the air conditioner. I could hear traffic outside. Did I leave a window open?

"Nice physique you got there, Mamoru."

A huge man sat on the couch under the windows. He was wearing a khaki work uniform under a climbing harness studded with carabiners.

"Mr. Kaneda? What are you doing here?"

"Sorry, didn't mean to scare you. I have to be discreet. I don't trust the net, so I brought you this in person." He held out a scrap of paper with a matrix bar code.

"Here's your data. Dry off. You've been spending too much time in Isamu's office. It's freezing in here."

"How'd you get in?"

"He gave me your room number. It was an easy climb. All these windows need is a little help and they pop right open."

"Why didn't you just call me? I could've picked this up."

"Yeah, but hotels at least try to keep out the riffraff. The city is crawling with camera crews, and I don't like being photographed. I hear World Reporting is after you."

He had a point. Who knew where the skinhead and her crew might be lurking. She would have the hotel staked out by now. A secret meeting with a shady-looking Kaneda would play right into her hands, and he'd end up getting the same treatment I got. I could see the headline: GENE MAPPER'S SECRET RENDEZVOUS WITH UNDERGROUND BIOCHEMIST.

"I swept the room for surveillance devices while you were showering. It seems clean. Your window looks out on the river. Isamu knew what he was doing when he put you here. It's hard to spy on."

I pulled on a T-shirt and jeans and sat on the bed. "Okay, what've you got?"

"I was going to give you this tomorrow in an easier format, but Isamu said it was urgent, so I had to improvise. Anyway, here's your grasshopper." He slapped the paper into my palm. "The server's on the local network. The URL is untraceable. Just be careful with this. Be *very* careful."

"Why?" I smoothed out the paper and studied the bar code. Kaneda brought his face close to mine. His sandpaper voice whispered in my ear.

"It's classified military. A new bioweapon straight out of DARPA. I don't know which branch of the military it's for, but I don't think it's more than a year or two from deployment."

He sat back. "Naturally, I didn't know any of that when I loaded the data into Gene Analytics the first time. If you don't open the genome with the right template, it turns around and bites you with a mil spec virus. Crashed my workspace before I could stop it and took the sequencer with it just for fun. Whoever designed this was very thorough."

"So how did you extract the data?"

Kaneda grinned and formed a key with his index finger. "I have the template. Got it from an old pal who deals in that sort of thing. Unfortunately I was a little lax about my security. I don't think the transaction was traced, but I'm going to disappear for a while. Your plant samples were dirty too. Two hundred gigabytes and no mistake."

"It looks like we've put you in some kind of danger. Can you take care of yourself?"

"Don't worry. Isamu's got my back." He stood up, pulled the window wide open and climbed onto the ledge. "That's it for me. Remember: open it with the template in the folder, *off*-line." He clipped a carabiner to a rope dangling from the roof. "Good luck."

He kicked off and disappeared into the darkness.

I sat down at the desk and sent a text message to Kurokawa with copies to Thep and Yagodo, telling them I had the grasshopper genome and that it might be weaponized.

Now to ID the grasshopper. It was going to be a long night. I faced the desk, blinked twice, and read the bar code into my workspace.

Download complete. Shall I open the folder?

Kaneda's folder held four files: the grasshopper genome, the template, and genomes for the intruder and the mutated SR06. I guessed that the last two files were identical. I decided to look at them later.

"Gene Analytics. Off-line. Open the insect genome with this template."

A bar appeared on the wall above the desk and started filling in with color-coded data—genome header, patents, compression codes, and a huge library of documentation. The genome itself was almost all artificial code.

"Holy shit. It's a designed animal."

When Kaneda told me the grasshopper was a bioweapon, I assumed we were dealing with an insect designed for pest resistance that could function as a nanomachine vector. But the data unrolling from Gene Analytics went way beyond anything I'd expected. This grasshopper hadn't been selectively modified with natural genes. Like SR06, it was a full-scratch, artificial life-form.

I felt the cold from the ceiling vent blowing on the nape of my neck. The hair on my body was rising into goose bumps.

A few, very simple members of kingdom *Animalia* had already been full-scratched. Everyone knew about the terrestrial corals that secreted sustainable cement. Universities and corporate labs were using worms and other unsegmented animals to transport nanomachines, but designing a viable organism as complex as a grasshopper was a staggering achievement.

Gene Analytics started flagging each color-coded data segment with drop-down index cards. Scrolling through the cards, I felt a new sense of unease. The genome itself was less than half the file. The rest was documentation and development tools. Release builds of distilled crops never went out the door with more than bare-bones documentation.

"It's almost a debug build. No—it's the whole developer's kit."

L&B's kits came with a ton of documentation and a complete toolbox. The non-genome section of the file I was looking at was just about the right size.

"This is hilarious. All we need is a Read Me file."

Shall I open VB01G-X W/E READ ME?

"No shit... Do it."

The file started off with boilerplate terms and conditions, followed by a summary of the documentation. Stuff like this never went out with the final deliverables. I was starting to understand what I was dealing with.

"Tutorials, by any chance?"

VB01G-X W/E Developer Tutorials is found. Shall I play them in order?

A green rectangle faded in above the desk. A deep, resonant voice began speaking.

"My Rifle: The Creed of a United States Marine. By Major General W. H. Rupertus, USMC.

"This is my rifle. There are many like it, but this one is mine.

"My rifle is my best friend. It is my life. I must master it as I must master my life.

"My rifle, without me, is useless. Without my rifle, I am useless. I must fire my rifle true. I must shoot straighter than my enemy who is trying to kill me. I must shoot him before he shoots me. I will..."

US Marine Corps? Kaneda said this was a DARPA project, but he'd also said it was close to deployment. The narration ended, and the green rectangle was replaced by an image of a physical manual cover.

USER MANUAL
VB01G-X W/E (1015-02-138-0001)
BIOLOGICAL TACTICS POD

The next page was a table of contents.

1. WARNING
2. BOOT, STOP, RESUME AND HALT
3. INSTALLATION AND OVERRIDE
4. TUTORIAL
    4.1 GENE TRANSPORTATION
    4.2 COMMUNICATIONS
    4.3 SUICIDE
    4.4 MORE...

It looked like I had the whole kit. The manual didn't just cover basic operations like deployment and withdrawal. There were even sections on instinct plug-ins to engineer new behavior.

I was still regretting not paying enough attention to the emotion settings in that biochem suit tutorial. This time I was determined to start at the top with WARNINGS and read through everything.

This first section was long. It started with a recitation of the dangers of using designed organisms. Luckily none of the content was over my head.

IF THE MISSION IS CANCELED, HALT
VB01G-X BEFORE LEAVING THE ZONE.

There were links to DEACTIVATION and FORCED DEACTIVATION.

"There you go. Isamu, you just saved our collective asses." I sat back and sighed with relief. The solution was somewhere in this manual. But what came first? Should I look for information that would protect L&B from World Reporting or forget that and concentrate on stopping the grasshoppers?

I was about to skip to DEACTIVATION when a dot appeared in my field of vision. It was a meeting request from Kurokawa.

"I read your message about the genome. Thanks for keeping me posted." Kurokawa popped in next to the sofa.

"I thought you were sleeping. It'll be a few more hours before anyone's on deck at L&B headquarters."

"I'm half asleep." Kurokawa put a raised index finger against his forehead and swept it to the right. That half of his brain was in sleep mode. With his conscious mind replacing the functions of his autonomic nervous system, I couldn't imagine what sleep was like for him.

"Are you looking at the genome now?"

"I'm reading the user manual. The grasshoppers are designed animals." I summarized what I'd discovered so far. Kurokawa was surprised to hear we were dealing with a designed animal but seemed to grasp everything quickly.

"As soon as you figure out how to stop them, tell me and Thep immediately. She'll be handling the extermination."

"Extermination?"

"Yes. I want to finish tomorrow morning if possible."

I couldn't believe it. "That soon? Are you authorized to do that?"

The question of terrorism hadn't even come up until a couple of hours before. L&B was asleep, and Mother Mekong's headquarters was closed for the day. It was too early to decide how and when to pull the trigger.

"I'm making the decision on my own authority as L&B's representative on the ground. I'll get Ms. Thep on board. I'll talk to

Barnhard in a few hours, but Mother Mekong will probably have to give us retroactive authorization."

This was crazy. Kurokawa didn't have that kind of authority, even if there was a biohazard.

"Hold on, Takashi. We've got to do something, but we can't destroy evidence in the process. If the grasshoppers are all dead—and we don't know if there's a way to spare some of them—then it just gets harder to identify the mutation mechanism. All we'll be left with is Purple Dusk—"

"Evidence is secondary. I don't care about saving face for L&B and Mother Mekong. I doubt we can do it with pesticides. Keeping the mutation from spreading is more important than anything else." Kurokawa had lost his gentle tone. His eyes burned into me.

"Taking action before everyone's had a chance to weigh in will have consequences, but there's no time. I alerted Mother Mekong about the biohazard. Unfortunately their reaction was not encouraging. They want to be the ones to notify the Cambodian government, but they won't lift a finger until they've touched base with L&B."

"Okay. I'll let you know what I find out."

"Thanks. Do that, please." Kurokawa bowed and logged off.

I couldn't shake my discomfort with Kurokawa's plan. His piercing stare had shut me down, but if we exterminated the grasshoppers, all we'd have left as evidence would be mutated vegetation. I still didn't know our options for terminating the grasshoppers or how fast it could be done. It was almost as if his goal was to take out these insects before World Reporting or anyone else could show them to the world. Yet the ultimate goal was the same: to terminate the biohazard.

I shrugged and turned back to the workspace. If the genome was from DARPA, it was stolen, which made terrorism a possibility. There was no way of knowing how far from the site the grasshoppers would try to go.

They had to be stopped.

*   *   *

"What a masterpiece..."

I was green with envy. DARPA's tools and GUI were absurdly user-friendly. After an hour reading the documentation and code for VB01G-X, I was almost ready to plan and launch my own operation. I could send swarms of insects to any location on a variety of missions with the full range of offensive and defensive measures and at any given time. I could use the grasshoppers to genetically modify food crops and starve out guerrilla forces in remote areas, or launch attacks from the air by combining their bioluminescent output.

I tried writing some code based on a few tutorials. One tutorial, named HELLO WORLD!, showed how to deploy swarms of grasshoppers in complicated, shifting formations. The coding sequences were far more straightforward than with SR06. The user had real-time control over complex movement. Mission parameters could even be reprogrammed on the fly, something that was structurally impossible with terrestrial coral, much less distilled crops. In terms of features and functionality, the whole approach was years ahead of any cutting edge I knew of.

But what really impressed me were the safety features. Maybe I shouldn't have been surprised, given that I was dealing with a bioweapon, but there were layers of protection against accidental deployment, with suicide codes for terminating the grasshoppers remotely. The user had a range of options: cell apoptosis, central nervous system shutdown, even physical disintegration. Any attempt to tamper with these modules instantly sterilized the insects to prevent further breeding. Breeding options were also strictly defined. The deployment area and the number of generations capable of breeding were limited. Extending the limits of viability required coded authorization from the president. It was a model of fail-safe design.

With so many safety features, I started to relax a bit. Even if we did nothing, the grasshoppers would die out long before they ravaged

Southeast Asia. We were facing a genuine crisis, but the survival of
humanity was not at stake.

I closed the documentation and studied the Gene Analytics data
bar. The top line data was beautifully organized. DARPA's engineers
had created a work of art that was almost fractal in its detail. This
wasn't just the product of a big defense budget and secret technology.
It was a labor of love. My first sight of SR06's clean design had given
me a similar feeling, but there was something almost ethereal about
the design philosophy behind this grasshopper.

So much for the user manual. Now I had to find the specific code
that was controlling the grasshoppers at Mother Mekong.

"Gene Analytics, show mission parameters."

MISSION: OPERATION MOTHER MARY
MISSION TYPE: GENE PROPAGATION
DEPLOYMENT ZONE: UNRESTRICTED
MISSION TERM: UNRESTRICTED
TARGET: UNRESTRICTED
BREEDING: UNRESTRICTED
PESTICIDE RESISTANCE: INFINITE

Operation Mother Mary? It looked like Yagodo was on target.
We were dealing with terrorism—unrestricted gene propagation
across time and space, for all plant species, with no vulnerability to
pesticides. The mission parameters were an elegant declaration of
intent to cause serious harm.

Still, I was baffled. According to the user manual, a mission like
this was impossible. The restrictions built into the genome kernel
could not be overridden by the user, which meant that the person
who coded this was an amateur. Hadn't they read the files? The
restrictions were spelled out in detail.

I decided to take a closer look at the code. Just as I thought,
it was amateurish, almost childish. Whoever did this was no

professional—giving variables names like "Variable A," or leaving comment fields empty except for "Begin iteration" or "Define variable," where even a cursory examination of the code made that obvious. Instead of selecting mission parameters from the drop-down menus, the coder had inserted invalid parameters by hand.

How people at this level got their hands on a DARPA development kit was a mystery. It looked like they'd grabbed the kit, skimmed the documentation, done a little slipshod coding, and unleashed the grasshoppers without even running a simulation.

"Who the hell wrote this, anyway?"

The coder's name is John McCauley.

"He left his *name*? Display profile."

JOHN MCCAULEY. BORN 2015. RESIDENT OF SYDNEY.
EDUCATION: OUTLANDS POLYTECHNIC. GRADUATED
2036. EMPLOYER: GUARDIANS OF THE LAND (NPO).

I looked up Guardians of the Land. They were an environmental protection group operating out of Sydney. It also looked like they were camped outside Mother Mekong. There were aerial photos of the site on their wall and a blog bragging about their links to World Reporting.

There is a message to you from John McCauley. Shall I play it?

"Come again?"

It is a handoff message with a request for the next editor.

Handoff message? What was he handing off, his terrorist plot?

"Play it. Use the translation engine."

A space opened in the wall above the desk. A man in a blue T-shirt sat against a green backdrop. The video was full 3D, which made no sense. I also wondered why he would bury a video in a genome. I grabbed the screen, resized it, and placed it over the sofa.

"Hi there. My name's John McCauley. I do genetic coding for Guardians of the Land, an eco-protection group. Well, I'm not sure

where I should start. Okay, why don't I try getting right to the point."
He brought his cupped palms together and held them out for a few
seconds, as if he was offering something. The gesture reminded me
of the statue of Mary in front of Saigon Cathedral.

"Operation Mother Mary is a blow against genetic engineering
overreach. One of our members came up with the name. It's really
cool. People all over the world love the Virgin Mary."

"Get to the point, please." I was already impatient.

"We're all together on Mother Mary. Some of the team are really
good at what they do—"

"Stop playback and summarize handoff."

There is one location with handoff content.

"Play it back. Forget the rest."

"So, um, I have this request?" This was twenty minutes into
the video. What did he have to talk about for so long? If that wasn't
enough, there was another hour left.

"I want you to disable the grasshoppers. Operation Mother Mary
is supposed to take all the SR06 at Mother Mekong and modify it
to be Purple Dusk, this old kind of rice. The operation will prove
distilled crops aren't controlled and stuff, like people say. Gough got
us this . . . this weapon from someplace, I don't know where, but I kind
of skimmed the tutorial, and, like, I just graduated last year, but even
I could use it. It was a piece of piss."

What a joke. Who was Gough and why would he hand a weapon
like VB01G-X to a kid fresh out of school?

"So I did just like he said—made it so all the grasshoppers
would die off after they changed SR06 to Purple Dusk. That way no
one could prove that the grasshoppers did it. Except when I ran the
debugger, I got all these error messages. Everything was unlimited or
something."

"No kidding," I said to the image floating over the sofa. "You
can't hand-code every parameter, even if the API lets you. The kernel
just ignores it."

"But we were running out of time, so I didn't want to say anything to Gough. I thought it would be simpler to just bung the whole kit into the genome. There must be something in there that tells how to stop the mission. I hope you can do it."

Huh? I can't do it, so here's all the tools, clean up my mess? What if the deactivation code wasn't *in* this version?

"Once the grasshoppers have disappeared, the damage will be done. I wonder who you are. Military? Cops? You don't have to agree with what we're up to, but you don't want the grasshoppers to keep spreading any more than we do, I guess. I'd say we share the same goal."

"What the fu—"

"At least I'm sure that L&B guy from Japan will be wrapped when this is all over. Gough says he's a real find. He's coming to the site to check out our work."

I almost fell out of my chair in mid-shout. What Japanese guy?

As McCauley droned on, I thought about Kurokawa's plan. Terminate the grasshoppers as soon as possible. "Once the grasshoppers have disappeared, the damage will be done."

But what other option was there? In the end it was the same. Even if Kurokawa was connected to "Gough," I had to find a way to put the grasshoppers out of business.

"Operation Mother Mary? What a load of crap."

I opened the user manual and started my search.

*   *   *

I was hungry. I checked the time. It was past eleven. That meant all I could get was the late-night room service menu. I pulled open the desk drawer and hauled the menu out. Sandwich and coffee.

You have a message from Shue Thep. Shall I open it?

"Go ahead."

"I just got back from the field. Kurokawa-san told me what he

wants. We need to talk. How are we going to exterminate the grasshop-
pers? Can we meet in half an hour?"

Thep had been out long past dark. We didn't know what would happen if a human was bitten, but all she had for protection was that worn-out jumpsuit. The lady was brave.

I texted her that I'd found a solution using the messenger towers. I hoped that would give her spirits a lift until we talked.

Terminating the insects didn't require specialized chemicals or equipment. DARPA's safety features covered every contingency. The user had multiple options—strobe lights with a specific wavelength, sound waves, even delivery of common chemicals by aerosol in dis-tilled crop environments. A solution for every tactical situation.

I decided to go with "Forced Deactivation: Chemical Messenger." This involved releasing a messenger compound, trans-2-hexenal, in a specific sequence to trigger suicide. I wondered why DARPA would include such an option, but then I remembered the distilled opium farms the Americans were always searching for.

Coding the pulse timing was more complicated than for distilled crops, but I'm a veteran. It wasn't long before I finished the dispersal code. The chemical would reach all the grasshoppers on-site and those within three kilometers of the perimeter.

I ordered coffee and a sandwich from room service. While I was waiting, I moved to the next step: simulation. I sized a 3D model of Mother Mekong to fit over the bed. It was hard to believe that only yesterday I had been walking the site while my suit played games with my emotions.

Just this morning we had no idea of the identity of the intruder or the cause of the mutation. We hadn't dreamt it was terrorism. Now we knew quite a bit about the terrorists, and I was testing a way to exterminate the grasshoppers causing the mutation. A day packed with surprises and discoveries was coming to an end.

"Run suicide simulation."

The two thousand messenger towers projecting from the landscape on my bed started releasing concentric yellow circles representing trans-2-hexenal in a sequence that varied from location to location. Gradually the entire site was blanketed. It was like drawing logos, just more complicated.

I was so satisfied with the first simulation that I threw myself on the bed before it finished. Coffee, a sandwich, and Thep would be arriving soon.

*   *   *

"Pretty impressive."

Thep showed up on time. She stared, palms upturned in surprise, at the 3D model over the bed and the long data bar suspended above the desk.

Her off-hours avatar sported the same cargo pants, but without the Mother Mekong jacket. She must've been worn out after hours in the field, but her avatar didn't show it.

"I know how to eradicate the grasshoppers. We don't need special chemicals or equipment. We'll just use the towers. I already have a first draft of the code." I handed her a copy of the user manual. "Our friends are designed animals. This is a bioweapon. We're actually lucky it's from DARPA. It's unbelievably well-designed. If I can't make it work with the towers, there are backup options."

Thep sat on the sofa and started paging through the manual. After a few minutes she nodded and looked up.

"A lot of this could be applied to agriculture. It would be revolutionary. It's sad we can't use it."

"I know. Well, at least we can stop them." I started the simulation. "I'll need you to load trans-2-hexenal into the towers. According to the manual, with the right timing the messenger will signal all the grasshoppers in range of the yellow concentric circles to self-destruct. They're programmed to decompose into soil."

Thep got up and sat on the bed. Her avatar merged with the

mountains around the site. "All right. I'll reprogram the towers. By morning there won't be a trace left—what's wrong?"

"There was a message buried in the code from one of the people behind this. He said 'the damage will be done' once the grasshoppers are exterminated." I gave her the gist of the message from Guardians of the Land.

"So the grasshoppers vanish and the mutated vegetation is heirloom rice. Is that their goal? Why haven't they issued some kind of statement?"

"A statement... Wait a minute!" I remembered the HELLO WORLD! tutorial. "Maybe this is what we need."

I pointed to the page in the manual that dealt with changing missions on the fly. "Before we terminate the grasshoppers, I want to alter the mission code."

"How would we signal the grasshoppers to change the mission? You know how hard it was to develop the signaling for SR06, and that was just to get the plants to change color."

"I know, but DARPA found a way. Let me explain." I showed Thep the tutorial.

Delivering new mission code to the grasshoppers with simple pulses from the towers would be impossible because the shortest pulse frequency was 0.2 seconds. Transmitting a megabyte of data that way would take nineteen days. During the entire time, every grasshopper would have to receive every byte of data with no errors or signal loss in an environment where constantly shifting winds were affecting the dispersion pattern. The wind also kept the rice stalks in motion, varying the precise distance between the grasshoppers and the towers.

DARPA's engineers solved this by loading the mission codes into the grasshopper genome itself. The user ran a 64-byte Secure Hash Algorithm to output a unique hash value—in effect, a mission activation signal using unbreakable encryption—and sent it to the grasshoppers along with a four-letter code indicating the precise length of the mission code. That was the whole message. Once the grasshoppers received the hash value, they used several hundred million code-breaking cells to run a brute-force attack on the hash value and look up the mission code.

As I was explaining this to Thep, I remembered Yagodo's molecular model. I didn't understand what he was doing at first, but now I realized that he and DARPA were after the same thing: a brute force approach to looking up specific data.

"I don't get it. The calculations would take millions of years."

"That's what I thought—at first. But the grasshoppers have a secret weapon: collaboration."

If the mission codes were written in an "alphabet" of 256 letters, there were 65,000 possible codes with two letters. An eight-letter code would have eighteen *quintillion* possible combinations. A one-megabyte code had more possible combinations than the number of particles in the universe. Even if a grasshopper had thousands of trillions of code-breaking cells, the odds of hitting the jackpot and finding the right mission code would be vanishingly small.

To solve a problem that would have taken one grasshopper the lifetime of the universe, DARPA's engineers used collaboration to zero in on the solution.

"The grasshoppers can communicate to avoid redundant calculations. In effect, one of them says, 'I'm only looking for codes starting with A.' Another will say, 'Okay, then I'll only look for codes starting with B.' When a search hits a dead end, that grasshopper sends out an alert. The first grasshopper to find the correct code tells the rest how to narrow their search, so they can confirm for themselves that the code is correct."

"How do they do that? They don't have transmitters."

"They can tap on each other's bodies to pass the message on."

"Sounds pretty primitive."

"They can also spread the message farther by signaling with light. I tried it myself. Let me show you."

I closed the suicide simulation and launched the mission I'd written to get a feel for the tutorial. The whole thing was just a few kilobytes of code. Each grasshopper acted as a search node, transmitting its results to the others with light signals from its bioluminescent wings.

"Unbelievable. It's like digital communication. But are you sure about this?"

"No problem. If wind patterns affect the distribution, all we need is for one grasshopper to get—"

"That's not what I mean. Do you really want to show this animal to the world?" The constant flashing of the grasshoppers signaling each other overlapped her avatar. "If I saw this on the news, the first thing I'd do is try to recreate it."

The thought had crossed my mind, but I'd been holding it at bay while I worked on my immediate problem.

"I mean, listening to your explanation, and reading this manual... I feel so inspired. If plants can communicate and designed animals can be sent into the fields to perform tasks, we can do almost anything, not just with agriculture. We could design insects with RealVu to image places that humans and robots can't. Soil restoration, energy production, terraforming... Imagination is the limit. If I saw one of these grasshoppers, I'd want to go right back to the lab and design something like it.

"But can anyone be trusted with organisms like this? DARPA's engineers did a fantastic job, but think about it. Even L&B—if their engineers see designed animals interacting with crops, do you think they'll be as careful with their fail-safe features as DARPA was?"

That didn't take much thought. "I don't see how they would."

I looked at the model. My mission was still in progress. Thep stood up and watched it pensively.

"So this is what you want to do before we exterminate?"

"I wrote the code while I was working my way through the tutorial. It's a rough first pass. I want to transmit it tomorrow for at least the few minutes when the satellite is overhead. We can exterminate afterward. I don't want to be the guy who just carries out their plan for them."

"I like the idea, but we should ask Kurokawa-san how he feels about showing the world these designed animals before we—"

"Sorry. I don't want to do that."

"Why not?"

I wasn't sure how much I should reveal to Thep. My suspicion that Kurokawa was involved with Guardians of the Land was just that, suspicion. Maybe Enrico was trying to screw up our investigation. The disappearing grasshopper sample might have been programmed suicide. There was no proof that the "Japanese guy" McCauley mentioned was Kurokawa. My guess that Kurokawa might want to eliminate evidence of an artificial origin for the mutation could be based on faulty reasoning. Maybe he just wanted to eliminate a potentially disastrous biohazard along with the grasshoppers that were spreading it.

But I couldn't forget the bar code on his shoulder and the wounds from his frenzied attempts to rip it off.

"All right, I understand."

"What?" I looked up. Thep was standing next to me.

"You disabled Behavior Correction, didn't you? I still think we should tell Kurokawa-san, but I can see you're conflicted about it. The grasshoppers slow down after sunset. I think we have a reprieve until morning. I'll think things over too. If it looks like we're running out of time, we can activate the suicide program. Agreed?" She took the folder with the suicide program off my desk and put it in a pocket of her cargo pants.

"Thanks, Shue."

"That's quite a face you're wearing. You haven't finished coding. You need to figure out the details of your mission too. Better get started."

"Yeah. Thanks."

"Blow my socks off." She gave me two thumbs up.

*   *   *

I'd ordered a whole pot of coffee. Now it was empty. It was almost the same as the drip brew I drank every day in Tokyo, but after the sweet taste of Vietnamese coffee, regular coffee left a bitter aftertaste.

It was four-thirty a.m. The horizon outside my window was starting to lighten.

I turned away from the window and watched the latest simulation unfold. Once again, the grasshoppers began to execute the mission I had designed for them.

I had finished the coding about an hour earlier using a HELLO WORLD! template and run the simulation using one of DARPA's testing tools. The code included the termination commands McCauley hadn't figured out. Even if Thep didn't launch the suicide program, the grasshoppers would all be reduced to dried soil before sundown tomorrow.

Now all I had to do was hand the code off to Thep. Mother Mekong's message towers would send it to the bugs, and the mission would go off just as I'd simulated it in my room.

Still, I was wavering. I'd spent the last hour running simulations. If the mission was a success—the digital message transmitted, brute-force decoded, and executed by the designed animals— engineers everywhere would be inspired to design their own organisms. They would see what was possible, not from an academic paper or a commercial concept model, but unfolding in reality before their eyes.

Any engineer worth his salt would salivate at the chance to be involved in something like this. Venture funds would bankroll any number of startups to develop "Mother Mekong-type" designed animals. The greatest risk of all—the question of whether or not designed animals of such complexity could actually be developed— would have been eliminated. They would know it was possible.

The outcome of all this would be a flood of designed animals of uneven quality and ultimately biohazards that would be impossible to cope with, unlike DARPA's grasshoppers.

I ran the simulation again. Everything went exactly as it had many times before. Once again, I was astounded at what I could do after only a few hours of familiarization. I couldn't buy into the concept of weaponized organisms, but as an engineer, I felt almost reverent toward the talent and concern for safety of the nameless men and women who had created this technology.

What if I *didn't* carry out the mission? The US would deploy the grasshoppers eventually. The user manual indicated that the Marines would be first to get them. What would happen then? Engineers working to create knockoff designs would have no way of knowing the lengths DARPA had gone to to make the weapon fail-safe.

Suddenly I had an idea.

It would work. It was the only way.

I called Thep.

*　*　*

"You finished the mission."

Thep was intently watching the simulation unfold across Mother Mekong.

"Yes. It's ready." I handed her the mission code and the chemical messenger release routine for the towers.

"What happens when the world finds out about the grasshoppers?"

I explained my idea. If I succeeded, banishment from the industry might be the least of my problems. I might have to go underground for the rest of my life.

"That's a coincidence. I was thinking about going underground myself." Her avatar gave me a beautiful, natural smile. "I turned off Behavior Correction. The tension feels good, doesn't it?"

14   Fear Report

I woke to Nguyen's voice ordering coffee. The morning sun bouncing off the stucco ceiling made me blink.

I'd made it to the office at eight to brief Yagodo and Kurokawa on Guardians of the Land's plans and the code Thep would transmit to trigger grasshopper suicide. I kept the rest to myself. After filling them in, I lay down on the sofa and fell asleep.

Nguyen hadn't been there when I arrived. How long had I been asleep?

I'd had another AR meeting with Thep at sunrise. I thought I'd just be handing her the code for my mission, but we ended up tweaking it together. With her stronger technical background and just a read-through of the user manual, she had pretty much figured out how to code a mission. It was after seven by the time we were through. I'd tried to get some sleep, but my mind was so focused on the coming operation that I had to give up.

I opened my workspace in my palm. It was nine. I'd only been asleep for half an hour.

"Hayashida-san, you can rest a bit longer. We're going to write up our report on the terrorists and the extermination of the grasshoppers later."

Kurokawa was sitting on the opposite sofa with several workspaces open and floating above the table. He must have been up all night dealing with L&B, but as his fingers flew over his virtual keyboard, he seemed fresh and rested.

"What are you working on so hard?" Yagodo got up from his desk to peer over Kurokawa's shoulder.

"Barnhard's presentation. He has to rebut that World Reporting teaser with a statement. I have to get this out right away."

"A presentation for the veep? Shouldn't his own people handle that?"

"Should, but can't. Anyway, he asked me to do it. World Reporting's preview already has him in hot water with the media. He has to say something, and we can't ask Mamoru to go on camera."

"The VP's ghost writer? There's a leash I wouldn't want to be at the end of," said Yagodo.

"Those two teasers have paralyzed L&B. All they have time for is damage control. We're on the front line, we know what's going on. I'm logically the one to handle this."

Kurokawa had turned his head to speak to Yagodo even as his fingers kept flying over the keyboard. He must have been using both of his avatars.

"Thanks to both of you, we know the identity of the intruder. We know that the grasshoppers are a designed bioweapon and that environmental activists are behind this attack. Our trip to the site gave us all the video we need. I don't think Barnhard will have any problem answering his critics."

I hadn't told Kurokawa everything about the grasshoppers. I couldn't shake my suspicion that he was carrying water for Guardians of the Land. I'd told him only that the goal was to undermine people's trust in distilled crops. I didn't mention Guardians of the Land, Operation Mother Mary, or McCauley's video message. When I told him that exterminating the grasshoppers was the final objective of the terrorists, all he'd said in response was, "Then our interests are aligned. I think we have more than enough evidence to prove this is terrorism. We don't need more."

This had convinced me that Kurokawa didn't want the TerraVu images to show the grasshoppers at all. At least I was certain that Thep hadn't told him about my little addition to the playbook.

"You've been pretty busy yourself," Yagodo said to me.

"Thanks for lighting a fire under Kaneda. I never dreamed we'd be dealing with a designed insect, but we can use Mother Mekong's infrastructure to wipe them out."

I was still stretched out on my back. Yagodo brandished a document in my face as he took his usual place on the sofa.

"I found something myself—where Purple Dusk comes from. You want to see this."

I put a hand on the table and levered myself into an upright position.

"I was filtering a list of Purple Dusk growers. Turns out this particular cultivar is associated with some very interesting people— a Japanese collective of rice farmers called The Hermitage." He waved a finger and an old-fashioned website popped in over the table.

"I ran across a site backup that was originally on someone's PC. Classic design, isn't it? Very nostalgic."

The web page showed a kindly looking older man cradling a bundle of harvested rice plants. Behind him spread a few acres of paddies hemmed in by mountains. "The Hermitage" was written in calligraphy along the left margin of the page. The photo was framed with slogans in fancy script: "Organically Grown," "Locally Grown and Consumed," "GM Free," and "Pest and Weed Control with Ducks." Maybe this sort of thing was interesting for people twenty years ago, but a lot of it went over my head. With only one harvest a year, it didn't look like they could've harvested much from such a small acreage.

"The collective had to disband when red rust broke out. Later the land was bought by a corporation that grows L&B seedlings. It seems there was some sort of disagreement over the terms of payment. The owner probably hated the spread of genetically modified rice, but there was no future for Purple Dusk."

"He must've held a grudge."

"If he did, it was a waste of energy. Import tariffs on rice were abolished in 2015. Small farmers just couldn't compete. Red rust isn't the only thing that killed The Hermitage."

Yagodo touched a link to a blog. "Here's the interesting part." He pointed to the last post, dated July 2016. It was in English: "Natural Farming Methods Know No Borders." There was a shot of the farmer surrounded by a group of young men and women, Europeans or North Americans. Two of them flanked him with their arms over his shoulders.

"That's Enrico!"

"Enrico? The missing project manager?" Yagodo seemed puzzled.

"Sure. Right here." I pointed to the man on the right. He was wearing a blue T-shirt stenciled with "natural" in white Japanese script. There was no mistaking the straw-colored hair and the eyes with their drooping corners. He looked relaxed and happy. There was no trace of the dark aura I saw in the cathedral.

"Enrico? Harvesting Purple Dusk? That's absurd," said Kurokawa. He kept typing away without even looking at the photo. "Enrico's twenty-eight, the same age as Thep. He was eight years old in 2016."

Yagodo nodded. "Mamoru, this is Gough Robertson. He's a veteran activist. His specialty is coordinating protests between green groups. He spent six years or so at The Hermitage and made it a magnet for foreign activists. His love and respect for the man who owned this place is clear from the blog—"

"Gough? Guardians of the Land Gough?"

Yagodo raised an eyebrow. "You do get around. He hasn't been a member of that group for very long either. Where did you hear about him?"

"His name was buried in the grasshopper genome."

"Then it's him for sure. He must be leading this operation. Just so you know, the man on the other side is Darrel MacCarthy. He was discharged from the Marines just last week—"

"Isamu, wait a minute. The day before we left for Cambodia, I met this guy calling himself Enrico."

"What? Where did you meet him? What did you talk about?" Yagodo lowered his eyebrows and leaned forward.

"In the cathedral. He was complaining about things at L&B..." I wasn't sure how much I could say. "He showed me old news footage about Takashi. World Reporting videoed me sitting there after he left."

"It looks like Guardians of the Land and World Reporting are plotting to frame—"

"No! It's not a frame-up!" Nguyen's voice was shrill. "We'd never stoop so low. You don't know anything about us!"

"Nguyen?" For a moment I wasn't sure it was the same woman. She was wearing a khaki field vest and her hair was pinned up. She stared daggers at Yagodo.

"People all over the world will finally see natural rice fighting back against your horrible distilled crops. Operation Mother Mary—"

"Where did you hear that name?" I stood up and took a step toward her. My blood was boiling.

"Duck, Mamoru!" I heard Yagodo shout, but something soft was already striking me in the face. I reflexively arched backward to avoid the blow. Something caught my heels and I lost my balance. I tripped over the table and fell flat on my back. The base of my spine felt numb.

"Did I hurt you?"

I looked up at Nguyen. She was blurred and surrounded by artifacts, then suddenly she was squatting next to me.

"Physical Mixed Activity. Aikido? No, Sanda. Where did you learn that? Mamoru, are you all right?" Yagodo peered at me with concern.

Nguyen's avatar had remained motionless while the real Nguyen faked a blow to my face and swept my feet out from under me when I flinched.

"Sit down. Next to Yagodo. I'm with Guardians of the Land. World Reporting will be here soon. They need footage of all you distilled crop people in one room.

"Today, TerraVu will photograph Mother Mekong in daylight. Glowing crops and disintegrating logos at night have impact, but it's not enough. High-def daytime images of Operation Mother Mary will shock the world. Everyone will see natural plants beating back that stupid L&B logo and advancing against distilled crops."

Nguyen held her cupped hands out in the same gesture McCauley used in his video.

"It's time for humanity to get back to safe, natural food, the kind that was good enough for our ancestors. You'll watch as it happens, and the world will be watching you, courtesy of World Reporting."

I stared at her in a daze. Everything was coming together.

"Images have such power. I'm sorry I had to trick you, Mamoru, but that footage of you in the cathedral was just one scene from our little movie. And if it makes any difference to you, which I guess it won't, I tried to stop them. But the director from World Reporting wouldn't budge. She said it would make great footage."

Someone knocked on the door and called out, "Master!" Were we going to sit around drinking coffee?

Nguyen stepped over me on her way to the door. "One more thing. I'm the one who named this operation." She took off her AR glasses and tossed them in Yagodo's lap. "I won't need these anymore," she said. I heard English.

For a second her avatar blurred, then disappeared. The real Nguyen opened the door.

"Hey guys! Nice to meet you!"

It was the skinhead again, wearing the same sunglasses. She gave us a stylish wave and walked to the table, stiletto heels clicking across the floor. Her shoes, expensive-looking beige jacket, and black slacks were a strange contrast to her shaved head and heavy sunglasses.

"Nice to see you again, Isamu."

Yagodo snorted dismissively. I felt suddenly disoriented. Did they know one another?

Two men followed her through the door. One was fat with long hair and carried a multi-camera array on a belt-mounted stabilizer. The face of the second man was concealed behind a mask and goggles. He carried an AK-74.

The cameraman stepped across me and waddled over to Yagodo's desk where he could cover the whole room with his array. He chose his position, brushed the hair out of his eyes, and unfolded a monopod to take the camera's weight.

The gunman shut the door and stood next to it, feet slightly wider than shoulder width, shoulders relaxed and loose. He kept the muzzle of his weapon trained on Yagodo. With his tinted goggles and the mask covering the lower half of his face, he was a sphinx, but his posture was that of a seasoned professional.

"Take it easy, everyone." The woman pointed to the gunman. "I like to travel with security. Jean over there is my c-man." She looked at Yagodo, put a hand on her hip, and cocked her head. "He needs to port in to your stage."

With the gun pointed at him, Yagodo wordlessly made the invitation gesture with an upright index finger against the corner of his eye. The three newcomers blurred and were replaced by avatars. The woman and the gunman hardly changed, but the cameraman's avatar was a complete makeover—slim and trim.

"As I said, nice to see you, Isamu," she said in Japanese this time. Yagodo frowned and squinted at her warily.

"I thought I'd see you again, but not in the flesh. *This* is unpleasant. You're welcome to turn tail and get out of here."

"My my. For someone so richly paid, you don't seem very grateful. You were worth it, you know. That old Internet footage of the Linux developers made for a great program."

"Yeah, except I didn't know you planned to use it that way. Anyway, I gave you back your damn money."

"You mean your donation? It's helping to pay for this report."

"You guys must be running out of dirt to dig. Then again, why report the news when you can make it up?"

"That's not nice, Isamu. We mostly tell the truth. Everyone knows genetic engineering and engineers are a danger to society, and dangers to society are what everyone wants to hear about. Don't you get it?"

"You're all bottom feeders."

"I wonder." She put her sunglasses on her head. Her eyes were ice blue. The pupils were like the vacuum of space. I watched as the red bob cut filled itself in under her sunglasses.

"People can't get enough of 'Sascha Leifens Reports: Engineers Gone Wild.'"

Sascha was in news program mode. She crossed one ankle lightly over the other and drew her shoulders back. "Do you know how many people saw our teaser? A hundred million!"

I forgot the numbness in my spine at the thought of so many people hearing my name.

"You're Mamoru Hayashida, aren't you? Could you sit on the couch? We can't shoot you lying on the floor." Sascha pointed to the sofa next to Yagodo. He moved over to make room for me.

I looked toward the door. The muzzle was pointed at me now. The masked man pointed to the sofa with his jaw. I sat down next to Yagodo.

"Wait, someone's missing. Nguyen, can't we rely on you for anything at all?" Sascha stamped with irritation and punched a hole in the parquet with a stiletto heel. Nguyen bit her lip and hung her head.

"I'm through asking you to do things. Which one of you is going to call our missing guest from Mother Mekong?"

Kurokawa said nothing but lifted his left hand in the telephone receiver gesture.

"You must be Takashi Kurokawa. Could you resize yourself? Otherwise there won't be as much impact." Sascha peered at Kurokawa through a thumb and forefinger frame. Kurokawa nodded. A second later, his legs were too short to reach the floor.

"That's it. Nice. Make the call. And be discreet."

Kurokawa pulled an address book from his breast pocket and riffled the pages.

"Hello? Ms. Thep? We need to meet right away. No, I'll explain when you log on."

He closed the address book. "She says she'll be a few minutes."

"I wonder if we have that much time...Well, that's all right. We can composite her in later."

"Composite her? You can't call that reporting— All right, all right!" Yagodo shrank from the gun muzzle jammed in the back of his head. The masked man had worked his way around behind the sofa. I hadn't even seen him moving.

Sascha clapped sharply. "Ready? We don't have much time, so I'll keep this simple." She opened a palm workspace and extracted a bookmark. "I'm going to put this real-time TerraVu feed on the table. We're set to zoom in when the satellite is over Mother Mekong, so you'll see all the details. You'll be looking at the feed with a serious expression."

Sascha tossed the bookmark on the table. It expanded to show the view from the satellite. A translucent pin labeled "Mother Mekong" peeked up just over the horizon.

"This whole thing is a put-up job. What a load— Stop jabbing me! The end of that thing is harder than my head." Yagodo grabbed the muzzle and glared at the masked man.

Sascha waved the gunman back. "A put-up job? You're just jealous. I'm sure you were planning to watch the TerraVu show anyway. I'm also sure you were going to look serious when you did it. That's reality. That's what I report on." Sascha wagged a finger at Yagodo. "Let's get back on track. I'll start at the door and walk slowly around the room. Every now and then I'll touch something. I know you're new at this, but don't look at me until I speak to you. Of course you can answer my questions any way you like. It's nonfiction— Welcome! You got here in time."

Thep's avatar stood next to Kurokawa. "Who are these people?
What's—"

Kurokawa cut her off. "Don't say anything! Please sit down."

Thep frowned and looked down at him. She jammed her hands
into the pockets of her Mother Mekong jacket but made no move
to sit down.

"Love the logo." Sascha smiled. "We'll have to be sure and get
that. Jean! Take a reading for her back. Do I have to tell you everything?" Sascha yelled at him.

The cameraman mumbled "Roger that." He shifted the array
from the monopod to his belt and started working his way around
the sofa.

Sascha turned to Thep. "You're from Mother Mekong, right?
Nice to meet you. Now sit down."

Thep looked around the office. Her eyes stopped between me
and Yagodo. She had noticed what the masked man was holding.

"That's an old-fashioned weapon. I saw a lot of those during the
revolution. Do you know how to use it?"

The gunman snorted with amusement.

"Care for a demonstration?" asked Sascha. "Don't get any silly
ideas just because he can't hurt your avatar. If you don't cooperate,
you know what will happen."

Thep scowled and sat next to Kurokawa.

"Good girl. Keep being good, otherwise you'll never see these
two again, not even in AR."

These two. Yagodo and me. That meant Kurokawa was one of the
terrorists. I'd already noticed that the gunman paid no attention to him.

Kurokawa had a right to hate L&B and genetic engineering. His
parents had been emotionally devastated. His health was permanently
damaged. If that weren't enough, he'd been trapped in a timeless
limbo, treated like a guinea pig, and branded with a bar code. I'd
seen the fresh welts on his shoulder, proof that his anger was still
very much alive.

"Five minutes. Ready to roll, Jean? Eyes on the table, everybo—What are you grinning at?"

I stood up. *I'm sorry, Takashi,* I thought to myself. *I wanted to fight by your side.*

"Sascha, if we're going to put on a show, let's do it right."

"Didn't you hear me? Sit down!"

I ignored her and grabbed the TerraVu feed. I threw my arms outward with a flick of the wrists. The image filled the entire office. At this huge magnification, the 3D image had a strange power. The floor was now an ocean. The image interpenetrated the desks and the furniture. The Mother Mekong pin was advancing over the horizon from the wall behind Kurokawa.

"What are you doing?"

"What do we have, four and a half minutes?" I pointed to the north side of the image, in Kurokawa's direction. The islands of Indonesia were directly below the satellite.

"Want to make your program even more gripping? How about a live feed? Nguyen, come over here and get in the frame. You should get Gough to join us."

Sascha gestured with her chin. I followed her line of sight to the masked man, who nodded once.

The right side of my head exploded and the back of it slammed against the wall. Something hard was shoved against my face, pinning me. My head felt hot above my right eye. A warmth was flowing down and pooling between my face and the gloved hand over my mouth.

I hadn't even seen him move. He had attacked me with Physical Mixed Activity.

"Hayashida-san!" Thep cried out, but her response was delayed. She must have seen me slammed against the wall before she saw who did it.

"Open your mouth," the gunman snapped. He could speak. His voice was oddly sweet and clear. He held up a clear capsule with his free hand. I could see the circuitry inside it. I didn't know what it was, but I knew I had to keep him from feeding it to me. I clenched my jaw.

"Nothing doing. I'll break your teeth for you." He pressed the heel of his hand on the tip of my jaw. I opened my mouth.

"Don't give him a jammer!" shouted Sascha. "He's the star of the show. He can't answer questions if he's immobilized."

Now I knew what the capsule was. I felt a chill run up my spine. With my feedback chips jammed, I'd be paralyzed.

"Listen, Mamoru. Avatars don't show injuries. Your bloody face won't affect our shoot. Before I ask him to hit you again, would you mind telling me what you're up to?"

The gunman took his hand away from my mouth. I glared at Sascha. The blood from my forehead ran into my eye and down my cheek.

"You know what I'm up to. The satellite will prove the Guardians of the Land are a bunch of unscrupulous terrorists."

"Hayashida-san, you're wrong." Nguyen got out of her chair. "You people are the ones with no ethics. Drawing a giant logo across the surface of the planet is perverted. Genetic engineering is inherently harmful. Why is it so difficult for you to accept that? You saw all those people in wheelchairs and crutches in the park. So many people are suffering. Agent Orange was developed by a genetic engineering company. Vietnam was used as a testing ground for chemical weapons!"

"Bullshit. What about the biological weapon you're using in Cambodia?"

"If it keeps corporations from doing even more damage to nature, who cares? It's the only way!"

"The only way? You unleashed those creatures without a plan to stop them. You don't even know what you're dealing with."

"That's enough!" Sascha clapped her hands. "It's almost time to roll camera. Nguyen, sit down and shut up. You're a broken record. Vietnam, the Americans, defoliants. It was more than sixty years ago. No one remembers it, but it's all *you* talk about."

"But, Sascha, I..." Nguyen's mouth trembled.

"I said shut up! Call Gough." Nguyen sat down and assumed the default pose. She was calling Gough in Private Mode.

Sascha sighed. "Working with civilians is such a pain in the ass. Mamoru, would you please just sit down?"

"Sorry, I'm not your fall guy."

"Neither am I. Why do I have to participate in your idiotic program?"

It was Kurokawa. His voice was quiet but firm. Sascha looked at him in astonishment.

"Wait a minute. Didn't Gough explain all this to you?"

Kurokawa shook his head. Suddenly I had forgotten the ache above my eye.

"*What*? Are you shitting me?" Sascha gaped for a second before jabbing a long index finger at Nguyen. She was opening her mouth to speak when Gough's avatar popped in, wearing a black safari jacket.

"Ready to roll, Sascha?"

"You!" Sascha took a step toward him. "I thought you recruited him. You said you'd deliver one of L&B's victims. That's the only reason I'm here. Who the hell do you think is paying you to camp out in Cambodia?"

Gough shrugged but didn't seem too perturbed. "I contacted him, okay? So what if I never got an answer?"

"Don't fuck with me!" Sascha brought a heel down on the floor. There was a snapping sound as it punched through the wood again. Yagodo put a hand over his face and sighed.

"Convince him. Now!" The masked man leveled his gun at Kurokawa.

"I don't think that's going to work, Sascha," said Gough. He and Sascha looked down at Kurokawa. "I sent you a message, Mr. Kurokawa. I invited you to join Guardians of the Land and help us make our case by appearing on World Reporting. Are you saying you didn't read it?"

"I get requests like that all the time, from all over the world—

to be interviewed as a victim of genetic engineering, or about the dangers of physical augmentation. They're all pretty much the same, and no, I don't read them in detail. If you sent me a message...Is it this one? From July fifteenth?"

Kurokawa pulled a video message from his jacket pocket and tossed it on the table. Yagodo picked it up and scanned it. "This is it. Amateurish."

"Is it? I thought it would be the perfect chance for you to get some justice," said Gough.

"I don't need your help," said Kurokawa. He leaned back and crossed his legs. Gough turned to Sascha with upturned palms.

"Gough, you can't wiggle out—" He cut her off and pointed to Kurokawa.

"Sascha, he's not like these other idiots. He has a mind of his own, that's all. Just do what you came to do. I'm handing you the scoop. A natural mutation proves the latest distilled crops are under no one's control. Nature is fighting back against the best that genetic engineers can throw at it. It's a story about nature's fury and vengeance against the arrogance of technology. It's perfect."

He snapped his fingers and pointed at the pin that marked Mother Mekong's location. It had topped the horizon and was advancing toward the center of the room.

"It's showtime. I'll give you an even better ringside seat. This should square things." Gough suspended a bookmark over the table. A section of the satellite image snapped into crystal-clear detail. A line joined the image to the pin, which kept advancing. The 3D view was probably from a kite-mounted camera. We could almost make out individual stalks of SR06 and Purple Dusk. It was a degree of magnitude more detailed than the satellite image.

Good, I thought. *We'll see the whole thing.*

"Yes, it's showtime." Everyone turned toward me. "But it won't be about a mysterious crop mutation. You're going to see Guardians of the Land claim responsibility for an act of terror."

"I'd watch your tongue," said Gough. I shook my head and motioned to the high-def image. Everyone leaned closer and peered at it.

Tiny pinpoints of light were appearing all along the divide between SR06 and Purple Dusk. "What is that?" Gough murmured.

Thep, who had been silent until now, gave a long sigh and sat back. "Beautiful."

Nguyen was indignant. "What's that supposed to be?"

Flashing points of light were spreading across the site. The mission's Call Phase was starting. Sascha glared at me. "Huang, make him."

Another blow to the face. My knees buckled and hit the table. I heard a popping sound. One of my contacts had been knocked free.

"Mamoru!" Thep and Kurokawa cried out after a slight delay. I touched my right eye and extracted the contact lens. The tiny chip embedded in the clear polymer was undamaged.

"Plant your ass on the sofa and stay there," Sascha barked in English. She reached out and gave me a sharp poke in the head with a long fingernail. The translation engine had cut out. I heard her unprocessed English. The satellite image, Gough's kite feed, and Thep's and Gough's avatars were gone. Huang grabbed me by the hair and dropped me like a sack on the sofa.

"You're going to jail for this, Sascha," said Yagodo.

"Should I worry about the police? Who's going to call them?" I could see her shrugging through my blurred vision.

I looked at my lap and tried to focus. Out of a corner of my eye I could see Yagodo wagging a finger. He opened his mouth and pointed to it. Was he telling me to put the lens in my mouth?

"No hand signals, old man. Keep your eyes on the map." Huang poked Yagodo in the back of the head again. He shrugged and concentrated on the center of the table.

I put the lens in my mouth and immediately felt feedback from the chips in my ears and throat. I was back in AR through my left eye. My right eye was practically swollen shut anyway.

Suddenly I heard Yagodo's voice in my ears. It was a private message. "Both lenses have to be in wet contact with your body. This isn't over yet. Don't do anything rash."

The man wasn't afraid of anything. He was right, it was time to watch and wait. I sat back and kept my left eye on the feed from the site. Mother Mekong was wrapped in softly glowing, flashing points of light. Tens of millions of grasshoppers were working through the Call Phase, searching for the mission code. Soon one of them would hit the jackpot.

Almost there.

Now the 3D satellite image spread across the floor showed Mother Mekong too. The fluorescent green of SR06 was stained by a duller hue at the north edge of the site and in the surrounding jungle. The whole site was enveloped in soft clusters of light, like luminous froth. The clusters pulsed slowly, like some gigantic creature breathing.

The communication between tens of millions of grasshoppers searching for the mission code was visible from the satellite too. Gough leaned over the feed for a better view. He looked up at me.

"What is that glowing down there? Is that the grasshoppers? What have you done?"

"I told you. You're going to tell the world what *you* did."

"Yes, damn it, but how—" He was about to grab me by the shoulders but stopped. A sharper light was flashing in the zoom view, a white light different from the rest. The brilliant point rose and flew over the site, flashing as it went. It dipped and rose again and again. Everyone held their breath.

"Jackpot," murmured Thep. One of the grasshoppers had found the answer among the astronomical number of possibilities. Now it was signaling the rest of the swarm. I hadn't expected the illumination to be so intense.

The grasshopper left a trail of lights in its wake, each new little star rising and flying in a different direction, spawning more lights. The glowing wakes spread like capillaries across the site.

Soon the 3D image looked like the center of a galaxy. The TerraVu image feed spread across the floor started picking up the new lights.

Yagodo exhaled in amazement. Kurokawa's eyes devoured the image. The whole site was bathed in a brighter glow. The different hues of SR06 and the intruder were no longer visible. All we could see was a field of pulsing light.

"It's starting," I whispered. The light at the north edge of the site faded quickly, leaving a bright slash of red across the dull green backdrop. When the glow had ebbed from half the site, I heard Nguyen gasp.

Two gigantic lines of red text emerged, topped by an even bigger bar code.

OPERATION MOTHER MARY
COURTESY OF GUARDIANS OF THE LAND

The edges of the letters flickered like fire.

"There you are, Gough. Your declaration of responsibility. I used your grasshoppers to spell it out."

"You did this? How did you figure out the software?"

"John McCauley was nice enough to leave me DARPA's development kit. That and a video message."

"McCauley? That little twit!"

"You're the twit. You let a kid fresh out of school play with a bioweapon. You must've been smoking something." I turned to Sascha, who was leaning against the wall with her arms folded. "Why don't you interview Gough and Nguyen? The ecoterrorists who caused the mutation at Mother Mekong. You've got the culprits right here. That's quite a scoop."

She glowered at me. "I don't need your advice. You don't know anything about reporting. You've no idea how much we spent to get this story."

"Here's a chance to recoup some of your investment."

"Don't bother, Mamoru. World Reporting is finished," said Thep quietly.

"What's that supposed to mean?" snapped Sascha. Thep stood up and pointed to the table.

"The message has two parts. The second part is coming."

Everyone's eyes returned to the image. Below the first message, another line of flaming red text started to materialize, beginning as a blur but coming quickly into focus.

SPONSORED BY SASCHA LIEFENS AND WORLD REPORTING, INC.

Yagodo clapped gleefully. Sascha's eyes flashed with rage.

"When did you do this?" I asked Thep.

"Just before you called me. Coding another line of text was easy. With plain text all you have to do is input it"—she typed on an invisible keyboard—"compile it, and you've got yourself a mission code. Kurokawa-san told me all about World Reporting."

"Wait, when did he do that?"

"Mamoru, I can deploy two avatars, you know. One was briefing her while the other one invited her here." He raised an index finger and swept it left and right across his forehead.

"Let's not forget the memorial photo." Yagodo pointed to the feed on the table, made the copy/paste gesture, and placed a screen shot on the wall next to Sascha. "Guardians of the Land didn't actually write this declaration, but the impact is the same. This is it for the Guardians and World Reporting too."

"Jean, we're out of here!" Sascha yelled. She sounded hurt. Jean already had his monopod folded and was running for the door.

"You might have a problem with that," said Yagodo.

"Sascha, we're trapped!" The cameraman tugged frantically at the handle. "It's no use! There's no latch."

Nguyen had stayed slumped in her chair, staring at the floor. Now she looked up. "It opens if you're registered."

"Huang! Take care of them all. Do her first." Sascha pointed to Nguyen.

Kurokawa and Yagodo both yelled "Down!" I hit the floor. Behind me the masked man growled, "Goddamn it, which one is which?" I saw a double image of Kurokawa, one small figure running toward Nguyen and another tugging at the legs of her chair. The first Kurokawa leaped on her and knocked her backward.

The air behind me exploded with gunfire and the shock wave from the muzzle. I shut my eyes tight.

"Huang, don't kill him yet! It might deactivate the stage." I heard a struggle behind me and opened my eyes. Yagodo was grappling with Huang for the submachine gun. The bodyguard knocked him to the floor, jammed the toe of his boot into Yagodo's back, and started kicking him toward the door. Sascha pointed at me.

"No, him!" Nguyen and Yagodo were still struggling on the floor. The gun butt struck me in the head again. Huang frog-marched me to the door.

"Jean, grab his hand and touch the handle with it," called Sascha. Huang shoved me toward the cameraman and swept the muzzle toward Nguyen.

"Paul! Here, boy!" Yagodo shouted.

I heard the unlock tone. The door sprang open. The scent of blossoms blew in from the terrace. How did Yagodo's avatar dog open a real door? I was trying to process this when something shoved me aside. A blur of golden fur sped past my feet.

"Hey, I know you." The familiar sandpaper voice. My knees buckled and I pitched forward against the door. Again the voice. "Sorry, you better stay down. Talk to you later."

"Shit! Who put the safety on?"

I heard the gunman swearing behind me and a man's pitiful squeal, followed by the sound of crashing metal. I steadied myself against the door and turned. The cameraman had toppled over and was pinned under his array. Sascha was struggling with Paul and a man in black combat gear. Paul was going for her throat, while the man had her in a headlock.

It was Kaneda. I was seeing him through my right eye and his avatar through my left, in augmented reality.

"Paul, four o'clock!" Yagodo yelled from behind the sofa. He sounded like he was enjoying himself.

"My name's not Paul!" Kaneda's avatar barked. He jerked Sascha's right arm behind her and pinned her in front of him, turning her toward the gunman. Huang couldn't decide who was real, Kaneda or the dog. The muzzle of his gun jerked up and down.

"Heads up!" Kaneda yelled and propelled Sascha straight toward him.

"Stop or I'll shoot!" Huang growled.

Kaneda put a huge hand on the nape of Sascha's neck and threw her at the gunman. Huang dodged her and moved toward Kaneda, but Kaneda was faster. He grabbed Huang's hands as they gripped the gun, and in one smooth movement stepped behind him and jerked them upward and back, folding Huang's wrists sharply in the wrong direction. There was a sound like ripping fabric. The bodyguard bellowed in agony.

Sascha was gasping half crumpled against the wall. Kaneda grabbed the back of her neck, brought her head back for momentum, and slammed it against Huang's goggles.

There was a crunching sound. Sascha shrieked. She and Huang collapsed in a heap on the floor.

"That was impressive," said Yagodo, rising to his feet.

"You've sure got some bad taste. What is it with you and dogs?" grumbled Kaneda.

"You saved us, my friend. Tie them up for me, okay?"

"You could learn to listen. Hey, your guest brought something useful with him." Kaneda stooped to pick up one of the jamming capsules scattered on the floor around the unconscious gunman. "Mamoru, help me feed these guys."

"Sure, but we still have him to deal with." I motioned to Gough, who had been watching everything from the sofa.

"Oh well, guess I have to do everything." Kaneda grinned. Paul the avatar wagged his tail. Kaneda pushed a capsule into the gunman's mouth. He gurgled and put his arms stiffly at his sides. His eyes bulged. Kaneda fed a capsule to Sascha and moved toward the cameraman.

"I have one last job for you," said Yagodo. "It's a piece of cake. Here's the location." He handed Kaneda a piece of paper.

"Piece of cake, right," said Kaneda, studying the paper. "That's what you said when we hijacked that ship off Singapore. All right. I'll handle this. Hope to see you again, Mamoru." He was already out the door.

Nguyen's feet peeked out from behind the sofa. Was she shot? I looked behind the sofa. Kurokawa was kneeling next to her.

"I think she just fainted."

"What about you, Takashi?"

"Oh, I'm fine." Through my right eye I could see that his jacket sleeve was ripped. His hair was spiking in all directions, but he wasn't hurt. Nguyen seemed to be asleep. There was no blood. "You look a little banged up, though."

I squatted next to him. "Listen, I have to apologize. I thought you were in with those guys."

He smiled. "I know. It's okay. But what about him?" He nodded toward Gough. I took a deep breath and stood in front of him. Gough squinted up at me.

"Congratulations, Mamoru. You really cocked this up. Mother Mary is a failure. Meanwhile the march of genetic engineering goes on, with no one in control, thanks to you. You're the terrorist." He gestured dismissively to the image floating above the table. "Our kites captured the whole thing in high def. Grasshoppers using bioluminescence to communicate digitally."

"So?" Kurokawa broke in.

"You don't get it." Gough sat back and lazily crossed his legs.

"Mamoru just showed the world that artificial animals aren't some unattainable dream. They weren't just munching on SR06, either. They were engaged in directed activity using digital signaling. You even demonstrated that missions can be reformatted on the fly." He jerked a thumb at the image Yagodo had pasted to the wall.

I'd thought of Gough as a naïve activist chasing an ideal world, but even without a background in science, he had grasped the significance of the Call Phase that Thep and I had coded.

"The boom in designed animals begins tomorrow. Engineers all over the world will be looking for backers. The big boys like L&B will be the tip of the iceberg. Tiny startups, totalitarian states, even high school students will be looking to make a killing because they know it can be done. Idiots like McCauley too."

Gough's point was the same one Thep had made the night before, a point I had overlooked. It was a shrewd insight. Even twenty years after losing his beloved Hermitage, genetic engineering and the fate of humanity remained his obsession.

"So what happens now?" said Gough. "The bugs we unleashed just happened to be a DARPA weapon, and you just happened to figure out how to hijack them for your own purposes. But the animals everyone is going to be scrambling to design? Some of them are going to be unstoppable breeders. You can bet on it." He stood up and poked me in the chest. "You've opened Pandora's box."

"I know. You don't need to explain it."

His face stiffened and broke into a smile. I stepped closer and spoke right into his phony smile.

"I understand your fears. That's why I'm publishing the source code. You saw the bar code over Mother Mekong. It's the download link for the kit."

"That's insane! You're going to put that tool in the hands of anyone who wants to play genetic engineer?" Gough took a step back in astonishment. His eyes opened as wide as Behavior Correction would let him.

"You got it."

"But—but look at Takashi! You know the world is full of fools like McCauley. How can you put your trust in them?"

"Because it's the best chance we have to move forward. Standing pat is not an option." I'd been thinking about this for some time, but it had only been last night, when I was with Thep, that I'd finally decided it was the only way.

"There must be—has to be—a way to handle designed animals safely. DARPA has given us the best textbook we could've hoped for. Now the amateurs can't do any damage." I took a step closer to Gough. "Why don't you help us find the way?"

I heard someone clapping. It was Yagodo, coming toward us with a folder under his arm. He had already downloaded the kit. The man didn't waste time.

"Mamoru, you're a hero. Audacious, but it was the right thing to do. This technology cost billions to develop. Giving humanity free access to a proven, safe path to designed animals will make sure no one is tempted to reinvent the wheel—the wrong way. Besides"—Yagodo opened the folder and riffled through the documents—"these files cover the whole range of things humanity has to start thinking about."

He put a hand on my shoulder. "After tomorrow, we'll be living in a different world. You did well."

"Have you both lost your minds? I swear, the first biohazard that comes out of this, they'll be gunning for you, Mamoru. You'll be on the run for the rest of your life."

"We won't let that happen," Kurokawa said. "I'll make sure L&B does everything it can to protect him. It's our responsibility to make the best use of the code he released."

"If you ever need a job, Mother Mekong is waiting," Thep said.

Gough snorted. "How long do you think that honeymoon will last? It'll be a matter of time before the world turns against you."

"The Hermitage is never coming back, Gough," said Yagodo.

Gough said nothing. For a moment he just stared at his lap. His avatar betrayed no change of expression, but Yagodo's words seemed to have touched a nerve.

"Mamoru's going to need more than a few allies to protect him from humanity's rage when this technology blows up in everyone's face. It's too bad, but it's the truth," he said finally.

Yagodo gave him a piercing look. "That's why everyone needs to own the code, and not just the 'big boys.' We want the whole world to get involved. Mamoru understood the necessity of this. I think you realize it too."

"Gough?" Kurokawa left Nguyen's side and sat beside him. "I want you to know something. Without tough critics like you, genetic engineering and distilled crops would be in trouble. Nothing devised by human beings is perfect. I'm living proof of that."

Gough was silent for a beat. "Takashi, be honest with me. You read my offer, didn't you? Why didn't you take me up on it?"

Kurokawa paused. "All right, I'll be honest. You nearly had me. Living in this body is a personal tragedy. But I believe in the future." He peered at Gough steadily. "So does Mamoru. That's why he released the code."

"You're willing to bet humanity's future on a bunch of idiots you can't control?"

"I'm sorry someone like you, with your dedication and commitment, is always looking backward to a time that's gone forever. This technology is real. Regarding it with fear solves nothing. So let me invite *you*. Work with us. Help us create a better future for humanity."

"I thought about it, once. But I am who I am. I'll keep resisting the overreach of technology."

"I'm sorry to hear that."

"I'm sorry it has to be that way." Gough turned to me. "I wonder if you really understand how much danger you've put the planet in."

"I stand by what I said."

"Then I'm going to dog you from here on out until you admit you're wrong." He put a raised index finger to his eye and logged out.

"So that leaves..." Yagodo looked down at Nguyen. She was still on the floor, eyes closed. "I guess it's time for the boss to say his piece." He squatted next to her and put a hand on her shoulder. She batted it away quickly and sat up.

"You heard everything then," said Yagodo. "It's all over. You've got a date with the police." Nguyen shuddered. "I knew you were a member all along. I never guessed you'd be willing to go so far though." Her eyes widened.

"I guess I should apologize. I thought I could stop you before you crossed the line," he said.

Kurokawa squatted next to them. "I'm sorry I had to get rough with you."

"No, I should thank you," she said. "I'm probably alive because you pushed me out of the way."

"Can I say one thing?"

Nguyen looked gravely at Kurokawa and nodded.

"I don't know why you hate genetic engineering. There was a time when I hated it too. All I could feel for L&B and the technology that did this to me was pure hate. It was years before I was ready to accept a world where distilled crops kept humanity from starvation. Super Rice Zero put twenty-six other people in a coma. Their families refused to give their consent for the modifications L&B performed on me. Today those people are still trapped in a world without time."

"But how did you..." Nguyen's voice faltered.

"I couldn't return to that world of endless dreaming. I could've immersed myself in memories of a world of real tastes and real sensations. I could've held on to the memories of my parents. In dreams."

Kurokawa unbuttoned his shirt and showed her the bar code on his shoulder.

"Time began seven years ago, when my body and brain were reconnected. The memories of my parents fade with every passing year. I had to learn to use my avatars to force this body to do my bidding. I won't tell you what the rehabilitation process was like. Let's just say that I hope no one else ever has to go through it.

"I can't taste, I can't sleep, I can't feel unless I decide to. I can't tell if I'm cold or hot except in terms of numbers. Whenever I see this bar code, it reminds me that augmented reality is keeping me alive."

Nguyen was transfixed by the softly pulsing tattoo.

"Still, I'm grateful for every day. I don't want to live in a past I can't change. If happiness is waiting for me, it's not waiting there." Kurokawa buttoned his shirt.

"Nguyen, it's time for you to choose. I'll respect whatever decision you make. If you choose to believe in the future, no one will be happier than me. I hope we'll meet again somewhere."

Kurokawa stood up, stretched, and sat next to Thep, who had a fingertip behind her ear. She looked off into space, then nodded and stood up. "Kurokawa-san, I'm sorry I tore up your shoulder getting you out of that suit."

"You had no choice." Kurokawa shrugged.

"Mission accomplished. Flawless," said Thep. "Nimol says the grasshoppers are dying. We've got a lot of cleanup to do. I'd better get back."

"L&B will cover half the damages. Just send me the bill." Kurokawa bowed.

I held out a hand to Thep. "Thank you." Thep's avatar put her hand over mine in the AR gesture for shaking hands.

"I can't see what they did to your face, but you should get some first aid. Listen, there's one thing. I ran a few simulations with the grasshoppers this morning. Every time, the jackpot hit around block C3. It might be random chance, but when you have time, why don't we figure it out together?"

The feedback chip gave me a momentary sensation of touching her hand.

Yagodo was back at his desk, eyes locked on his workspace as he pecked away at his virtual keyboard. "Everybody's leaving. I'm starting to feel lonely. Wait a minute... Mamoru, Takashi—if you get over to the Ambassador, you'll have a ringside seat for the arrest of Gough Robertson. Kaneda just gave me a heads-up. Says he collared Gough himself."

"At the Ambassador? He was staying at the same hotel!"

"His message to Takashi came from a suite on the eleventh floor. Nguyen could've been a little more careful with her hotel arrangements." Yagodo glanced at her and chuckled. "I'll contact the police and the media. They'll be right on top of it. Except..." Yagodo rubbed his jaw and looked at me and Kurokawa.

"You two are a mess. Especially Mamoru. That bloody shirt is too conspicuous. Don't worry, I have something for you." He reached under the desk and pulled out a pair of aloha shirts and baseball caps. The shirts were fluorescent green with a pattern of purple flowers. The caps were pink, with appliqué catfish. He handed a set to each of us. Kurokawa groaned.

Kaneda was right. Yagodo had unbelievably bad taste.

15   And Then...

The eleven-story Ambassador Hotel cast a sharp shadow over the traffic circle. It was noon, the hottest time of the day. The first traffic jam of the afternoon was gearing up.

The street and sidewalk around the hotel entrance swarmed with reporters and camera crews. Alerted by Yagodo's tweet, they were there to cover the arrest of ecoterrorist Gough Robertson. The local news crews had been pushed out to the periphery of the circle and were arguing with a team from Qatar, who were setting up a huge camera array. Police in body armor stood in a ring on the steps above the sidewalk to keep the journalists from pouring into the lobby. Ho Chi Minh City was about to become the center of a story that would rock the world.

Kurokawa and I were watching the commotion from a coffee stand on the opposite side of the circle.

"Cà phê sữa đá."

I ordered iced coffee using one of the handful of phrases Nguyen had taught me. I'd learned that adjectives follow nouns in Vietnamese. "Coffee" was *cà phê,* "milk" was *sữa,* and *đá* meant "ice." Cà phê đá was iced coffee, Cà phê sữa đá was iced coffee with condensed milk.

"Cùng một, xin vui lòng."

Kurokawa ordered the same thing. With his aloha shirt and flawless Vietnamese accent, I almost thought for a moment that I was looking at one of the locals.

"When did you learn Vietnamese?"

"I have an onboard translation engine. L&B's engineers don't fool around." Kurokawa grinned and pushed up the brim of his baseball cap. The cap was too large and kept slipping over his eyes.

"So what was the deal with the English you were speaking to Nguyen?"

"Oh, that's how my father used to talk. It fits the Japanese salaryman image. Maybe I pushed it a little too far."

More vans were pulling up outside the hotel, disgorging more news crews.

"Barnhard is about to make his statement. Let's watch it while we wait." Kurokawa gave the invitation gesture. I blinked twice and closed my right eye.

A tiny, three-dimensional press conference setup popped into place on the white plastic table. A few seconds later, an eight-inch-tall Barnhard walked to the long table, lit by strobing cameras. The table was draped with a banner sporting the L&B logo.

"Ladies and gentlemen. I am Lintz Barnhard, vice president of L&B Corporation. For twenty years, I've been helping to feed the world with genetically modified crops. As you know, I've been a champion of distilled crops for many years. I'm here today to make a statement regarding recent events."

Using a three-dimensional model on the table in front of him, Barnhard traced the events that led to the mutation of SR06 at Mother Mekong. He walked his audience through the development of DARPA's bioweapon and Guardians of the Land's plot to fake a "spontaneous" revolt by nature against distilled crops. He didn't have a firm grip on the technology, but the passion driving him was undeniable.

"This attack on a technology that feeds billions is absolutely unforgivable. Completely and totally unforgivable. I also find it utterly reprehensible that World Reporting would subject an innocent engineer to what amounts to a witch hunt and a frame-up when all along they were in bed with terrorists."

"Barnhard?" I chuckled. "More like blowhard."

"Everything's off the cuff. His people keep telling him to use the Presentation settings in Behavior Correction, but he hates the whole idea. Says he won't work with a safety net."

"Cám ơn."

The owner thanked us as she brought the tray to the table: the now-familiar chrome filters filled with ground coffee and hot water atop ceramic cups, and plastic glasses filled with small ice cubes. She set the tray down next to mini-Barnhard, then squatted by the ice box out on the sidewalk, keeping an eye on the buzzing crowd.

"All right, I think he's getting to the point." Kurokawa gestured toward Barnhard, who was just catching his breath after a long burst of invective against Sascha Leifens and Guardians of the Land.

"There's one more thing I must tell you. Today, for the first time, I learned of the existence of a new life-form, one designed by man. This new creature...Please forgive me, I'm not used to this terminology."

He leaned forward, hands on the table, and paused.

"This new animal is a completely artificial life-form. Its DNA was designed from the ground up by genetic engineers. It is not a single-celled organism, nor a worm or some other simple creature. It is an insect with a much more complex structure. It is capable of rapid movement and can reproduce in a natural environment. Furthermore, it can be programmed dynamically to display various behaviors. Earlier today I witnessed its ability to use bioluminescence and digital communication to solve complex calculations."

The legs of my plastic chair squeaked on the concrete. I was unconsciously trying to distance myself from Barnhard. It would probably be a while before I could listen to laypeople talk about this subject without cringing.

"This is an astonishing development. I thought it would be ten—no, at least twenty years before animals like this walked the earth."

Kurokawa stretched out his hand and paused the feed. "Sorry. They're bringing him out. We can watch the rest later."

He pointed to the hotel. A few seconds later, a fusillade of camera strobes lit the entrance under the awning like a sunburst.

The wings of the revolving door turned and Gough emerged, flanked by two police officers. He stopped at the top of the steps and surveyed the waiting journalists with jaw set and head held high, as though he could dominate them through sheer will.

I wondered how he felt about the relentless advance of genetic technology over the last twenty years. I wished I could've had the chance to ask him.

"He looks pretty defiant," I said.

"Prison won't change him. He'll be back on the front line as soon as he's out. It's in his blood, unfortunately."

One of the cops prodded Gough. He walked down the steps and into the sea of reporters. The crowd flowed around him as the camera strobes traced his progress. The traffic circle was ringed with curious locals.

"That's it. Our investigation of the mutation at Mother Mekong is over. It's been a busy four days."

"Four days. That's all..."

Less than a week had passed since I had met Kurokawa in the flesh for the first time. A project we thought might last a month was suddenly over.

A breeze lifted the sweet smell of local coffee to my nostrils. On either side of the frozen Barnhard, the dark brew was dripping from chrome filters, filling our cups.

"Shall we catch the rest?" said Kurokawa. He swiped his hand over the frozen image of Barnhard.

"—like this would walk the earth. At first, I found this frightening. What would happen if these creatures escaped into nature and out of man's control? What if they displaced natural life-forms and took over the planet? These thoughts occurred to me as I watched the swarm of grasshoppers at the Mother Mekong SR06 site."

I enjoyed Barnhard's verbal attack on Gough, but his warning about the dangers of designed animals was making me nervous. The decision to turn potential danger into real danger had been mine and mine alone.

*   *   *

"More than twenty years ago, humanity was locked out of the Internet. This disaster was caused by the massive proliferation of computer programs. I'm sure many of you remember the chaos that followed." Barnhard straightened up and folded his hands over his spherical gut.

"We succeeded in replacing the Internet, which was hijacked by computer programs, with TrueNet. But designed animals are not computer programs. They are not bits and bytes stored in memory. They breathe the air we do. They feed and reproduce just as we do. We will have to share the planet with them. How should we deal with this new form of life?"

I felt the urge to say something, but my lips and tongue were stuck together. Whatever I said would sound defensive anyway. I decided to keep quiet.

"Fortunately the engineer who uncovered the genome of these insects, which were being used as a weapon of terror, has released the development kit used to create them. His act of courage is an affirmation of faith in humanity's capacity to make the right decision. For this I would like to thank him."

I relaxed a little.

"To ensure that this courageous act was not in vain, L&B Corporation has decided to establish a new laboratory that will use the designed animal genome as a platform for research and development. We will solicit participation from everyone—not just genetic engineers, but engineers in other disciplines as well as architects, artists, religious leaders, and even those who oppose genetic engineering. We want to create a conversation that is as inclusive as possible, to consider how designed life-forms should be used and controlled. We will appoint the senior directors of this new laboratory shortly."

Kurokawa swiped his hand over the image and Barnhard disappeared.

"Takashi, was this new lab your idea?"

"I made them promise to back us up, but the lab was Barnhard's idea."

"I didn't have that image of him. I thought he was more—"

"More of a pushy, calculating businessman? That's what he is." Kurokawa laughed. "He's also one of the industry's deepest thinkers about the future. He has to be—one of the victims of genetically modified rice is a relative of his."

"What? You're joking." Other than the people affected by Super Rice Zero, I had never heard of any GMO crop victims.

"Yes. That relative is me. As soon as they were finished modifying me, Barnhard adopted me. His support was the only thing that got me through the rehabilitation work. He was there for me the whole time, day and night." He pushed the slipping brim of his cap back on his head.

"I'll tell you more about it sometime. Right now—" He pulled out a one-page document and handed it to me. "I have another request."

I read the first sentence of the document and blanched.

"Would you be interested in becoming the first Chief Technology Officer of L&B's Designed Animal Laboratory?"

"Come on, Takashi. I'm nowhere near qualified."

"Last night, with no one to help you, you faced two possible tomorrows. In one, the world is overrun by designed animals. In the other, humanity collaborates to guarantee the responsible use of those animals. You had the courage to trust the future. That's the kind of CTO that L&B needs. That's not just what I think. It's what Barnhard thinks. He's right. Please join us."

"You're giving me too much credit. You should ask Thep instead."

"I talked to her. She told me she wasn't sure she would've had the courage to make the decision you did. Neither am I. I really don't know if I could've done it."

Kurokawa looked straight into my eyes.

"Please accept this position, Mamoru. Of course I'll be involved too. Let's build a team. We'll meet with Thep and get her on board. Unless I miss my bet, Yagodo will be too curious to turn us down. Let's talk to him." His eyes blurred. It wasn't an artifact. "Do you remember what Gough said? You've opened Pandora's box."

I nodded and looked at my lap, embarrassed for all kinds of reasons.

"Let's find the spirit of hope in the technology you unleashed on the world."

Working with Thep and Yagodo again sounded like a dream. And Kurokawa would be by our side.

"Mamoru, your ice is melting." I must've been staring wordlessly at my lap for longer than I thought. There was a glass of iced coffee in front of me. It held a healthy dose of condensed milk.

"It's not good to drink too much of the water," I said finally.

"That's what Nguyen said. Come on, cheer up. I made this for you. Just the way Yagodo likes it. Let's drink a toast." His eyes were smiling.

"All right, but no fair turning your taste buds off."

"You don't miss a trick, Mamoru." He smiled, pushed his cap back, and took off his glasses. He looked like a kid who'd been caught playing a prank. "This isn't fair."

"Of course it is. I wouldn't want to enjoy it all by myself. *Kanpai!*"

"Kanpai!"

I took a long sip. The taste of bitter coffee grounds and condensed milk filled my mouth, followed by the sweetness of the coffee. I massaged my temples as the cloying aroma flooded my sinuses. Kurokawa's lips puckered. He stuck his tongue out.

It was truly awful. How did Yagodo drink this every day?

"See? Told you."

"It's even worse than I expected. Let's lose the condensed milk."

The owner noticed something was wrong with her Japanese customers. She got up and came over to our table quickly, looking concerned. I smiled at her as if to say *It's not your fault*. Kurokawa and I nodded to each other.

"Cà phê đá!"

Six Months Later

I watched Thep push through the undergrowth ahead of me. She stopped at the edge of the field, planted the big tripod in the grass, and looked back down the slope. The wind rising from the southwest whipped her ponytail across her face.

A memory came back to me from my first visit to Mother Mekong—sitting with Thep at the base of a messenger tower while she filled me in on the distilled crop business. The wind had whipped her hair across her face then too, but it had just been my mil-spec AR stage putting on a show. She hadn't felt a thing.

"What are you staring at, Mamoru?"

Thep brushed the hair from her face with work-roughened fingers. They were patched with bandages. A few strands of hair clung to her smooth forehead. She pushed them away impatiently.

"I was just thinking how much nicer it is to see the real thing."

"This isn't me." Thep grinned. "It's RealVu." Behavior Correction would never have let me hear that nasal laugh.

"It's *almost* as good as the real thing."

She smiled and nodded. Yagodo had configured his stage to blanket the entire site. His AR was nearly indistinguishable from reality.

"Nothing's as good as the real thing," she said. "Anyway, here we go."

She quickly surveyed the terraces falling away behind her before turning back to her setup. I paused to take in the view. It was the same vista I'd been staring at for the last three months in my workspace.

The sparkling sea of green spread out under the noon sun, rippling in the breeze that caressed us. Mother Mekong had been reborn as a designed-animal test site.

Barnhard had kept his word.

L&B had set up the Institute for Gene Mapping Research in Singapore at the Nankai Institute of Technology, Thep's alma mater. Barnhard had also licensed the code for VB01G-X from the US government. Yagodo's network of freelance engineers had taken a bioweapon designed for the US Marines Corps and completely refactored the code. Kurokawa handled the negotiations with a reluctant DARPA, wearing them down with sheer tenacity until they capitulated.

Now L&B was on the cusp of releasing the first of its INAGO— "grasshopper" in Japanese—series of designed animals.

I had supervised the grand scheme for the enhanced organism. Over the past six months, I'd made the transition from gene mapper and style sheet specialist to the world's foremost commercial animal designer. There had been an overwhelming amount to learn and adapt to, but Kurokawa's superhuman management of the research institute let me focus all my energy on developing INAGO.

Now we were about to field-test it for the first time.

The first animal in the series was a grasshopper programmed to operate within a predefined area and eat only XSR01 rice, which now covered the site. Using code from L&B, Thep reengineered Super Rice into the ideal food for INAGO series insects.

Thep cocked her head and called to me as she went on setting up the camera.

"Feel like a little wager?"

"On what?"

"On whether it hits in sector C3. I'm betting it will."

"I'm not that dumb. I didn't check the latest tweaks with a simulation, but they always hit the jackpot in C3. You know that."

Thep just smiled and hoisted the camera into place.

Six months ago, when the grasshoppers cracked the mission

code to draw the Guardians of the Land logo in giant letters across the site, the one that hit the jackpot had been in sector C3, in the southeast corner of Mother Mekong. There was no particular reason that we knew of that it happened there rather than anywhere else; it was just where that particular grasshopper happened to be. Yet each time I simulated the brute force decryption later, the same thing happened—the first insect to crack the code was always in sector C3. After Yagoda joined the institute as my chief engineer, he became so intrigued by the unlikely phenomenon that he spent weeks on the mystery, but he never came up with a solution. I remembered the look on his face when he told me, "If it comes up C3 again, your simulation is buggy."

I reached into my leg pouch and drew out a clear acrylic tube. "Ready when you are," I called to Thep.

The tube held a single large grasshopper curled quietly like some museum specimen. Born ten days earlier from an embryo printer, it was an omega-class INAGO—in sleep mode, thanks to 500 ppm trans-2-hexenal.

As I studied the inert INAGO, Thep stood up.

"All right, I'm good to go."

I put a fingertip on the latch at the end of the tube and took a closer look at the omega. With wings folded it looked pretty much like a natural grasshopper, except for the rhythm of its respiration and the calm pulsing of its bioluminescent wings.

I designed this life-form.

Now our world was its world. Artificial life was about to take its place in the scheme of things.

Thep's giggle drifted down the slope.

"Getting cold feet?" She spread her arms joyously and spun around to survey the terraces of green that dropped away below us. "There are two billion alphas out there already, just waiting for a mission."

"That's true." I popped the lid of the tube. The scent of trans-2-hexenal reached me, a smell of ripe apples.

The omega detected the GPS signal and twitched its antennae sharply, twice. The light from its wings pulsed brighter.

Power up.

Thep peered into the workspace in her palm. "I'm used to working with alphas. The omega signal is much stronger."

"It needs to reach as many alphas as possible. That's why its life span is so much shorter."

Thep nodded gravely. "Until tomorrow morning."

"Right. The alphas have eighteen hours to find the solution. If they don't, I go back to the drawing board."

"Come on. They get better every time."

As if wanting to prove Thep right, the omega poked its head out of the tube and moved tentatively into the sunlight. Its tiny spurs pricked my palm lightly, leaving a slight tingling as it moved toward my fingers.

I raised my hand toward the sea of green, and the omega quickly clambered up my fingers. With typical insect behavior, it was aiming for the highest point to launch. Now its luminescent wings were bright enough to light up my fingers, even in daylight.

Ready, steady...

The grasshopper reached the tip of my index finger and spread its wings, flexing them. Their network of veins was filled with dense clusters of bioluminescent cells emitting a rainbow of colors—a signaling organ unique to the omegas, designed by me, implemented by Yagodo, and capable of transmitting up to several hundred megabytes of information to two billion alphas.

I felt the little kick as the omega launched with a low drone. It flew arrow-straight out over the field, a dazzling point of strobing color. The rice plants left and right of its path seemed to stir with life, and the soft glow from millions of points of light rose and spread outward like blue-white foam. The bio-nanomachines in the alphas' thoraxes were already working to crack the code.

"Find it." Thep's voice was taut with anticipation. "Just once. Find the answer, and you'll find your place in our world."

I had no words, but my heart was sending the same message.

Find it.

You'll have to find a way to coexist with us on a planet with limited resources. You'll have to discover the rules of survival for designed animals. Not even your designers know what they are, or if they even exist.

The rules for survival of Life.

That was the institute's mission. It was my mission too. I unleashed DARPA's grasshopper on the world.

The omega was a point of light now, a rainbow flame in the sun-drenched sky.

"Do you think they'll find it?" Thep murmured. She leaned close to me. The back of her hand brushed mine. A lean hand, toughened by the work to convert Mother Mekong into a petri dish for designed life.

"I don't know." I laced her fingers into mine. "We're a foolish species, Shue. We have the power to destroy our environment many times over. Yet here we are, still surviving. We don't need to be perfect. We just have to find a way to do the best we can."

She squeezed my hand. This time, her warmth was real.

About the Author

Taiyo Fujii was born on Amami Oshima Island—that is, between Kyushu and Okinawa. He worked in stage design, desktop publishing, exhibition graphic design, and software development.

In 2012, Fujii self-published *Gene Mapper* serially in a digital format of his own design and was Amazon.co.jp's number one Kindle best seller of the year. The novel was revised and republished in both print and digital as *Gene Mapper–full build–* by Hayakawa Publishing in 2013 and was nominated for the Japan SF Award and Seiun Award. His second novel, *Orbital Cloud,* won the 2014 Japan SF Award and took first prize in the "Best SF of 2014" in *SF Magazine*. His recent works include *Underground Market* and *Bigdata Connect*.

HAIKASORU

THE FUTURE IS JAPANESE

ASURA GIRL— OTARO MAIJO

Seventeen-year-old Aiko lives a life of casual sex and casual violence, though at heart she remains a schoolgirl with an unrequited crush on her old class-mate Yoji Kaneda. Life is about to get harder for Aiko, as a recent fling, Sano, has been kidnapped, and the serial killer Round-and-Round Devil has begun slaughtering children. The youth are rioting in the streets, egged on by the underground Internet bulletin board known as the Voice from Heaven. Expecting that Yoji will come and save her from the madness, Aiko posts a demand for her own murder on the V of H, but will she be left waiting... or worse?

DENDERA—YUYA SATO

When Kayu Saitoh wakes up, she is in an unfamiliar place. Taken to a snowy mountainside, she was left there by her family and her village according to the tradition of sacrificing the lives of the elderly for the benefit of the young. Kayu was supposed to have passed quickly into the afterlife. Instead, she finds herself in Dendera, a utopian community built over decades by old women who, like her, were abandoned. Together, they must now face a new threat: a hungry mother bear.

RED GIRLS: THE LEGEND OF THE AKAKUCHIBAS—KAZUKI SAKURABA

When the outlanders abandoned a baby girl on the outskirts of a village, few imagined that she would grow up to marry into the illustrious Akakuchiba family, much less that she would develop clairvoyant abilities and become matriarch of the illustrious ironworking clan. Her daughter shocks the village further by joining a motorcycle gang and becoming a famous manga artist. The outlanders' granddaughter Toko—well, she's nobody at all. A nobody worth entrusting with the secret that her grandmother was a murderer.

This is Toko's story.